Tame My
RACING
HEART

KELLY DUFF

TAME MY RACING HEART

Cover Design and Interior Format

© KILLION
THE
GROUP, INC.

DEDICATION

While the writing process is a solitary act, it takes a village to create a well-rounded story and I'm indebted to everyone who helped me complete this novel.

To my wonderful husband Ryan, you're my knight in shining armor and my happy ever after.

To my sister Michelle, for making me laugh every time she'd tell her kids "she's still writing!"

To Brian, my brother from another mother, who gave me a metric ton of information on the world of racing.

To my editor, Megan Records, for inspiring me and helping me make this story the best it could be.

To my romance writing friends, especially Tameri Etherton who helped me figure out the publishing side (and I thought the writing was hard!) and all the other awesome people out there who made me a better writer.

To my beta readers for being the first set of eyes on it besides my own.

And finally, to my dad, who incited the writer in me through music.

If everything seems under control,

you're just not going fast enough.

—Mario Andretti

LAP ONE

S AMI JO MCLEAN WAS LATE as usual.
Parking her vintage Mustang on the circular driveway of her uncle's oceanfront Myrtle Beach home, she
killed the stereo blasting Motley Crue's "Kickstart My
Heart," and realized the irony of a professional race car
driver not having a better handle on her time.

Fresh ink on the inside of her right wrist stung under
a gauze pad.

It wasn't her first tattoo, and it wouldn't be her last.
The sentiment behind the tribal symbol for *strength* was
there to keep her focused. It was also the reason she was
running late. She'd woken up and decided today was the
day, and luckily, Zach from Zach's Tats agreed to the early
morning session. He'd done most of the intricate work
on her upper arm and although this one was quick and
easy, she'd ended up spending more time at his shop than
she'd anticipated.

When Sami Jo opened her car door, a familiar voice
pierced the salty ocean air.

"Samantha Josephine, what's it gonna take for you to
ever be on time?"

Melanie McLean-Burton tapped a flip-flop on the
threshold of the open doorway as an Atlantic breeze

whipped her straight brown hair into a frenzy.

Sami Jo glanced at a black Escalade parked by the garage as she took the stairs to the front door and sighed as she followed her cousin inside. The smell of chocolate chip cookies filled the air, which meant one thing—Melanie was trying to impress whoever owned that Escalade.

"Why does Royce always insist on scheduling a meeting the day after a race? He knows this is my only downtime," Sami Jo said, thinking of the last time her uncle had sprung a meeting with a potential sponsor on her. She wasn't in the mood today, regardless of this being her first time out in the NASCAR series. She just wanted to relax before the merry-go-round of practice, qualifying, and another race started all over again.

"Mel, what the hell is going on?"

"*Mel, what the hell is going on?*" Sami Jo's eight-year-old nephew mimicked from the living room.

"James, go clean your room!" Melanie stomped her foot and retrieved a pitcher of lemonade from the refrigerator.

Sami Jo spotted the tray of cookies on the counter and reached for one.

"Stop right there. Those are for our guest. Make yourself useful and bring them outside," Melanie said, then pushed through the door leading to the porch.

"Who's here?" Sami Jo asked, but before she could get an answer, the door slammed.

She raised a brow and stuffed a cookie into her mouth. "*Some man.*"

The small voice that came from the living room made Sami Jo smile. She picked up the tray of cookies and carried it into the brightly-decorated room to find her six-year-old niece, Emma, sitting on the floor next to the leather sofa. Coloring books were splayed out on the coffee table.

"What's up, Emma-roo?"

"Looking for pink." Emma frowned as she probed a shoebox full of crayons that sat by her side.

Sami Jo craned her neck to see the picture Emma was working on. "A—*pink* cactus? Are you sure about that, Em?"

Emma pulled a carnation-pink crayon from the box and looked up at Sami Jo, wide-eyed and serious. "It's a *girl* cactus."

"Of course. Silly me." Sami Jo selected a cookie and handed it to her niece. "Who's the man outside?"

Emma shrugged and stuffed the cookie in her mouth. "I don't know him," she said as pieces of cookie fell from her lips.

"Hey, don't get crumbs all over the place or your mom will kill us both." She reached down and tousled the little girl's light brown hair.

Straightening, Sami Jo headed back through the kitchen and out the door to the porch.

"There's my girl!" Royce McLean called out from across the open-air, covered deck.

He leaned against the wood railing in his McLean Racing embroidered polo, the breeze ruffling his salt-and-pepper hair. His handsome face showed delight, but those smoky eyes of his pierced right through her. He was pissed she was late and calling Sami Jo his *girl* meant he was showing off to someone.

Royce's guest stood by the stairs that led down to the beach. Sami Jo caught her breath, releasing the cookie tray as if it had burned her hand, and it clattered onto the low table.

"Morning, Sami Jo."

The sound of Grayson Finch's voice sent a shiver through her as infuriating memories bubbled to the surface. Her first love, her first heartbreak, all rolled into one gorgeous package.

"Sami Jo, this is Grayson Finch." Royce crossed to a

cushioned wicker chair and sat down. He had no idea who Gray was to her, but she certainly wasn't about to get into it. "Weren't you friends with Grayson's cousin?"

"Gemma," Sami Jo and Gray answered simultaneously and it caused her to stiffen. His answer sounded low and calm while hers felt borderline hysterical.

"Here, Mr. Finch, let me top off your drink." Melanie hurried over with the pitcher of lemonade.

Damn, he looks good, Sami Jo thought as he lifted his glass for Melanie to fill it.

Under his sport coat, he was still built like a tank. He'd grown out his crewcut and long layers of dark blonde hair framed his face. Then there was the short beard. She'd only ever seen him clean-shaven. How any of it could be such a vast improvement on someone who was already ridiculously good-looking was, well—ridiculous.

Sami Jo broke from her trance and adjusted the tray of cookies on the table.

"Come, Grayson, take a seat. Sami Jo?" Royce pointed at her and then gestured to the chair next to his own. "Sit."

Her uncle always had a knack for making situations seem dire. Nonetheless, she obeyed as her heart did synchronized somersaults with her stomach.

"Melanie, would you be a doll and make sure the kids stay inside until we're done? And, let me know when Matt gets here." Royce gave his daughter a wink.

"Sure, Daddy." Melanie put the pitcher on the table in front of them and headed inside.

"Melanie reminds me so much of her mother. I don't know what I would've done without her after Trudy passed away last year. Having her and Matt living here with the kids has brought life back into this place. Matt has been negotiating for two new cars all morning, but I'm optimistic he'll get us a good deal." Royce stuck his thumb out and jerked it toward Sami Jo. "Meanwhile, this one is costing me an arm and a leg in tires every single time she races."

It was Royce's attempt at humor and yet Sami Jo had no sarcastic comeback to diffuse it—that was a first. Out of the corner of her eye, she swore Gray was smiling and nodding.

"But, she's already had a helluva season," Royce continued. "When she won Daytona right out of the gate, we knew she'd be a force to reckon with. Hell, her daddy didn't even make the top twenty his first series race."

Royce's gaze shifted down to his hands folded in his lap. "We lost my brother, Chase, at a race in Charlotte almost twenty years ago. I'll never forget watching his car come apart."

Sami Jo stilled. Royce rarely talked about her father's death. She barely recalled the details because she'd been eight at the time, only remembering the commotion on the track and in the viewing suite, where she and Melanie had been playing. Even the aftermath of being told her daddy had died was a blur.

"There've been lots of improvements with safety measures since then, so my concern for my niece's well-being lies mostly off the track," Royce said.

"Royce, what's this all about?" Sami Jo asked.

She had dispensed with *Uncle* years ago—the business had seen to that. Royce was her boss. He had been her crew chief, calling the shots into her headset when she raced in the local circuits. Now he was her team manager so it just made sense for her to drop the formality and make their relationship less about the obvious nepotism.

Royce picked up a blue file folder from the table and passed it to her. When she tried to take it, he didn't let go. "I want you to take this seriously. Especially after what happened last month."

She had hoped they were past the incident in Vegas. God knew she was trying to forget about it.

Tugging the folder out of his hand, she opened it. Inside were color photocopies of her at races and other appearances. Each had lewd words and images drawn over them in red marker.

She shrugged, trying to think of a way to lessen her uncle's concern. "I wish I had a dollar for every time some crazy fan sent me something like this."

That much was true. She'd had plenty of deranged individuals try to contact her. She always blew it off, knowing it was part of being in the public eye. But now she had to wonder if this might be tied to the episode she'd endured last month.

"You're not the only one getting these," Royce said. "Turns out drivers in the other pro series are getting them too. Mainly, Naomi St. James and Angela Guthrie. And after everything that happened, it just doesn't sit right with me. That's why I asked Grayson here. His company provides VIP protection and he's here to make sure nothing happens to you."

Sami Jo blinked at her uncle for a few moments, his intention sinking in. She closed the folder, tossed it onto the table, and stared at Gray. She struggled to keep her cool at his rigid posture, his gaze giving her the feeling he was judging her.

"Well, this is all very unnecessary," she said. "I don't need a bodyguard."

Gray's face made it clear he disagreed.

"Sami Jo, did you hear me when I said other female race car drivers are being targeted?" Royce asked.

"There's always some jerk who has an ax to grind about women in racing. This shit comes with the job," she replied as she stood. "I'm sorry if we wasted your time, Gray."

She slipped out of her sandals and took the stairs going down to the beach as Royce called after her. A cacophony of gulls drowned him out as she headed through the smooth sand leading toward the water.

Up and down the coast, young children were build-ing sandcastles as adults sat under colorful umbrellas. Just another day in the life of her uncle's Myrtle Beach neighbors.

Sami Jo let out a deep breath and her pace slowed.

Of all people, her uncle could've reached out to, why Gray? The last time they had even spoken—more like screamed at each other—he was breaking up with her.

Of course, Royce was clueless about all that. For all he and her Aunt Trudy knew, she'd been hanging out with her friends, enjoying one last summer together before most of her crowd shipped off to college.

How far from the truth that was.

From the minute she met Grayson Finch, she'd done everything in her power to spend time with him. She'd alienated her friends, including Gray's cousin Gemma, who had been her best friend. All because Sami Jo had been determined to lose her virginity that summer to the hottest man she'd ever met.

Gray, however, had kept making excuses. Telling her that she was too young—she was eighteen and he was twenty-four. That he wasn't going to screw his cousin's bestie and then leave Gemma to clean up the mess after he'd left for good.

She had practically begged for it that last night they were together, only to have Gray break her heart when he told her to *"go find someone who cares about you enough to want to pop your cherry."*

That ugliness he'd spewed at her came flooding back as waves licked at Sami Jo's feet.

It felt like it was just yesterday, not seven years ago.

When she glanced back at the house, Gray was approaching her with the blue folder in his hand.

"Sami Jo, come back so we can discuss this."

"Why are you here, Gray?"

"Your uncle hired me," he said without missing a beat.

"No," she said. "Why are *you* here?"

"I'm an expert when comes to things like this," he said, not lowering his gaze from hers.

She picked up a shell, casting it into the waves. A seagull overhead dive-bombed toward it in search of food. "It's nothing I haven't seen before, Gray. I can take care of myself."

"Considering you're a rather high-profile celebrity who makes public appearances, your uncle insists—"

Sami Jo spun to face him. His rugged features under the bright sun caught her off guard. The years had weathered him a bit, yet he was still arrestingly handsome.

"Give me a break. I wouldn't be surprised if this was just some stunt the media created to get extra coverage."

"I think you do fine getting it on your own." Gray stepped toward her, risking the waves hitting his leather shoes. "Why don't you tell me about what happened in Vegas last month."

A shudder ran through her but she did her best to conceal it.

"Well, obviously you know about it if you're asking."

"Yes, but I want to hear it from you," he said.

She studied him for a moment. Uncharacteristic scruff covered the dimples she knew existed in both his cheeks and the sun off the waves reflected in his intense stare, making her insides flutter a bit.

"It was a month ago after I won a race. There was an after-party at the Monte Carlo where we were staying." Sami Jo poked at the sand with her foot. She'd repeated the story often enough it sounded exactly like the statement she'd given the police and admittedly, it was the only way she could get through it. "Since it wasn't a private party, we mingled with the crowd at the nightclub. Sometime after two in the morning, a large group of us left together. Several people got off the elevator on the same floor. By the time I realized one of the guys from the crowd had followed me and that we were alone in the elevator, it was too late."

Sami Jo's mouth went desert-dry at the memory. She decided to leave out the shame of how drunk she'd been and how she feared she'd coaxed the guy by flirting with him earlier in the night. Although the police insisted none of that mattered, she wasn't about to admit her guilt to Gray. She also omitted the part where he'd forced himself into her room and how she could still smell the beer on his breath when he'd shoved her up against the wall. Gray could read that in the police report if he wanted the gory details.

"Sami Jo—"

It made her angry to hear the pity in his voice.

"I never saw his face clearly but I was able to fend him off. I clocked him with a bottle of champagne and ran out of the room. When the police got there, he was gone. They couldn't obtain a blood sample off the bottle so nothing became of it."

"I'm sorry that happened, Sami Jo." Gray closed the gap between them.

"Yeah, well, I still think Royce is over-reacting."

"He's concerned for your safety. I don't blame him, but you're not the only one. The person is targeting a specific group of women."

Sami Jo didn't want to show him how much his physical presence agitated her but he was so close, she could smell his woodsy cologne. She zeroed in on the short whiskers surrounding his mouth, remembering how his lips had felt—

She crossed her arms over her chest. "I'll be more careful. This whole thing is unnecessary."

Gray opened the blue folder, producing an item she had missed.

It was a color photocopy of her hiking alone in the

Blue Ridge mountains last week. She'd driven up the day after the race at Talladega to get away and clear her head.

The photo was covered in red ink, simulating blood splatter, with the words, *"Your death would've been so easy."*

The alarming thing was she hadn't told anyone she was there. Not even her family.

LAP TWO

SAMI JO CRUSHED THE PHOTOCOPY in her trembling hand as she and Gray returned to the porch.

Their footfalls on the stairs drew Royce's attention.

"Sorry, kiddo. I told you this was serious," Royce said. "As soon as Matt gets here, we'll discuss a plan to move forward."

Sami Jo looked toward the door to the house. No wonder Melanie had joked about her tardiness. If she'd known about the photo, she would've gone ballistic.

"What about the police? Why aren't they involved?" Sami Jo asked.

"I already spoke to the sheriff and they're sending someone over," Royce answered.

"The original photo is on its way to a local lab," Gray said, taking a seat.

Sami Jo looked at the image again and a wave of nausea hit her. "I think I need a drink."

She handed the piece of paper to Gray, blindly headed into the house and thankfully, into an empty kitchen.

Retrieving a highball glass from one cabinet and Royce's special reserve bourbon from another, Sami Jo poured a shot and knocked it back.

It instantly set her throat ablaze.

Someone had followed her to the mountains. They had taken her picture, written threats insinuating they could've likely followed through with had they decided to do so. Walking through the Blue Ridge was just one of many ways she decompressed after a race and it angered her that someone had taken that freedom of solitude away from her. But mostly, it scared the shit out of her.

She'd had her earbuds in that day. She'd been listening to the Allman Brothers—a band her daddy had loved. It was one of the few things Sami Jo remembered about him. Despite the stereotype of a southern race car driver loving the country-blues ensemble, Chase's appreciation of the band ran deep. The album "Eat A Peach" had played throughout the house when she was little and listening to it seemed to fill the void her father had left after he'd died.

"Is it five o'clock already?"

Sami Jo jumped at the sound of her cousin's voice but Melanie didn't seem to notice.

"He looks good," Melanie remarked.

"Who?" She knew *exactly* who her cousin referred to.

"Gray. I didn't recognize him at first, then I remembered meeting him at one of the Finch family picnics ages ago." Melanie busied herself with washing the baking pans in the sink. "Daddy was pretty mysterious about why he's here."

Sami Jo couldn't even look at her cousin for fear Melanie would see the concern on her face. Luckily, the kids bounded through the kitchen, causing their usual ruckus. James cruised by, barely offering a hello as he grabbed a juice box from the fridge, and escaped to the living room, dodging a reprimand from his mother.

Emma grabbed Sami Jo around her leg and hugged her.

Sami Jo had driven at speeds of two-hundred miles per hour but the experience of being in the room to witness Emma being born had been one of the greatest thrills of her life. The little girl's innocence now tugged at her heart.

The sudden chime for the front door startled Sami Jo and she blinked away the tears that had sprung to her eyes.

"There's Matt. Sami Jo, can you go tell Daddy he's home?" Melanie walked out to the foyer to greet her husband as Emma released Sami Jo's leg and ran after James.

In a haze, Sami Jo exited to the porch.

"Matt's here." She took the seat she'd vacated earlier and slipped back into her sandals.

"Sami Jo, do you have any reason to believe this person might be someone at the track?" Gray asked.

"I don't think so. I mean, I've had a few drivers and mechanics pissed at me on occasion. But no, no one I can think of."

"Even though our other drivers aren't doing quite as well as Sami Jo, I don't think anyone would begrudge her any of the wins she's had," Royce said.

Sami Jo frowned. "Shouldn't the police be guarding my house? Or yours, Royce?"

"The Sheriff's office will send someone over to take your statement but they don't owe any citizen protection, regardless of celebrity status," Gray said. "Trust me, they'll tell you the same thing."

She opened her mouth to argue but the doors to the porch exploded open as James and Emma rushed out of the house and onto the sand just beyond the stairs. Their father, Matt Burton, was in tow, along with Melanie.

It was barely the middle of the day and Matt looked exhausted, which seemed to be the norm lately. He'd taken over helping Royce run the business—between managing the drivers, reviewing race tapes with them, and making sure all the cars stayed in top form, he had his hands full. He gave Sami Jo a faint smile and ran a hand through his graying hair.

"Matt, this is Grayson Finch. John Finch's nephew. He owns a company called Alliance Security." Royce nodded toward Gray.

Matt shook Gray's hand and sat on the sofa.

"Mel, honey? Don't leave. You should hear this too." Royce waved her over. "Go ahead, Grayson."

"Sami Jo has been receiving threatening photos," Gray said.

"What? Why didn't you tell me?" Melanie's head spun toward Sami Jo as she sat next to her husband.

"I've gotten them before and it hasn't been a big deal," Sami Jo said.

"Still, with what happened in Vegas, we have to be careful," Royce said. "Especially since the guy got away and Sami Jo isn't the only one receiving threats like this. St. James and Guthrie got them too. Grayson, tell them what we discussed."

Gray nodded. "For starters, I'd advise installing badge readers at McLean Racing to make sure the right people have access. I haven't had a chance to inspect Sami Jo's residence yet, but it sounds like her house could stand to have cameras and alarms installed. And with her public appearances, we can minimize risk by assessing any threats in advance, having her escorted at all times, and establishing backup plans to avert any incidents. "

"Well, if her safety is a concern, I'm all for doing whatever it takes. But, and don't take this the wrong way, Sami Jo—that all sounds expensive." Matt grimaced.

"That's why I trust you'll help me figure out a way to make it work, Matthew." Royce cleared his throat and looked over at Gray. "Tell them about the other thing."

"An item that concerns us is a photograph of Sami Jo hiking in the mountains last week. As you may know, she was alone and no one had known she'd gone there. It's clear someone followed her."

Melanie inhaled sharply and Matt's face turned pallid as Gray handed the photo over to them.

The couple stared at it for some time before the sound of the kids' squeals caused Melanie to shoot up from her seat. The panic in her face only slightly subsided when she realized James and Emma were merely playing, kicking through large piles of sand. She put a hand to her mouth as her eyes flooded with tears then she turned sharply to face Sami Jo.

"I knew this would happen. You bring this type of behavior on yourself."

Sami Jo gasped. "Mel, how could you say that—"

"Sami Jo, you're one of the most reckless people I know," Melanie said. "I don't even get why I'm surprised. Between the partying and clashes with the paparazzi, your carelessness in Vegas…"

"Mel, come on. Don't be like that. I didn't ask for this." Sami Jo felt all eyes on her and she shifted in her seat.

"You're impulsive," Mel continued. "You disappear for days without telling us where you've gone off to."

"I need my downtime. You know that." Sami Jo crossed her arms across her chest.

"Yes, I know. Your precious 'downtime.' Meanwhile, you have no regard for your own safety," Melanie spat out. "You're always running around, shooting your mouth off, saying things they have to bleep on television. You may be winning races but your behavior is an embarrassment. I don't care if you and Daddy think any coverage is good coverage, you need to think about more than just yourself. You already risk your life on the track chasing your father's ghost, you need to start thinking about how your actions could affect this family."

Sami Jo went to respond but Melanie held up her hand to stop her. "What if that picture was you with the kids?"

The possibility forced Sami Jo's mouth shut.

Her cousin wasn't wrong but she had never spoken to

her like that before. She'd always been like a protective older sister, but this was an outright reprimand.

In front of Gray made it even worse.

It took every ounce of her will to not run from the porch, race up the coast, and disappear until the dust settled. Her disappearing acts were the only way she could find a sense of harmony in her life. Being amped up the days around races and being pulled in so many directions to keep her sponsors happy, she needed that solitude. But that was exactly why she was in this predicament.

"How about you bring the kids inside, sweetheart?" Royce suggested to Melanie.

Melanie got up and walked to the stairs to call James and Emma into the house.

Matt stood. "Thanks, Mr. Finch. Let me know what you need."

"Please, call me Gray. I'd like to meet at your headquarters later and discuss the security improvements if you don't mind."

As James and Emma stomped onto the porch to shake off the sand, Matt wrangled them by their shoulders and presented them to Gray. "James, Emma, this is Mr. Finch. He's going to be working for me and Grandpa."

"Hi, James." Gray stood and stuck out his hand. James took a moment to check Gray out, scanning his six-foot frame before offering his hand.

"Are you a race car driver like my aunt?" James gave Gray a suspicious look.

"No, but I've flown in a helicopter."

The answer seemed to satisfy James. "Maybe you can help us fix the Lego chopper I built. It keeps falling apart."

Emma reached out for Gray's hand. "Come on, Mr. Finch, we'll show you. Did you know your name is a type of bird?" she remarked as she led him to the door.

"Come on, sweetie." Matt put his arm around his wife and led her inside.

Sami Jo was so dumbfounded by the sight of Gray holding Emma's hand, Royce had to say her name twice to get her attention.

"Look, honey, I want you to cooperate with Grayson."

Sami Jo sighed, feeling the weight of the situation. "Royce, how did you connect with him? And why not someone local?"

"I ran into John Finch at Myrtle's Tavern last week. We got to talking about you and I told him about the Vegas incident. John mentioned Grayson's company specializes in providing security for celebrities and politicians, so they're familiar with handling public appearances. Honestly, I'm glad I called Grayson, especially with that photo showing up."

"I can't believe this is happening." Sami Jo looked out across the beach where James and Emma had been playing. The thought that someone was watching her was one thing, but realizing the kids could've been at risk made her sick.

"I know, sweetheart, but you're in good hands. Grayson has impeccable references." Royce's face turned grim. "John did say something happened during a mission in Afghanistan and that Grayson had to retire from the SEALs due to an injury. I half-expected him to show up with a prosthetic leg, but honestly, I didn't notice anything."

Sami Jo thought about the next few weeks leading up to the only race that mattered—the AWOL Energy Drink 600 in Charlotte.

She had worked so hard to make it this far and that race was important because she'd be racing in the same competition that killed her father. Yet as dangerous as the sport was, she was confident in her skill.

Still, this stalker business, and the potential link it had to Vegas, sent a chill through her despite the warm breeze off the ocean.

She ran her hands up and down her arms. "I've got a lot of events coming up. I can't flake out and lose my sponsors."

"I know, honey. No one is asking you to give anything up. We just need you to be careful."

"What about you guys?" Sami Jo looked solemnly at the man who'd served as her replacement father for two decades.

"We'll be fine, kiddo." Royce lowered his gaze. "You know, you may want to inform Alec. Just as a precaution. Wouldn't want anything bad to happen to that young man."

Sami Jo's shoulders dropped at the thought of Alec Clarke's safety.

Whatever sliver of hope she had that this situation wouldn't affect anyone else she loved was suddenly lost.

LAP THREE

BOOKS, BOARD GAMES, AND TOYS filled the ornate shelves that lined the brightly painted walls of the kids' playroom. Emma and James sat on the oversized rug that depicted Harry Potter playing Quidditch and Legos were scattered in every direction.

Gray was right in the thick of it, crouched on one knee as he inspected the piece Emma had handed him. He scoured the floor, selected a few more pieces, and when he clicked them together, a joyful squeal erupted from Emma.

The little girl resembled her mother for sure but Gray was convinced the six-year-old behaved more like her Aunt Sami Jo. She certainly had a similar streak of confidence in her.

That defiant mask of the wild child he'd once known had visibly cracked when Sami Jo had noticed him standing on the porch. Her glare would've sliced right through him if he hadn't been distracted by her beauty. And while he'd expected the chilly greeting and the dismissive remarks, he hadn't expected how striking she'd be up close and personal. The photos and videos he'd recently perused online didn't do her justice.

Her long dark hair seemed to spill in waves over her

shoulders. She was tanned and toned yet he could still make out the curves under her loose-fitting dress. The fact that she was wearing a dress had caught him off-guard. When he'd met her years ago, she'd been a fresh-faced spitfire in t-shirts and sneakers. Now, she was all woman.

He'd quickly learned in his online search that she'd not only raced her way to the top of the male-dominated sport and garnered national sponsorships her first year out professionally but she'd also become a celebrity with a pretty volatile reputation. It was no secret men wanted to bed her and women most likely wanted to be her—or maybe kick her ass.

What gave him pause were the numerous gossip rag photos of Sami Jo on the arm of Alec Clarke. Clarke was your typical ass-shaking pop star who made teenage girls and their mothers scream in his presence. His songs were always on the top of the charts and he'd sold out his most recent tour.

Seeing Sami Jo with Clarke like that solidified that she'd gotten on with her life.

He'd chided himself for allowing it to bother him. What else could he expect? Anything less was downright silly.

Still, his initial reaction to seeing her now, mainly the stirring it caused in him, was starting to make him rethink why he took the job. It wasn't like Alliance was hurting for contract work. Hell, he couldn't even delegate the job to anyone on the team because they were so busy. He had no choice but to personally handle it.

Which was exactly what his uncle had requested when he had called with the heads-up that Royce McLean would be reaching out.

"Royce is a good friend. I wouldn't trust anyone but you to deal with it, Gray. Plus, it would be good to see you. It's been too long," John had said.

That was true. The last time he'd been in Myrtle Beach was the last time he'd not only seen Sami Jo but the last time he'd seen his relatives.

And how could he refuse his uncle? John had been financially and mentally supportive in Gray's recovery after the incident in Afghanistan five years ago when his team's peaceful withdrawal from the region ended with a missile taking out their helicopter. The impact had thrown Gray and several of his men into the water below. He could still feel the concussion of the air as the chopper exploded, the weight of his gear pulling him under as he had struggled to unload all of it, the panic of looking for the other men and only finding body parts among the blood-red water, along with the sound of enemy fire and the searing pain of the slug as it hit his shoulder.

John had orchestrated funding for Gray's hospitalization and rehab. He'd personally visited Gray for weeks at a time as he convalesced, keeping him from spiraling into a dark depression from losing most of his team. He'd even helped Gray start Alliance.

He owed Uncle John everything.

And he owed it to himself to make peace with the past. It had been years since he'd abandoned Sami Jo and yet his heart was still heavy with the way he'd left things.

All the time he'd spent in recovery had given him time to think about his transgressions toward a lot of people in his life—his relationship with his father, for one. But that would take some work to make right. And though he was slow to repair things in general, the one thing he could focus on was right here in front of him. The least he could do was keep Sami Jo and her family safe.

Movement in the doorway brought him back to reality.

He looked up to find Sami Jo watching them. She leaned against the doorjamb with her arms crossed as if she'd been there a while.

It was hard not to stare at her tattoos. The ink that snaked around her upper arm was damn sexy and sent signals south—signals he'd rather mind their own business.

"Aunt Sami Jo, look. It's a boat!" Emma ran up to her aunt.

James raced past Sami Jo with his helicopter, shouting behind him as he left the room. "Thanks, Mr. Finch."

Emma walked back to Gray and hugged him around his neck. "Thank you, Mr. Birdy." She giggled at her cleverness and skipped after James.

"Well, it looks like you're a hit with them," Sami Jo mused.

"I just snapped a few bricks together." He got up and brushed off his pants.

She stepped into the room and surveyed the toys on the floor. "Think you can make me a fort I can hide inside until this all blows over? Melanie is pretty pissed at me."

"I don't think we have enough pieces." He chuckled, then gave a sympathetic smile. "And your cousin is scared. Her way of dealing with it is to project her anger."

He crossed the room, assessing Sami Jo's concern, and squeezed her bare arm where the ink slid under the fabric of her dress.

"Don't worry, Hot Shot, we'll figure it out."

Touching her sent a surge of electricity through his body. Her skin was soft and warm, yet she seemed to tremble under his hand. He instantly released her, surprising himself by speaking the nickname he'd once given her. Even more so, that he'd thought it okay to use it or to touch her.

He stuffed his hands in his pockets.

"What's with the bandage?" he asked, nodding at her wrist.

"New ink," she said, her hazel eyes hypnotizing him.

He glanced away and got down to business before he asked where else she might have tattoos. "Someone from the sheriff's office will be here soon. Then I'd like to assess your home security system."

He left her standing there and went to find Royce.

———————

When Sheriff Ed Kovach arrived, Gray realized just how small-town Myrtle Beach could feel despite its population. The older lawman seemed to know Royce personally and practically treated him and Sami Jo like royalty.

There was no doubt McLean Racing was a big deal. The company employed over three dozen people, most holding positions as engine specialists, pit crew, or transportation services for the team and their cars. He'd learned as much from Royce that morning before Sami Jo arrived. The rest of the racing lifestyle, however, was a bit of a mystery to him.

The sheriff took Sami Jo's statement and got details from Gray on the lab that would perform forensics on the original photo. He gave the family some safety tips and was out the door in under an hour.

Gray then followed Sami Jo in his rented Escalade to her home just a few miles away. He was thankful for the V8 engine under the hood as he stepped on the gas pedal to keep up with her sports car over the winding highway to her place.

They arrived at her three-story beachfront home ten minutes later. Far from other houses, it featured yellow clapboard siding with decorative white storm shutters and wrap-around balconies with spectacular views of the ocean. It sat on top of a two-car garage and when the automatic door opened, Sami Jo pulled her Mustang next to a black SUV parked in the other spot.

Gray pulled onto the driveway and followed her up the stairs leading to the main door on the second level.

The open layout of her home was cozier than he'd expected.

Chocolate-colored furnishings in the living room were accented with gold and burgundy pillows. White pillars separated the area that opened to a country kitchen. A granite-top island was centered among stainless steel appliances and white wood cabinets.

"Do you want anything to drink?" Sami Jo opened her refrigerator. "I have bottled water and—well, bourbon, I guess."

"No thanks," Gray said, inspecting the main entrance.

"Suit yourself, I'm having the bourbon."

Gray walked to the balcony doors overlooking the beach. It was empty except for a few gulls picking food from the sand. He made a mental note of the lock on the French doors. "No alarm system?"

"Just the keypad on the garage entry door and the main door has a deadbolt. Never thought about it since the house is listed under an LLC. That way no one can look me up online and find out where I live."

"Mind if I take a look upstairs?"

"Go ahead," Sami Jo replied and swirled the liquor in her glass.

Gray headed up to the second floor. There were two guest bedrooms at the back of the house. One had been converted into a workout room complete with a treadmill and free weights. The other was simply decorated with sage-painted walls and a queen-sized bed with a matching dresser and armoire.

He briefly studied the surrealistic paintings that lined the hallway leading to the master suite before heading to her bedroom. It was painted in golden hues and he could smell the floral notes of perfume as he entered. Pillows of different sizes were stacked against the wrought-iron headboard of the king-sized bed and on the dresser were several framed photos.

In one, a racing suit-clad Chase McLean held a young Sami Jo on his shoulders as she raised a trophy over her

head. In another, a teenage Sami Jo hung out the window of a race car, flashing a thumbs up.

He scanned the various stages of her life in the photo-
graphs and couldn't help but notice the one of Royce's
late wife, Trudy, holding a young Sami Jo in her arms.
He didn't have to research the story there. He knew
the background. It was one of the first things Sami Jo
had shared with him when they'd met. Her mother had
died from cancer when she was three and when Chase
McLean had been killed in the accident, custody had
been given to Royce and Trudy.

His gaze was dragged away by another photo. One he'd
seen online. One that made him bristle.

In the photo, Sami Jo smiled seductively from the arm
of Alec Clarke at the American Music Awards. What she
wore made Jennifer Lopez's infamous Versace dress look
like a winter coat. It had been the talk of the internet for
weeks. Material that barely covered her was connected by
delicate golden chains that crisscrossed across her midriff.
The hem of the sheer skirt fell to her mid-thigh so her
legs seemed to go on for miles.

Clarke's mischievous expression corroborated every
hot-blooded male's secret fantasy. A fantasy Gray had
once had the chance to fulfill but hadn't.

He shook off the feeling and headed back downstairs,
where he found Sami Jo had taken up residence on the
leather sofa. Her legs were tucked to the side and the
dress she wore swirled high on her thighs.

Look away, pervert.

"You have a beautiful home, Sami Jo," he said as he
approached one of the accent chairs and sat.

"Thanks. It used to belong to my dad. I lived here as a
kid but Royce sold it after I went to live with him and
Trudy."

"Yes, I remember you telling me—"

—all about your life the night we met. The night you took

me for a ride around your uncle's dirt track and I kissed you for the first time.

She gave a gentle shrug. "I probably paid three times what my dad bought it for thirty years ago but it was worth it. I've always loved it here."

"The view is pretty amazing." He pulled out his phone to take notes on it. "Let's talk about your schedule. What do most days look like?"

"Depends. Fridays and Saturdays are for activities leading to Sunday's race. During the week, I try to take a day or two to decompress, but sometimes I have appearances. Our PR department—well, Diane—she handles everything for the team. This week I have a meet-and-greet in Miami and then we're off to Kansas City for a race but Diane would have all the details."

"Normally, I'd advise against public appearances because they can be a security nightmare but your uncle has made it clear you have obligations to your sponsors. I'll meet with Diane when I head over to your uncle's office. We can go over the itinerary and sync up my flight arrangements."

"*Your* flight?"

"You can't go alone, Sami Jo."

He could tell she was working through what that meant.

"The purpose of security detail is to follow you around and keep you safe," Gray said.

"And *you're* going with me? You don't have someone else at your company to do those sorts of things?"

"Your uncle hired me personally."

"Yeah, well, he doesn't know that we—" She stopped mid-sentence as if she was searching for the right words.

"Sami Jo, it was a couple of weeks of watching movies and making out. I think we can put it behind us, don't you?"

That didn't quite come out as he'd intended and it was

clear his words had agitated her.

She threw her hands up. "You're right. It was a blip on the radar. I'm just surprised you'd volunteer."

Gray proceeded to type a few notes on his phone, surprised by how easy it was to convince her. *A blip—*

"Royce said you were forced to retire from the military. What happened?"

Gray's thumbs stilled over his cellphone. "I was injured coming back from a mission."

Her silence indicated she wanted to hear more but he wasn't about to dive into that clusterfuck of a story. He tucked the phone in his pocket and stood.

"I need to head over to your uncle's office. Don't go anywhere unless I'm with you. Got it?"

"What if I have plans later?"

Gray headed for the door and produced a business card.

"Call me first." He set the card on the kitchen island. "And, it better not to be to go shoe shopping or something trivial like that."

He didn't even look back at her as he walked out the door but he imagined she was glaring at him again.

LAP FOUR

"SHE'S AT MCLEAN RACING, MR. Finch."
Diane Quaid, the PR Director, had called Gray the next morning just as he'd requested.

He couldn't say he was surprised Sami Jo had gone against his instructions to call him if she needed to leave the house—he'd almost expected it.

Typical indifference to authority—he could write a book on it. He could appreciate the resilience and self-confidence some athletes had; he'd felt it as a SEAL.

Plus, he knew Sami Jo.

Determined was a word that came to mind when describing her. Even in the short time they'd spent together back when she was barely eighteen, he'd witnessed how headstrong she could be and not much had changed. Now, she was in the big leagues for the first time in her life, and despite the Vegas incident and the threatening photos, he figured she must still be feeling pretty untouchable right now.

When Gray arrived at McLean Racing, he entered through the showroom where two display vehicles were parked. He pushed through the glass doors into the reception area, nodded to the girl behind the desk, and made his way into the main office. A few heads popped up from the low-walled cubicles that filled most of the room.

Diane's desk was closest to the doors and the middle-aged woman sat in a McLean Racing button-down typing away at her computer as she cradled a phone between her ear and shoulder. She smiled up at him as he passed by.

Yesterday afternoon, she'd been very helpful with scheduling time for him to interview most of the employees. Thanks to some background assistance from his partner, Cole Donovan, who was back in Alliance's Chicago office, Gray was able to weed out most of the internal threats that might be on the business side. Today, he planned on meeting with the two other drivers on the team.

But first, he had to deal with *Little Miss I-Don't-Follow-The-Rules*.

The hallway that led to McLean Racing's main conference room was lined with framed headshots of the current and past team members. As Gray approached the room, Matt Burton's voice could be heard through the open door.

Gray had spent some time with Burton yesterday as well. Once a leading driver for McLean Racing, he had been sidelined from his racing career by multiple concussions as a result of several accidents on the track.

Matt had admitted his relationship with Royce had experienced some friction when he and Melanie first started dating—she was, after all, the boss's daughter. Now, the trust between the two men was as strong as ever. Matt was fully invested in the task of running the organization once Royce retired. He indicated, however, that the past several years had been hard on the business. Attendance at the tracks had gone down—the cost of tickets and travel for a typical fan was extraordinary, especially if they had a family to support. And while many tracks had recently innovated the experience by installing new in-field courses to attract fans again, other factors weighed heavily on McLean Racing.

One of their drivers had jumped to another team at the end of their contract last year because they'd been unable to command big-name sponsorships. They'd also seen a dip in bonus money due to the team slipping in rank.

Some of that was changing for the better, thanks to Sami Jo. Her wins coupled with her popularity were helping move the needle but it wouldn't completely turn the business around for another two to three years.

"See number forty and six?" Matt asked. "They always catch up with you in the last ten laps because you're not paying attention even though we're shouting into your headset. You gotta think, Sami Jo."

"The minute I start thinking, I'll slow down," she responded.

Gray rounded the corner to see Sami Jo's high pony-tail peeking over the top of the high-back leather chair closest to the door.

"Well, they almost passed you because you left that opening. You got lucky." Burton paused the video and pointed to the area on the big screen with the remote. When he turned around, he spotted Gray standing in the doorway. "Oh, hey, Gray."

Sami Jo didn't budge.

That's right, you're busted.

"Morning, Matt. Mind if I take a few minutes of Sami Jo's time?" he asked. "And can you tell Ray Skinner I'm here?"

"Sure thing," Matt replied. "I think we're done here anyway."

Matt exited and Gray shut the door.

He rounded the eight-foot laminate table to see Sami Jo slouched in the chair. In a faded Guns 'N Roses shirt and worn-out jeans, she looked like the eighteen-year-old girl he'd met many summers ago. She studied her manicure as if she hadn't a care in the world.

He crossed his arms. "Is this how it's gonna be?"

"How what's 'gonna be?'"

"I told you not to leave your house without letting me know."

"What can I say, Gray? I forgot. I'm not used to having my every move approved."

He held his breath for a second and dug the tips of his fingers into the area where he'd been shot to massage the ache. He knew damn well she didn't forget and based on Matt's comments, her life on and off the track was scrutinized.

"Is there something wrong with your shoulder?" she asked, surprising him with the question. "You seem to rub it a lot."

Who's busted now?

He looked down and pulled his hand away. It was practically second nature; half the time he didn't realize he was doing it.

"It's where I was wounded."

Bullshit. That slug almost took your arm clean off.

"Listen, I have a few interviews while I'm here then the alarm system technicians are meeting us back at your place," he said.

"I have to go over the itinerary with Diane for Miami anyway." She stood and turned to leave.

"Sami Jo?"

She slowly faced him.

Yep, eighteen and obstinate all over again.

"Listen, I understand you think the idea of a bodyguard is silly. I'm sure the last thing you want is someone following you around. Until we figure out some things, how about you let me do my job?" he asked. "For this to work, I need to be able to trust you."

She stared at him for several moments, then her shoulders dropped slightly. "Fine."

Gray tempered his desire to produce an exasperated sigh as she exited the conference room. She'd already proved to be a handful and he was not looking forward to this Miami trip with her. Maybe he'd talk to Royce about it. Get him to convince her to stay locked in her room for the entire trip.

Fat chance and you know it.

No one probably told Sami Jo what to do.

A knock on the doorframe diverted his thoughts.

"Mr. Finch? I'm Ray Skinner."

Lanky and tan in a t-shirt and jeans, Skinner had a face that showed three decades of hard living. Deep creases surrounded his eyes and thin lips, and inches of gray collected at his temples. Cole's research had provided some truth behind the race car driver's *good old boy* reputation—an endearing quality if you asked his fans. However, Skinner had been prone to fist-fights with other drivers, even with some of his teammates. He'd also been married and divorced three times due to his inability to keep it in his pants. Still, he had been unbeatable in his early years, had helped build McLean's empire, and was a considerable talent on the tracks.

Skinner extended his hand to Gray as they sat down.

"Thanks for taking the time," Gray said.

"Not a problem. I have to tell you, word has gotten around that you're investigating some pictures sent to Sami Jo. I imagine that's why we're here."

"It is. I didn't think it would be kept a secret for very long, but if you wouldn't mind keeping our conversation to yourself and not talking to the press about any of this, I'd surely appreciate it."

"Absolutely." Skinner held his hands up in submission. "Wouldn't want to put Sami Jo in any danger."

"How would you describe your relationship with Sami Jo?"

"It's good. We're not the best of buds if that's what you're asking." The right side of Skinner's mouth turned up. "Hell, I'm almost fifty. It's not like we hang in the same circles."

"You've been driving with McLean for most of your career?" Gray asked, already knowing the answer.

"Yes, sir. In my early days, I ran with a small outfit that was bought out. I didn't like the way the new owners were running things and I guess you could say I was pretty vocal about it. Around that same time, I met Chase McLean. He invited me to meet with him and his brother, Royce, to talk about joining their team."

Gray nodded. "You knew Chase well, then?"

"Sure did." Skinner's expression turned somber. "Was actually on the track the day he lost his life."

"You've known Sami Jo since she was little?"

"I used to watch her drive around the dirt track behind the building here. She has the same racing bug her daddy did."

"And how do you feel about her surpassing you on the track and winning all the awards?"

"Are you asking if I'm pissed about it?" He chuckled. "Well sure, I'm pissed. I'm being unseated by a younger driver—a younger *woman* driver to boot. No one likes to lose, no matter how many times they've won because victories never get old. But I'll tell you something, I couldn't be happier to see Chase's kid out there. It's a testament to his legacy and I'm sure he's smiling down on her from heaven right now."

Gray asked a few more pointed questions but Skinner's body language and answers indicated he didn't know much. He wrapped up the interview asking Skinner to keep an eye out for anything suspicious and gave him his card.

As Skinner went to leave the conference room, a younger man in a bright blue McLean Racing polo and khakis entered.

Skinner clapped him on the shoulder. "Hey Luke, good timing. This is Mr. Finch." Skinner nodded toward Gray and headed out the door.

Where Skinner may have looked rough and worn, Luke Dillon was quite the opposite. Baby-faced and clean-shaven, he was the type the ladies fell all over themselves for. According to Cole, he had a clean record but certainly wasn't a top performer on the team.

"Mr. Finch, let me start by saying I'm concerned about Sami Jo. Whatever you need me to do, you can count on it." Dillon's teeth gleamed as he spoke.

"Thanks, Luke. How about you tell me who's sending her pictures?"

Dillon's response was textbook shock. It seemed genuine as far as Gray could tell.

"I—I have no idea."

It was also obvious that Dillon wasn't necessarily the brightest bulb on the team.

"Take a seat, Mr. Dillon. Tell me, are you close with Sami Jo?" Gray asked.

"We're friends, but she keeps mostly to herself these days. She's super focused so I think she's aiming for rookie of the year." Dillon paused, and looked down at his shoes, stuffing his hands into the pockets of his pants. "I should probably come clean and tell you because you'll find out eventually, but Sami Jo and I used to date."

Gray stiffened. This wasn't in any of the research.

"It was a few years ago," Dillon said.

"Who broke up with who?" Gray asked more out of curiosity than to uncover a motive.

"It was amicable—I think that's the word. We were both busy working our way up through the lower series races. Neither one of us could put the effort into the relationship. Plus, she's with that singer now. He's probably much more her type."

Gray pushed past the desire to ask Dillon more questions about their relationship and focused on some of the same things he had asked Skinner. Once he'd finished with Dillon and sent him on his way, he reached into his pocket to retrieve his cellphone.

The text he sent Cole Donovan was short and sweet.

Skinner and Dillon interviews complete. Text you when we get to Miami.

———

"Diane, why did you have to call him?"

Sami Jo sat on top of the desk across the aisle from her PR director and swung her legs.

The defiance of leaving her house that morning without Gray's permission had worn off. It wasn't as liberating as she'd hoped and now if anything, she felt childish for doing it. She just couldn't find the courage to call him and had allowed herself this one indiscretion because she was only coming here to meet with Matt.

"Try not to give Mr. Finch a hard time, Sami Jo." Diane tucked a pen behind her ear and stacked some papers on her desk.

Sami Jo studied the silver strands that had weaved their way through Diane's dark-blonde bob. Other than a few wrinkles around her eyes, the woman looked the same as she did when she started working as a secretary for McLean Racing over three decades ago. Never married, Diane's life was running the office. She operated it like a well-oiled machine and had been managing Sami Jo's schedule since her days on the amateur circuit. She'd remained a close friend of the family and was a confidant to Royce. Of course, she tattled when Sami Jo had shown up at the office without her bodyguard.

"I hope you at least put him in coach and on another floor at the hotel." Sami stretched her legs out in front of her.

"Seats 4 A and B and you have an adjoining suite."

"You're joking, right?"

"Afraid not."

Gray's voice made her jump but Diane was all smiles.

As Gray walked toward them it drummed up a memory of his arrival in Myrtle Beach years back when she and Gemma had been sitting on one of the town square benches, chatting about how they were going to spend their summer. Gemma had leaped into Gray's arms when he'd approached them, while Sami Jo could only sit there with her mouth hanging open.

He was gorgeous. Tall and muscular, he'd made all her high school guy friends look like children. His angled features and massive chest had drawn her in but it was his smile and mesmerizing eyes that had hooked her.

When Gemma had introduced him as her cousin who was staying in Myrtle Beach for a few weeks while he was on leave, Sami Jo had barely squeaked out a hello. His half-smile had sent butterflies coursing through her veins as he had stared directly at her under that warm Carolina sun.

His current expression, however, was quite the opposite. They conveyed his annoyance with her.

He walked past her and claimed a folder from Diane's outstretched hand. His eyes scanned the papers inside before he tucked it under his arm.

"Thank you, Diane. Everything looks perfect. Can you please email a copy of everything to my office?"

"Sure thing, Mr. Finch. Just make sure you're both at the airport by nine a.m. tomorrow. You both have TSA pre-check but you can't be certain the lines won't be long. And the car service will pick you up in Miami when you land."

Diane's voice was syrupy sweet, and Sami Jo wanted to crawl under the desk and barf.

"I'll make sure we're on time." He turned to Sami Jo.

"Shall we?"

Sami Jo slid off the desk and followed him to the door without a word.

"I'll be right behind you in my truck," Gray said, holding the door open for her.

"Are you sure you can keep up?" she quipped and put on her sunglasses.

He gave her the slightest smirk and walked to his vehicle.

The rumble of her Mustang didn't come close to her race car, but she welcomed the focus and the solitude for the ride home.

As she pulled onto the highway, she glanced into the rear-view mirror and saw the black escalade behind her. Her finger jabbed at the button to turn on the stereo. Heavy drum beats filled the interior of her car along with Nicki Minaj's rapped lyrics she knew by heart. It was a song she and Melanie would often sing along to and it reminded her that her cousin still wasn't answering her calls or texts.

The two had grown up like sisters, and while back in the day they'd fought as all families do, it was over borrowed clothes and which movie to see. Nothing quite as severe as this situation. She missed having her "girlfriend"—a role Mel had filled after Sami Jo's friendship with Gemma had dissolved, ruined that summer several years ago by her raging hormones, and messed up priorities to be with Gray.

And what an ugly fallout it had been with Gemma. Sami Jo had run right to her with her broken heart and was met with such disdain—Gemma pretty much slammed the door in her face and that was the last time they'd spoken.

She had to wonder what Gemma would think about her being involved with Gray again.

You're not involved, he's just working for Royce.

As Sami Jo pulled up to her house, several men were exiting two vans with alarm system company logos on the side. Royce's pickup was parked in the driveway and he paced the length of his truck as he talked on the phone.

After parking in the garage, she stepped out onto the driveway and shielded her eyes from the sun. "Who's with Mel and the kids?" she asked Royce, who had just pocketed his cell.

"Matt just got there. Go on inside, I'll be up in a minute," Royce said.

Uninterested in spending any more time with Gray than necessary, she headed upstairs and into her kitchen.

While the bourbon bottle tempted her, it wasn't quite noon, so she opted for the sweet tea she'd made late last night. It wasn't like she could sleep. The red-splotched photo had tormented her every time she'd closed her eyes. Plus, seeing Gray looking the way he did wasn't helping either. Her mind had insisted on going places she didn't want to revisit.

After Gray had stalked out of her house yesterday, she'd called Alec Clarke as Royce had suggested. She told him what was going on and would've called him now to calm her nerves but he was probably sleeping off last night's show.

Alec was her best friend outside of Melanie. Possibly, her only real friend.

No one has ever made my toes curl like Grayson Finch, she'd admitted to him early on in their relationship because truth be told, as much as she loved Alec, he wasn't her boyfriend.

It had been a setup. A blind date of sorts. A business proposal between Alec's team and Royce. At first, she was against the idea. But, after meeting Alec on their first "date" two years ago, they'd hit it off over dinner then went back to his hotel room. While she'd admit he was good-looking, she hadn't felt a romantic connection, so nothing had happened that night. With her lifestyle, she didn't want the complexity of a man in her life. At least that's what she told herself and that was why Alec was perfect.

If anything, they'd realized almost immediately they were kindred spirits and talked into the early morning hours about family dramas, what motivated them to succeed, and how they manage their celebrity lifestyles. They'd connected as friends because, in their industries, people you could trust were few and far between.

Still, her undeserved "walk of shame" for the cameras parked outside the hotel the next morning sent the media into a frenzy. They'd agreed to play along. Their non-romance would be their little secret.

The front door opened and Royce let himself in.

"Want some?" she asked, holding up the pitcher as he entered the kitchen.

"Please. It's hotter than Hades out there." Royce pulled out a stool at the island and sat. He removed his sunglasses and pulled a bandana from his back pocket to wipe his face. "Can't believe those boys are gonna install anything in this heat."

"You don't remember it being a hundred and thirty degrees inside a damn race car?"

"Good point," he replied and reached for the glass she'd poured.

She set the pitcher by the sink and turned back to the island to sit across from him. "How's Mel?"

Royce took a long drink and let out an exasperated sigh. "Oh, well, you know Mel. She's worrying."

"I tried calling her."

"She'll come around. Just give her some time to assimilate the situation, Sami Jo. Now, let's talk about Miami." Royce paused and focused on the glass in front of him. "Sweetheart, I know how you like to go and hang out with your people—"

"I won't have *people* there. I'm the only driver. Everyone else will be representing other sports."

"Yes but you and I both know you tend to, well, gravitate toward the spotlight. Just get in and get out of there without causing too much trouble for Grayson."

"Did Gray say something to you? Because I don't need him getting in the way of me trying to do my job."

"Partying isn't your job," he said sharply. "Racing is. Nowhere in the contract does it say you need to stay after the event. I don't want a repeat of Vegas."

"Well, neither do I. And with that six-foot shadow you have me tied to I don't think you have anything to worry about."

"Good." Royce set down his glass. "Talk to me about your time with Matt this morning."

Gladly.

She updated him on the videos they'd reviewed and Matt's suggestions.

Royce nodded in agreement with the strategies for the next race. "His approach is aggressive but with the way we're tuning the car, I have no doubt you'll qualify top five for sure."

"Top five?" Her mouth hung open.

"You'll do fine, kiddo." Royce winked.

Just as she started to rebuke her uncle for patronizing her, the front door opened and Gray entered.

Her face flushed at the sight of him walking through her kitchen as if it were commonplace.

"Grayson, you have to have some of Sami Jo's sweet tea." Royce lifted his glass. "It's just like her Aunt Trudy used to make."

"That sounds great," Gray replied.

Sami Jo slid reluctantly from her seat and retrieved another glass while Royce made small talk. All she could hear was her heart pounding in her ears as she opened the freezer and managed to put a few ice cubes in the glass.

The race. The photo. The Vegas incident. It all flashed in her mind like a flipbook of pictures and when she turned around, she bumped right into Gray who was standing behind her holding the pitcher.

Clumsily, she tried to swap with him and their hands touched briefly. She hoped her reaction didn't look like she'd just been electrocuted as she poured tea into his glass.

"Grayson, have you had a chance to spend time with your uncle and the rest of the family yet?" Royce asked.

"Not yet," he answered before he took a drink. "This is good."

"Thank you," she said. "What are those guys going to do to my house?"

"They're installing a few cameras with motion sensors, access point alarms, and a keypad by your entry doors. You'll be able to access the cameras on your cellphone."

"Hi-tech. That's good," Royce chimed in.

"How long will it take?" she asked.

"It won't all be done today but they'll be here at least a few hours. Any chance you have more of this?" Gray held up his glass. "It would be a nice gesture since they fit you in on such short notice."

"I'm sure Sami Jo would be happy to make more." Royce smiled widely.

"Royce, I can show you some of the technology they use if you want to come down to the van," Gray said.

Royce got up from his seat. "Sami Jo, you get to that tea. I might need another glass when we come back in."

After they left, Sami Jo gave them a snarky two-fingered salute. As much as she wanted to bark back at his orders, she'd rather stay busy making sweet tea than learn the ins and outs of security systems—or have to talk to Gray.

How the hell was she gonna make it through the next few days in Miami with him?

LAP FIVE

I N ALL HONESTY, NOT EVEN the bright Florida sun could temper Sami Jo's tensions.

The humidity was a suffocating blanket as she stepped through the sliding doors of Miami International's departure gate but it sure was good to get out and do something after being trapped on a plane for two hours with Grayson Finch.

"The car should be waiting for us just ahead." Gray put his sunglasses on as he walked alongside her with his carry-on in tow.

It was the most he'd said to her all morning but in his defense, she'd kept her earbuds in since they'd left the house. Just because they were traveling together didn't mean she had to make small talk. She was perfectly fine playing her part as the client.

When he had shown up at her place earlier that morning in a polo and jeans, she assumed he attempted to blend in as her companion. The expanse of his chest alone would scare away anyone interested in harming her, no matter what he wore. And it unnerved her because he also looked every bit as handsome as he had the other day.

They approached a black Lincoln Navigator parked

alongside the arrivals curb and Sami Jo smiled politely at the driver as he helped her with her bag. She then took a seat in the back of the SUV and sent a quick text to Diane letting her know they were on their way to the hotel.

Premium Sports had reserved rooms at the South Beach Loews and she couldn't wait to slip out of her yoga pants and go have a drink by the pool. The butter-flies she'd had around Gray at eighteen-years-old were rookies compared to the giant hummingbirds wreaking havoc in her stomach and she needed to unwind.

To distract herself, she called Alec.

"Hey, babe," he answered.

"Hey, I just wanted to let you know I made it to Miami. Pretty steamy here."

"Ah, you jumped into bed with him as I suggested," Alec snickered.

"Alec!" Her gaze darted over to Gray who seemed preoccupied with his phone. When she'd spoken to Alec yesterday about her anxiety traveling with Gray, he'd pro-posed she pursue what she'd missed out on and finally have sex with him.

"I'm kidding," he said, laughing.

"How was the show last night?"

"It was good. Great crowd. Hey, I'm sorry to cut this short but I'm about to get on the bus to—ah, hell, I have no idea where our next stop is. Everything else okay?"

"Yes, fine. I'll text you later," she said. "Miss you."

"Same here," Alec said and hung up.

Sami Jo turned her music back on and checked her watch. In twenty-four hours from now, they'd be heading back to the airport. It seemed like such a long time from now and she prayed it went fast.

After Gray checked them in at the hotel, they headed to their rooms. He entered her suite first and did a quick sweep of the spacious room. The living room was sectioned off by a partial wall and beyond it was the bed-room. Sami Jo entered went and set her carry-on on top of the folding luggage rack next to the foot of the king-sized bed.

"I'm going to head next door and get settled," he said, pausing by the adjoining door to unlock it.

She grunted in response and unzipped her bag.

Once he'd left, she exhaled and processed just how sur-real things were.

She needed that drink.

She grabbed some things out of her carry-on bag and stepped into the bathroom. A large jacuzzi tub took up half the room and she instantly envisioned Gray in it, naked and surrounded by foamy bubbles.

Furious with herself for even going there, she busied herself by organizing her makeup and hair products on the counter next to the sink. She pulled her hair up in a clip and changed into her one-piece black bathing suit and a sheer cover-up. When she exited the bathroom, she found Gray standing in the living area by the sofa, still dressed in his jeans and polo.

"I'd like to go to the pool," Sami Jo announced as she slipped into black and white checkered flip-flops.

"This isn't a vacation, Sami Jo. You're here for business."

"Business starts later. I want to have lunch and I need some fresh air."

Without waiting for him to comment, Sami Jo picked up her tote and walked toward the suite door.

Gray caught up with her and his arm shot out to hold the door shut.

"Come on, Gray. I need this. I've been locked in the house for the last two days." She held his gaze as she put on her oversized sunglasses. "No one will even recognize me."

He slowly removed his hand from the door. "I'll just be a few minutes."

The suffocating feeling he provoked in her lifted as he stalked into his room.

Adjusting the strap of her tote, she opened her door and headed to the elevator.

The Loews' outdoor pool was filled with people enjoying the beautiful Miami weather as high-energy dance music played through speakers scattered around the patio area.

A young man from the pool concierge greeted her at the entrance and offered to find her a seat. She asked for two, knowing Gray would join her eventually and the attendant directed her over to a pair of chaise lounge chairs covered with extra-large towels.

Sami Jo inhaled the warm ocean air, tossed her tote on the ground, and sat down.

"Well, look who's here," a male voice said.

Sami Jo turned to see Danny Welliver, from TV's *Sports Scoop*, walking up behind her. Welliver hosted the number-one sports talk show on the Victory Network, and despite his tough questions, he was well-respected by his peers and the athletes he interviewed. He was casually dressed in a polo, his show's logo on the chest pocket peeking out from behind the strap of his messenger bag.

"Hey, Danny. Here for the event?" she asked.

"Wouldn't miss it," he said, running a hand through his wavy brown hair. "Would you like to join me for lunch?"

"Thanks, Danny. But I'm waiting for someone. Guess I'll see you tonight."

"You bet. Good to see you, Sami Jo. Don't forget to use your sunscreen," he said, smiling as he waved and walked away.

Sami Jo laid back on the chaise and closed her eyes.

Welliver was nice but he always had an agenda. No doubt he'd turn their casual lunch into some sort of interview and she didn't have the brain capacity to deal with it before tonight's event.

While she'd done enough meet and greets over the last year to know tonight should be a no-brainer, she was distracted by Gray's presence and worried he would affect her ability to be herself with the attendees. The last thing she wanted was for Gray to see her off her game. She wanted to show him she wasn't the wayward teen who once fell all over him. She'd grown up. She was successful. She was winning races, owned her own home, and had her shit together—well, sort of.

So why did she feel like at any second all her vulnerabilities would be revealed? Was it the photo? PTSD from Vegas? Could Gray see right through her tough image? Could he tell how fragile she felt right now?

"Penny for your thoughts." Gray's deep voice startled her.

Her eyes shot open to find him towering over her in beige shorts and a blue t-shirt, his large frame blocking out the sun. She ignored his remark as well as his muscular legs.

"You must be working through something. That deep crease between your eyebrows was always was a telltale sign." Gray took a seat on the other chaise.

"It's just bright out here," she remarked and raised her finger at a slim, blonde waitress in a Loew's uniform.

The waitress took their orders, and while Gray asked for water with a lime, Sami Jo ordered a run-based frozen drink and considered asking to make it a double.

"Who was the guy you were talking to?" Gray nodded in the direction Welliver had walked.

"He hosts a show on one of the racing channels. He's here to cover the event and stopped by to say hello."

"So much for being unrecognizable. Going forward, I'd like you to wait for me," he muttered.

She ignored his comment. "Anything come up with that photo yet?"

"No, I didn't expect them to find anything," he said.

"These days most people know how to avoid getting caught. You'd be surprised how many of these things go unsolved."

"Well, that's reassuring. You know, I don't think the company can afford your services indefinitely. What's the plan?"

"One of two things will happen, Sami Jo. Either this guy will get bored and go away or he'll do something stupid and get caught."

The waitress dropped off their drinks as Sami Jo contemplated what he'd said.

"Like what, accidentally leave prints on the next photo?" She sipped her drink and tasted the sweetness of the rum.

"No," Gray answered. "More like he'll come after you."

Sami Jo swallowed quickly. The icy drink scratched her throat on the way down.

"Jesus, Gray. Do you have to be dramatic?"

"I've seen it happen. This is why I keep telling you to stay put and stop running off without me. This isn't some sort of game, Sami Jo. The guy followed you to the mountains. Why you went alone is beyond me but you should just assume you're always being watched."

Behind his dark sunglasses, his furrowed brow suggested his seriousness.

Man, he had an uncanny way of making her feel like a senseless teen.

"Did you inform your boyfriend?" Gray asked.

She had wondered how long it would take for that topic to come up.

"Yes, Alec knows. He's on tour, but his security detail is always with him."

After a few moments, Gray said, "That's got to be an interesting relationship."

"How so?"

"I imagine when two people's lives are that publicized,

it's got to be hard to have any semblance of a normal relationship. Not to mention the long-distance thing. With your schedules, when do you have time to see each other?"

"We do just fine."

"I'm just saying, you're doing your thing, he's on tour. How do you know he's not out there screwing around?"

She sat up and swung her legs over the side of the chaise to face him. She wasn't about to give him the benefit of explaining things. "Our relationship isn't as complicated as everyone likes to think."

"And how about Luke Dillon? Was that one complicated? Is that why it ended?" Gray asked.

She glared at him, feeling her blood boil.

"Wow, you've done your homework on me. Let's just say Luke was only good for one thing—and that got old."

She yanked the clip out of her hair, chucked it into her tote, and stood. Pulling off her sunglasses and coverup, she left them on the chaise and walked over to the edge of the pool. As she dove in, the cool water was a slap to her warmed skin, but she quickly acclimated to the water. When she resurfaced, she pushed the water from her face and waded over to the shallow side, opposite from their seats.

What the serious hell?

Leaning back against the ledge, she closed her eyes and let the sun bathe over her still-heated face.

Where did he get off talking to her like that? And how did she find out about Luke?

Knowing Dillon, he probably bragged about it to Gray. There was still some regret in her heart that Luke ended up being the one to take her virginity right after Gray had left. Luke had just joined her uncle's team and she'd been feeling pretty vulnerable.

She'd lied to Gray about Luke being "good for one thing"—sex with him was mediocre at best. That wasn't why she broke up with him. Luke just wasn't mentally stimulating enough for her. Sure, he was good-looking but she couldn't stand trying to have a conversation with him. It was like talking to a lane marker on the track.

Sami Jo had also seen pretty quickly that when it came to Luke, it would be impossible to be in a relationship with him and be dominating on the track. Which was exactly what she was doing now. Luckily, Luke seemed supportive of her wins as a fellow teammate but she knew if she'd still been dating him, he would've tried to undermine her determination to win.

When she opened her eyes, she scanned over to an elevated deck across the patio where a group of twenty-somethings chatted excitedly. Among their smiling faces was a man whose muscles bulging under his tank top. His thick blonde hair was pulled back and based on his looks, she surmised he was also there for the event.

He caught her eye and it didn't take long for him to make his way over to her. As he neared, he became vaguely familiar, she just couldn't place his face.

"Hi there." He crouched by the edge of the pool, the corner of his mouth turned up.

"Hello." She smiled back and wondered if Gray was monitoring the interaction and contemplating her safety.

Of course, he is. It's his job to "make sure nothing happens."

"Would you like to join us? We have more food than we know what to do with."

Sami Jo headed over to the shallow end's set of stairs and grasped the railing. "Are you here for the Premium Sports event?"

"I am." He retrieved a clean towel from a nearby bin and handed it to her. "Chris Stevens."

"The wrestler?"

He chuckled. "You've heard of me?"

"My nephew is a huge fan."

Recognition spread across his face. "Wait a sec, you're

that race car driver."

"Sami Jo McLean." She extended her hand.

Chris took it and didn't let go. "Oh my God, no way." He turned and led her to the deck. "You guys, look who this is!"

As they entered the area, he grabbed a beer out of a cooler and handed it to her.

"My nephew is going to freak out when he finds out I met you," she said to Chris after he had introduced her to some of the others.

"We'll have to get a picture together." He glanced across the pool and lowered his voice. "Did I take you away from your boyfriend?"

"No. It's embarrassing to admit but that's my body-guard."

Chris put his hand up to his massive chest. "Oh, well, pardon me. I didn't realize you were *that* big of a deal."

"It's sort of ridiculous."

"I could see why someone would want to protect you." Chris grinned and stepped closer to her. "I wouldn't let you out of my sight for a minute."

"Now *you're* ridiculous," she laughed.

As she made small talk with everyone, she discovered most of the group were athletes there for the event or guests of someone attending. The women were especially interested in her career in racing and she shared a few amusing anecdotes about her mostly-male teammates.

"Why don't you go ask your friend there if he'd like to join us?" Chris said to her and nodded toward Gray. "I mean, the man has to eat, right?"

She had wanted to grab her cover-up anyway so she left the deck and made her way over to Gray.

"Come join us. They have food." She slipped the cov-er-up over her head.

"I'm fine here."

Sami Jo put on her sunglasses. "Get over yourself, Finch,

and come eat."

To her surprise, Gray joined them. When Chris shook Gray's hand, Sami Jo had to wonder if Gray could take him. They were both imposing men but Chris was huge.

As she scarfed down a mini-burger, she watched two blonde women in bikinis approach Gray as he filled his plate. They tried to make small talk but something he said drove them away pretty quickly.

"Hey, man, you don't mind taking our picture, do you?" Chris presented his phone to Gray. "Hang on, I have an idea."

Chris scooped Sami Jo up in his arms. She let out a squeal and put her arm around his broad shoulders.

"Okay, now we're ready," Chris laughed.

There was no mistaking the scowl on Gray's face as he took the picture but Stevens didn't seem to notice.

"You're such a handful," Chris whispered into her ear before setting her down. "What's your number? I'll text you the pictures." Chris retrieved his phone from Gray and punched at the screen as she told him.

Sami Jo pulled her phone out of her tote as it buzzed in her hand. The text from Chris popped up along with an appointment reminder. "Damn, I have to meet with the stylist soon. I better get going."

"I'll see you tonight then?" Chris grinned and his gaze slid from her eyes down to her lips.

"I'll look for you."

She waved goodbye to the others and led Gray toward the hotel.

Inside the elevator, she scrolled to the picture Chris sent. "James is going to lose his mind when he sees this. Chris is one of his favorite wrestlers."

Gray grunted his acknowledgment and followed her off the elevator. He did a quick sweep once they were back in her room.

"I'll be back at seven-fifteen to get you." He turned and

left through the adjoining door without even a goodbye.

Sami Jo stared after him.

Let it go. He's just doing his job.

If his job were to be a massive jerk, he was killing it.

For a minute, she thought that maybe she should just behave. Maybe his attitude would change.

The invisible devil on her shoulder nudged her a bit.

LAP SIX

FAMILIAR CHIMES EMITTED FROM GRAY'S cell on the bedside table in his hotel room.

He hit a button to put the call on speaker and continued dressing.

"Hey, buddy. How's Miami?" Cole Donovan's friendly tone barely cracked Gray's frown.

"Hot as hell," he remarked as he put on his crisp black dress shirt.

"Yeah, well, try to remember the lure of tropical locations is part of the business plan. Florida is just one step away from a detail in the Bahamas. I already have the press release written up just in case it happens." Cole altered his voice to that of an announcer. *"Handsome co-owners of Alliance Security take company international by opening a new office in Nassau."*

Gray ignored Cole's chatter and got down to business. "Anything I should know?"

"I dug deeper into Premium Sports. They're legit and pretty successful at putting together these meet-and-greets. And the venue is basically like a small warehouse. Hey, did you know people will pay a thousand bucks just to press the flesh with their favorite sports celebs?"

Gray grunted his opinion but it certainly astounded

him that anyone would spend that much money just to meet another human being. He didn't see the draw. He'd worked with celebrities, had gotten a peek inside their crazy lives. They certainly weren't like the rest of the world. The majority of them were unable to handle the repercussions of wealth and he'd seen first-hand what it could do to a person.

"Did you find anything on the wrestler?" he asked as he stepped into slate-colored dress pants.

"Stevens? He's pretty clean. Been on the circuit for about five years. He's one of their bigger stars if that's what you'd call them. No arrests, although, he's got a bit of a reputation."

Gray's fingers stilled on the zipper of his pants. "Reputation?"

"He's a bit of a man-whore when it comes to the ladies. Recently, a girlfriend caught Stevens *in flagrante delicto* with another woman, went ape shit on his new Corvette, and landed herself in jail. He didn't press charges, though. Nice of him, I guess."

Yeah, a real humanitarian.

Gray shrugged into his shoulder holster. "He's showed interest in our client. Thanks for checking."

"I mean, you guys have only been there, what, like a few hours?" Cole laughed. "Damn, he works fast."

"Yeah, well, our client isn't exactly an angel." Gray pushed his fingers through his hair.

Based on the looks she was sharing with Stevens, Sami Jo was quite the opposite of angelic. So far he'd learned having a boyfriend might not be a deterrent to amusing herself with some 'roid junkie who'd been sizing her up like she was his next conquest.

This was exactly what he wanted to avoid.

Protecting clients who interacted with the public could be a tricky business. It made it more difficult when the client had no regard for their own safety. And if they were combative about following his rules, it flat out pissed him off.

"Gray?" Cole said, interrupting his thoughts.

"Yeah?" Gray answered as he tucked his Glock into the holster.

"You can stop referring to Sami Jo as 'our client.' You and I both know who she is and what she means to you—"

"Anything else, Cole?"

"You tell me."

Gray stared at the phone and internally reprimanded himself for telling Cole about his past with Sami Jo. When they'd been recovering after Afghanistan, he and Cole had nothing else but conversation to get them through recovery. Cole, with a broken back and some pretty severe internal injuries, had especially needed the distraction. Gray had assisted his teammate by telling him all of the stories he had to share. The ones about Sami Jo came up a lot. But it was all part of Gray's desire to purge the guilt from his past while muddling through the survivor's guilt a therapist had diagnosed him with. Cole did his part to help him work through things but he could be worse than Gray's own mother with his attempts to get him to talk about his feelings.

Gray wasn't falling for it. Not today.

"I gotta run. Text me if you need me." Gray ended the call and tucked his room's keycard in his chest pocket.

He took one last look in the mirror above the dresser. His skin was slightly browned by the sun he'd gotten by the pool. Nowhere near the tan he'd had when he'd been on a mission in the desert. His reflection also showed his apprehension of the evening.

He just had to get through the next couple of hours.

He prayed the night went by fast and Stevens would leave Sami Jo alone. It was pretty obvious where his interests lay when it came to her. Could he blame the guy?

Gray had damn-near pleasured himself in the shower not thirty minutes ago imagining Sami Jo peeling out of that excuse for a swimsuit.

That damn thing had nearly wrecked him. The sheer shoulder straps and side panels of black fabric were glued to her curves, and from behind, the open back made her look topless. Had her rack been that impressive seven years ago?

And then while she mingled with Stevens, he'd noticed the droplets of water on the back of her neck and had fought the urge to whisk them off and touch her skin. Her wet hair had produced a thin stream of water that slid under her cover-up and it had just about sent him over the edge. Especially when he thought about it slipping inside the waistband of her suit, no doubt curving over the top of her ass. An ass he should've appreciated more when he'd had the chance.

Pulling on his sport coat, he reminded himself that his carnal desires could not interfere with his work. His personal feelings shouldn't even be part of the equation. He needed to be professional, just like his assignments with the politician last year who had the anti-*everything* platform, the millionaire socialite with the trust fund and angry ex-husband, and the couple from New Jersey who'd won the lottery and feared going out in public without protection. While he didn't agree with the politician's campaign, knew the socialite was a flake, and the newly rich couple was showing off a little by hiring a bodyguard, Gray did his job and kept his mouth shut.

He should be able to keep it in his pants even if Sami Jo stood before him buck naked.

The thought made parts of him twitch.

He checked his watch and headed for the adjoining door.

As he stepped into her suite, he found Sami Jo bending slightly over her bed, looking amazing in a low-cut dress of black lace and high heels.

Fuck, it's going to be a long night.

For the second time that day, Sami Jo bristled when Gray let himself into her suite.

She had just picked up her handbag from the bed and when she turned around, he was standing there, gawking at her. His hand was still on the door that connected their rooms and in his dark suit, he very much resembled the role of a bodyguard. Emanating the strength of a brick wall, he looked even a bit deadly if she based it solely on his expression. Professional despite the lack of a tie.

Her eyes were drawn to his exposed neck as he swallowed hard, sending a wave of heat to her cheeks.

"We should head downstairs," she said as she adjusted the strap of her black handbag over her shoulder.

"Before we go," Gray said and crossed the room toward her. "There are going to be a lot of people there tonight, Sami Jo. A lot of people who paid good money to attend this event and mingle with the likes of you and every other major sports figure there."

She crossed her arms in front of her chest. "This isn't my first rodeo."

"You need to keep in mind that these people may feel entitled to your time and attention. They've spent some serious coin to rub elbows with you and they may expect more than just photos, autographs, and some light chitchat. If someone starts getting out of line, I want you to signal me. And just so know, I don't intend to let you out of my sight."

Sami Jo rolled her eyes and turned to go. Gray caught her arm and the heat from her cheeks echoed where he touched her.

"Hot Shot, you can't trust anyone."

His insinuation that she was some sort of idiot caused

her to stiffen and she jerked her arm from his grasp. And he'd used her nickname again.

"Come on, I don't want to be late."

On the elevator, Sami Jo pulled her phone from her purse so she wouldn't have to make conversation but where he'd touched her arm still tingled, as did her insides.

Why couldn't she just move on?

Over the years, as most of the bitterness over their breakup had dissipated, Sami Jo had daydreamed of running into Gray one day. Maybe he would've apologized for being a royal jerk and she would've joked about being young and naive. Maybe they would've even laughed about their summer fling.

The reality, however, was that his arrival at Royce's had caught her off guard, and any nonchalant attitude she'd hoped to have disappeared at the sight of his chiseled jaw and piercing stare.

As the elevator doors opened, Sami Jo headed toward the lobby entrance where a crowd of Premium Sports staffers in purple polos corralled the other sports celebs. She recognized several baseball players, Olympic gymnasts, and a few golfers who were part of the night's event, but it was Chris Stevens and three other professional wrestlers who stood out.

A large silk-screened X stretched across Chris's hulking chest. From the few times she'd watched wrestling with her nephew, Sami Jo knew it represented his nickname in the ring, X-Factor, and his intent to "X" out the competition.

Chris's eyes lit up when he noticed her and he waved her over.

"Want to ride with us?" Chris smiled as he put an arm around her and glanced at Gray, who followed a few steps behind. "We have room for your bodyguard."

"Lead the way," she replied, grateful to be included and

not left alone with Gray.

Outside the hotel entrance, the heat had subsided, but only slightly. The setting sun cast a glow over several black stretch limousines lined against the curb. More Premium Sports staff with clipboards conducted the boarding process.

A staff member with a name tag that said, "Hi friend, I'm Joseph" approached and directed them toward the nearest car. The other wrestlers piled in first.

"You can ride up front with the driver," Chris told Gray and proceeded to help Sami Jo inside the vehicle.

The spacious interior was accented with neon lighting around the roof and bar. The smoke-tinted windows gave passengers complete concealment except for the narrow space between the rear compartment and the chauffeur.

"Hey, driver, can we put the privacy shield up?" Chris asked.

Sami Jo saw Gray's jaw move but she couldn't hear what he said.

The driver turned his head. "Sorry, sir. The switch isn't working."

Chris gave a response that called bullshit on the driver's claim and grabbed the champagne from the stocked bar.

"How was the rest of your afternoon?" Sami Jo asked him.

"Filled with illicit thoughts." Chris lifted a brow as he popped the bottle open and poured champagne into a glass.

Sami Jo knew this game. She'd grown up in a world of men and had heard it all. Stevens' charming yet dirty demeanor wasn't new territory but maybe it would help her forget about the man in the front seat watching her every move.

When their limo pulled up to the nondescript building on South Beach's popular Lincoln Road, over five hundred fans cheered from their place in line. Chris stepped out of the limo onto the red carpet and presented his hand to Sami Jo.

The crowd craned for a better look from behind velvet ropes as the paparazzi shouted for them to pose together. The other wrestlers flanked them and Sami Jo genuinely laughed at the wall of muscle surrounding her. Maybe this was all the protection she needed.

"Sami Jo," Danny Welliver called from the area where the press had been stationed. "Are you and Chris Stevens here together?"

Chris answered before she could. "Just escorting the lovely lady, Danny."

She waved to Danny and glanced over at Gray who stood a few feet away, scanning the crowd.

They followed the line slowly and when they reached the doorway, a Premium Sports staffer escorted them inside the club.

The interior of the place was lit up in red and blue hues. Seating areas made up of long sofas and low tables rimmed the outer edge of the large room and sheer tapestries hung end to end along the ceiling, muting the overhead spotlights like linen clouds.

As the last few sports celebrities arrived and gathered on the massive dance floor, the upbeat music was lowered and the president of Premium Sports welcomed them by speaking into a microphone. He proceeded to outline the next few hours. It was a routine Sami Jo was familiar with, having done a dozen of these fan events, so she took the opportunity to sneak a peek at Gray.

He stood rigidly a few feet away and her eyes were again drawn to the open collar of his shirt. His Adam's apple bobbed every time he swallowed. Then her gaze fell upon his hands hanging by his side. The same hands that had once curved around her face and fingertips that had brushed across her lips.

Sami Jo had had plenty of hot nights with men over

the years, yet these innocent memories stirred feelings
she wanted to forget.

"You ready for this?" Chris whispered in her ear.

Sami Jo forced a smile. "Yep."

"Promise me you'll find me when it's over." He winked
and squeezed her shoulder before heading over to the
other wrestlers.

After the doors opened, Gray moved in closer to her as
fans began to flock to their favorite sports stars and the
room came alive with conversation.

Instantly, Sami Jo had her hands full with several middle-aged men who wanted their pictures taken with her.
Privately, she had her little nicknames for each type of
attendee. There was the Buddy-Buddy who acted as if
they knew her because they came to every race or followed her career closely, making them feel like she was
part of their lives. There was the Shy Guy who could
barely form complete sentences around her. They usually
stared at her in awe and seemed to lack basic personal
hygiene, but were otherwise pretty harmless. Then there
was the Creeper. This was the type of fan she avoided as
much as possible. They just seemed—off.

There was always one in the crowd.

Tonight's Creeper approached her in the second hour
of the event. His hair was matted on one side, his clothes
looked like they hadn't been washed in months, and he
was clearly drunk.

When the Creeper came up to introduce himself, the
smell of the alcohol on his breath burned her nostrils, but
she smiled through it.

Martin told her he'd flown in from Vegas to see her.

A flash memory of the guy that attacked her told her
this wasn't *her* Vegas guy. Not only was he too short, but
he also didn't seem sophisticated enough to send threatening photos without putting his slimy DNA all over
them. He was, however, getting uncomfortably close.

Sami Jo glanced down at a retractable pen Martin clicked open and closed repeatedly. She swore she could hear it over the music and every time he leaned toward her, the stench of booze along with a foul mix of body odor and sweat was enough to knock her over.

Click click click. Click click click.

She inched away but Martin inched with her. If she moved over any more, she'd be on top of the guy next to her.

Click click click. Click click click.

People were crowding around them and his arm grazed hers repeatedly. When she didn't think she could take anymore, she politely excused herself from the group and made a beeline for the ladies' restroom, ignoring Gray's massive form walking right behind her.

Inside, the tiled room, Sami Jo took three large breaths and studied her reflection in the mirror over the sink. Her face was pale and a light sheen of sweat covered her forehead.

She yanked a paper towel from the dispenser next to the sink and dabbed at her face.

Had this been any other event, Sami Jo would've been able to handle this guy and anyone else out there. But between the Vegas incident, the photos, and the buzz of champagne coursing through her, she didn't know if she had it in her to keep smiling at the strangers clinging to her.

Her phone chimed in her purse.

It was Stevens.

Where are you? I'm done answering the same questions over and over.

Sami Jo typed back.

Hiding in the ladies' room. Weirdo in my group. I'll meet you by the bar for a drink when we're done.

Sami Jo tucked her phone back in her purse, fluffed out her hair, and reapplied her lip gloss.

When the door to the ladies' room flew open, Sami Jo flinched. She recognized the woman as one of her peers and felt a slight relief.

The woman let out an embittered sigh.

"You have a weirdo in your group too?" Sami Jo asked.

The woman checked under the three stalls, making sure they were empty, and walked to the mirror, looking entirely disgusted.

"Yep. Always one who gets a little too handsy." The woman checked her teeth then glanced at Sami Jo's reflection. "You're that race car driver, right?"

"Sami Jo McLean."

"Right. Monica Newton. Glad it's you in here and not one of them out there. I can't take much more with these people." She looked Sami Jo up and down. "Nice dress."

"Thanks. I like yours too." Sami Jo regarded the sheath dress Monica was wearing. She recalled Monica played professional tennis, which explained her athletic build.

"I think I'm gonna hide out in here until it's over." Monica went into one of the stalls and shut the door. "Good luck out there," she called out.

"Thanks," Sami Jo replied and wished she could stay hidden in the bathroom. But she was the rarity in the group—the girl that beat all the boys at their sport. She'd be missed and she didn't want to be known as someone who flaked out on her obligations. She couldn't afford to. McLean Racing couldn't afford her to either.

She just had to get through this and then she intended to have a stiff drink at the bar.

She stepped out of the restroom to find Gray standing with his back to the wall.

"Everything okay?" He followed her toward the dance floor.

"It's fine." Sami Jo forced a bright smile as she approached a group of fans waiting for her to sign autographs. There was no sign of the Creeper anywhere.

Normally, Sami Jo would be the life of the party but she spent the remainder of the hour still as a statue as each fan leaned in for a picture.

She checked her watch and saw that in ten more minutes, the event would be over. Relief loosened her shoulders.

Another flash of a camera and an autograph and a sudden, familiar aroma caused the hair on the back of Sami Jo's neck to prickle.

LAP SEVEN

RIGHT AWAY, GRAY HAD KNOWN there'd been something squirrelly about the man standing inappropriately close to Sami Jo, but most of the people in this place seemed strange. If he had to bounce any one of them based on their peculiarity alone, the whole club would have been emptied.

He had to admit, Sami Jo handled herself pretty well. In a male-dominated sport, she not only had to live down a lot of stereotypes, she most likely had to deal with her share of weirdos. But she appeared genuinely interested in what everyone had to say. She flashed a smile when they took pictures with her and worked the crowd to make them all feel special.

When she retreated to the restroom, Gray figured she'd needed a break. But her expression as she exited through the ladies' room door caused him some concern.

She looked—afraid.

About damn time.

Maybe now she'd take him seriously. But someone had spooked her.

He'd noticed her whole body stiffen when the disheveled man walked up behind her for the second time that night.

When the man's hand came down onto her shoulder, Gray propelled into action. He swiftly put himself between them and with one fluid movement, twisted the man's arm behind his back and shuffled him toward the main entrance.

It took all of ten seconds and they were outside. Gray reached inside the man's back pocket and retrieved his wallet before shoving him toward the sidewalk.

"Hey!" The man stumbled.

Gray opened the worn brown leather wallet and checked the driver's license. Martin Zink from Las Vegas. He tossed the wallet back at the Zink, who fumbled the catch.

"You don't put your hands on a woman, Mr. Zink," Gray said.

Zink picked up his wallet off the ground and took a step toward the entrance but Gray blocked his path. "I paid money—"

"He's done for the night, fellas." Gray looked toward the two bouncers near the door, who reacted immediately by stepping toward Zink.

Zink sneered at the imposing men in black suits and smoothed his hair. "I hope that bitch loses." He spat onto the ground before he stormed off.

"Thanks, guys." Gray nodded at the men. "Appreciate the assist."

No one laid a hand on his clients. Ever.

This time, though, it felt different. He'd felt possessive and he didn't care if he was getting paid to protect her or not, no one touched Sami Jo like that.

The boyfriend touches her. Luke Dillon touched her. No doubt that Stevens asshole wants to touch her. Shit, you'd touch her if you had the chance.

Sometimes he wished the voice inside his head would just shut the hell up.

He paused at the entry doors. He didn't think Martin Zink was their guy but he texted his name to Cole anyway. He tucked his phone in his pocket and took a last look up and down the street. The general public was already lined up behind the velvet rope against the club's outer wall, waiting to get inside.

Gray straightened his jacket before reentering the club where back inside, Sami Jo was waiting for him with her hands on her hips, looking extremely pissed off and sexy as hell.

So different from the eighteen-year-old who used to wear her hair in braids with her face devoid of makeup. Back then she was adorable but innocent. Now she was delectable and womanly and—

"Thanks for stepping in, but did you have to make such a scene?"

"It was time for him to go."

Sami Jo threw her hands up and turned to walk away but he grabbed her arm.

"Hang on, Sami Jo."

Her eyes blazed but all Gray could feel was the softness of her skin under his touch.

She shouted over the music. "You didn't have to toss him out on his ass like that, Gray. I don't need the bad press."

"Bad press? Sami Jo, you gotta stop thinking about your brand. That guy laid his hand on you."

"Oh my god, he was just being creepy."

"Is that why you escaped to the restroom? Because he was creepy?" Gray asked. "Or was it because you felt unsafe?"

Sami Jo's mouth slammed shut and he released her arm.

"You know, I might be watching all of the people around you, Sami Jo. But I'm also watching you. Reading your reactions."

"Well, maybe if you didn't make me feel like everyone was out to get me, I wouldn't be on edge." She frowned and rubbed her temples. "You've gotten into my head, Gray. And I don't appreciate it."

Out of the corner of his eye, Gray spotted someone walking toward them. He looked over and saw it was the guy from the pool earlier in the day, the host from the sports show who'd asked the question on the red carpet outside the nightclub.

"Hey, Sami Jo? Everything okay?" The guy had a look of concern on his face that was no doubt an example of his television-host charisma.

"Hey, Danny. Everything is fine," Sami Jo responded.

Danny looked from her to Gray several times. "Is this guy bothering you?"

Gray stiffened, but Sami Jo laughed. "Oh, heck no. He's my bodyguard."

Danny's brows raised. "I didn't know you traveled with a bodyguard."

Sami Jo laughed weakly and waved off the remark. "Are you enjoying yourself? Get any good scoops?"

"Just the usual networking for the show." Danny's smile widened. "You know, I've been trying to get on your schedule. I would love to have an exclusive with the terror on the tracks."

"Is that what they're calling me now?" She brought her hand to her chest and laughed. "Well, reach out to our PR person at the office and we'll see what we can do. I should get back in there."

Danny looked Gray up and down then nodded at Sami Jo before walking away.

Gray followed closely as she pushed her way through the herd toward the back wall where Stevens stood at the corner of the bar. The wrestler put his arm around Sami Jo as he leaned in to say something that made her laugh.

How he'd like to toss Stevens on his ass too, Gray thought as he moved to an open spot next to them.

The music ended abruptly as the president of Premium Sports took to the microphone again to thank the fans for attending, then high-energy dance music began to thump through the club as the attendees filed out and the public began to fill the place.

In the mirrored wall above the bottles of booze, Gray watched as the bartender slid two shot glasses toward Sami Jo and Stevens. They downed their drinks quickly and Stevens ordered another round.

Gray, insistent on never babysitting a drunk client, decided he'd give her ten minutes then escort her back to the hotel whether she liked it or not.

He watched as Stevens waved over a tall blonde in a red dress who interlaced her fingers with Sami Jo's and pulled her toward the dance floor.

Shit.

Gray turned around to keep an eye on them. The woman was talking excitedly to Sami Jo as they began to move. Watching Sami Jo's hips tilting side to side brought up inappropriate thoughts he had to shut down.

One dance and then he was taking her out of there.

"That's Sasha. She's a fan." Stevens had come up alongside Gray with his cocky *hey bro* attitude. "I told Sami Jo to watch out, Sasha's a bit of a hellcat."

As if on cue, Sasha leaned in and her hand curved around Sami Jo's ass. Sami Jo didn't seem to mind and the two women continued to move in unison, torsos slightly brushing together.

Stevens bellowed in laughter, elbowing him. "Told ya."

It took every ounce of Gray's resolve not to reach out and strangle the asshole.

The wrestler walked—more like stalked away—toward the dance floor and inserted himself between the two women. He put his arms around Sami Jo and leaned into Sasha, tilting his head toward Gray.

Fuck me.

The Sasha woman moved like a snake through the

crowd, her eyes trained on him. She attempted a sexy smile but Gray knew a phony when he saw one.

"You can turn right around. Not interested," Gray stated when she got closer.

Sasha leaned into his chest and slid her hands around his torso coming dangerously close to his sidearm. Gray looked down at her with a scowl and firmly grabbed her arms, pushing her away.

When he looked back at the dance floor, the crowd had filled in the empty spaces and Sami Jo and Chris Stevens were gone.

———

A giddy surge of freedom hit Sami Jo as Chris rushed her off the dance floor and out the back exit where one of the black limos seemed to be waiting for them.

The shots had gone straight to her head but she didn't care. She wanted to blow off some steam.

"Let's have some fun, shall we?" Stevens popped the cork on a bottle of champagne.

Sami Jo's laughter filled the interior of the limousine as he took a swig straight from the bottle and passed it to her. She took a quick sip and the bubbles tickled her nose.

"If Sasha is good at anything, it's the art of distraction." He placed his hand on her thigh. "By now, she's probably got your bodyguard wrapped around her little finger."

Sami Jo dismissed the twinge of jealousy she felt. Why should she care what Gray did with the other woman? She needed to forget about him and all the crap that was going on in her life right now.

The car soon deposited them at the hotel's lobby entrance and before they even reached the elevator, Chris had his hands on her.

"Oh my god, control yourself," she giggled.

He disregarded her comment and as soon as the elevator doors closed them inside, his lips were on hers.

She melted against his powerful frame that seemed to consume her. She eschewed all the warnings that should have been going off in her head. Even the recollection of what had happened in Vegas wasn't going to sour this, not if she could help it.

Stevens was good-looking, a hell of a distraction, and maybe part of her wanted to stick it to Gray.

The doors to the elevator opened and they fumbled their way to his room. He produced the keycard and she snatched it from his hand. She tried sliding the card into the panel over the door handle a few times but the light on the panel kept blinking red.

"Come on, baby, hurry up." He slid his hands up the backs of her thighs as she tried the card again.

"Give me a second here." She pushed her butt toward him, making him step back a little.

Once the tiny light above the door handle turned green, the door opened easily. Stevens picked her up around her waist, making her squeal, and pushed the door shut behind them.

Somewhere along the way, her shoes and her handbag dropped onto the thick carpeting as he took her straight to the bed. He was on top of her before she could even blink, pushing her dress up. His tongue slid along her neck as his hands covered her breasts. The tight muscles under his shirt contracted under her fingers.

He rolled onto his back, taking her with him.

Sami Jo laughed and straddled him, pushing her hair from her eyes. For a brief moment, the face below didn't belong to Stevens. Her laughter subsided when the smoldering expression that gazed up at her was Gray's. She blinked to focus and it was Chris again.

Too many drinks, she surmised and place her hands on his chest.

His hands settled on her hips and he moaned, but it was

Gray's voice she heard.

Sami Jo stiffened and pulled her hands away.

"What's wrong, baby?" His grip slid around to grab her ass.

"Nothing. I just need a minute." She dismounted and slipped off the bed. Feeling the effects of the booze in her legs, she wobbled her way into the bathroom and shut the door.

Leaning against it, she took a few deep breaths.

As the alcohol coursed through her system, the reality that this was a bad idea stabbed at her conscience. Where did she think this was going to end up? This was a one-and-done kind of thing and despite what she might want Gray to believe, one-night-stands were not how she operated.

If she were being completely honest with herself, this was exactly why Mel was mad at her. Alone, with a legitimate stranger, in his bed? Regrets seeped into her thoughts.

What the hell was she doing here?

Just go back to your room, text Gray an apology, and go to sleep.

Sami Jo walked to the sink and stared at her reflection.

At first glance, she didn't recognize herself. Too much makeup, her hair was a wild mess, and her eyes were slightly red-rimmed.

She reached for the knobs and ran the faucet. Dipping her fingers under the stream, she brought the cool water to her face. She swiped the towel off the rack next to the sink and patted her face dry.

Tell Chris you're not feeling well and get the hell out of here.

She opened the door and stepped into the bedroom. The wrestler was not alone. Sasha, the girl she had danced with, the one who had been dispensed to deal with Gray, was lying on the bed.

Stevens was shirtless and standing by the edge of the

bed, pouring a tiny bottle of vodka into a glass. He smiled mischievously at Sami Jo.

"Sasha said she liked you so much she wanted to party with us. That okay, baby? You're cool like that, right?"

Before Sami Jo could answer, Sasha parted her legs, revealing her lack of panties.

Sami Jo turned away. "Where's Gray?"

"He was no fun at all." Sasha got onto her knees and pouted. "Someone that hot must be gay or something."

"I have to go," Sami Jo said.

"Sasha just wants to watch, baby. You don't have to do anything you don't want to." Stevens staggered a bit as he set the bottle down. "Or we can watch her."

The booze began to swill inside her stomach. Yep, this was a mistake.

"I'm sorry, this just isn't my scene," she said as she looked for her handbag.

"Come on, don't go. Have another drink," Stevens pleaded.

"No, actually, I think I've had a little too much."

Sami Jo located her shoes and bent over to pick them up but Stevens grabbed at her from behind. "I think you just need to lie down and let us play with you."

Sami Jo started to panic and struggled against him, knowing he was strong enough to force her to do whatever he wanted. It was Vegas all over again, and it was her fault this was happening—again.

She wished she hadn't been so foolish. She wished Gray were there.

Thankfully, she was able to squirm from Chris's grasp and grab her shoes. She hurried out of the room, leaving Stevens and Sasha laughing as the door shut behind her.

Sami Jo's hands shook as she stood in the elevator. The ride seemed to crawl, the floor was spinning a bit, and she prayed she'd make it to her room before the alcohol bubbled up. When the doors finally opened, she bolted down the hall.

As she slid the card against the lock and opened the door, a wave of nausea hit her, but the sight of Gray standing in her room by the window was a blinding jab to her stomach.

Sami Jo covered her mouth and raced into the bathroom just in time to spill the results of her evening into the toilet.

—————

Gray woke the next morning on the sofa in Sami Jo's hotel room. He'd spent the night there just to make sure she didn't try to disappear again but also to intercept Stevens if he made a surprise visit.

Slight relief filled him when he heard movement from the bedroom as blankets shifted, followed by Sami Jo's footsteps to the bathroom.

You should have taken her out of the nightclub as soon as the event was over.

That one brief moment he'd looked down to tell that—what had Stevens called her? *Hellcat*—to get lost last night had cost him. He knew too well that all it took was that *one brief moment.* It could mean the difference between life or death. One second, you're in a chopper with your buddies, and the next, you're treading water, several of your friends are dead, and your shoulder is split in two.

Okay, maybe the situation with Sami Jo wasn't the same, but he'd felt that same dread when he'd realized she was gone. Luckily, the limo driver he'd buddied up to on the ride over to the club had called Gray as soon as Stevens and Sami Jo had been deposited back at the hotel. Thank God for small favors.

He had stopped by Sami Jo's room first to see if she was there and was about to find Stevens' room when she'd burst in, looking green around the gills.

Something had happened with Stevens and it had happened quickly, whatever it was. Only about thirty minutes had passed from the time she'd left the club to when she'd erupted through her hotel room door. He didn't get the chance to ask her anything since she'd immediately retreated to the bathroom to retch into the toilet. And she'd gone straight to bed after that.

Gray heard the shower turn on in her bathroom and checked his watch. A car was coming to get them in an hour so he headed through the adjoining door into his room for a quick shower and to pack.

Just as he was zipping up his carry-on, his phone rang. *Mom* appeared on the screen.

"Hi, Mom—" Gray barely got the words out before Peggy Finch spoke over him.

"Grayson, you know it would be nice if you'd call occasionally."

"Yes, Mom. I'm sorry, I know it's been a while."

"A while?" She laughed into the phone. "I don't care how old you are, I'm always going to worry about you. I take it you made it to Myrtle Beach okay."

"Yes, I got in a few days ago. But now I'm in Miami with my client."

"You say 'my client' like I don't know who you're with, Grayson."

He cringed. Time for some evasive maneuvers. "How are you, Mom? How's your knee?"

"Oh, not great. Looks like I'll need a replacement. I just don't know when I'll have the time. We have a lot going on here." He listened to his mom rattle off a list of events she was in charge of at the Scottsdale community center. "Plus, I started delivering for Meals on Wheels and I can't let them down. Some of the ladies in my water aerobics class swear by some new herbal candy that's supposed to help with pain management. Tomorrow, a bunch of us are going to see if we can buy some at the pharmacy."

Herbal—

"Mom, those are called edibles and they have cannabis in them. They sell them at a dispensary, not a pharmacy. It's medical marijuana. You know that, right?"

"How do *you* know about it, Grayson?" Her tone sent him right back to adolescence.

"Mom, I mean, come on." He rubbed his forehead.

"I'm just saying, you still have shoulder pain, maybe it would do *you* some good—"

"How's Dad?" He never asked about his father but he'd do anything not to talk about weed or his chronic shoulder pain with his mother.

It caught her off guard and she stammered a bit. "He's doing well. Should I tell him you asked about him?"

"Look, I have to go, Mom, I'm heading to the airport."

"Well, it's nice to hear your voice. You know, your dad turns sixty next month. It would be nice if you could come to the party we're having here at the house. I'll email you the info."

"Yeah, okay, Mom. I gotta run. I'll call you in a few days." Gray ended the call before she could speak again and grimaced. She'd find a way to make him feel guilty for that the next time they spoke.

He ran a hand over his face and pulled his carry-on over to the adjoining door.

Instead of barging in, he decided to politely knock.

Sami Jo opened it dressed in faded jeans, a cotton shirt with a faded Allman Brothers logo on the front, and a black suede baseball hat over a low ponytail. He saw the puffiness around her eyes before she turned away.

"Is that your incognito look?"

"It's my hung-over look." Sami Jo slipped her sunglasses on. "I need coffee before we go."

"Okay, sure."

Sami Jo hesitated as she picked up her carry-on, like she wanted to say something, but seemed to decide against it and dragged her bag over to the door.

He followed her down to the hotel lobby and stood to the side as she ordered from the Starbucks counter. Across the beige marble floor, Gray spied Chris Stevens standing at the checkout desk with the Hellcat who'd succeeded in distracting him last night; and she was all over the wrestler.

Breathing through the urge to go over and beat the shit out of Stevens, Gray glanced at Sami Jo. She either didn't see the couple or didn't care, because she had put her earbuds in to take a phone call.

"Alec? Hey, babe."

The boyfriend.

Sami Jo's tone was casual like she hadn't just flirted with another guy and gone back to his room. She'd snuck away like that eighteen-year-old girl he once knew— except back then, she was sneaking away to be with *him*.

He heard her say "love you" into the phone and decided they couldn't get on that plane fast enough.

Due to inclement weather, the flights back to Myrtle Beach were bumpy, which only added to Gray's aggravation. The entire ride he'd considered Sami Jo's schedule. She had a busy couple of weeks ahead outside of practices, qualifying, and the races themselves. At least when she was on the track, she could only stay in one place— not that racing didn't come with its own set of liabilities. Maybe when they got back to Myrtle Beach, he'd talk to Royce, see if the uncle could talk some sense into her because their one-day trip felt like three and if this was what the future held...

It was on the ride back to her house in his Escalade that Gray finally broke his silence.

"Next time we do this, let's keep your socializing to a minimum." He'd hoped she could hear him over the music in her earbuds.

She removed them and he repeated himself. The words

hung between them, filled with accusations and blame but frankly, he didn't care how he sounded. His job was to minimize risk and she was being blatantly uncooperative.

"Just go ahead, Gray. I mean, you're dying to tell me off, right?" she said.

"I think your cousin was right—you're reckless."

"Why? Because I had a couple of cocktails and hung out with a colleague?"

Gray laughed in shock. "Don't give me that shit. Stevens is no colleague of yours. He only had one goal in mind from the second he saw you."

"Well, not that my sex life is any of your business, but obviously I drank too much and ended the night early."

"*My business* is to keep you safe. I won't have you sabotage it by disappearing, no matter how harmless you might think someone is."

As he pulled into her driveway, she unfastened her seat belt before he brought the truck to a stop. She pushed the passenger door open in a huff and stormed to the back of the truck to collect her suitcase. Gray met her there to find her pulling on the tailgate that wouldn't open.

He hit the button on his key ring to unlock it and opened it for her. She yanked her bag out, and he suddenly felt like the biggest jerk.

"Sami Jo," he began.

She spun quickly to face him. "Do you think this is easy for me? Having you here?"

Her lip quivered and his anger dissolved.

"Sami Jo," he said, reaching out to touch her shoulder.

She pulled away. "Look, I fucked up. Okay? I fucked up in Vegas, and I fucked up last night. And I'm—I'm tired. I just want to go upstairs and get some rest before practice tomorrow. I promise not to go anywhere."

"Okay," he said.

She sniffed back what he assumed were tears. "I take it that you'll be flying out with us?"

"Diane already sent me the itinerary," he said. "I'll be there."

She exhaled and her shoulders dropped. "Okay. I'll see you in the morning."

He watched her head to the stairs that led to her front door as he stood at the back of the truck and silently recited every curse word he knew. He was getting too personal and had crossed a line. If he'd only come clean in the beginning and apologized for the way he'd ended things. Explained why he'd been in Myrtle Beach years ago and the real reason he hadn't slept with her. Maybe this might have all gone a lot smoother.

The cellphone in his pocket buzzed and he pulled it out.

Cole was calling him.

Another photo had arrived at McLean Racing.

LAP EIGHT

SHERIFF KOVACH WAS ALREADY ONSITE at McLean Racing when Gray arrived with a stunned Sami Jo in tow.

Royce and the sheriff stood in the large conference room with a second officer who was handling an envelope with latex gloves. He held it by the tips of his fingers as he dropped it into a thin, clear plastic sleeve and secured it with red evidence tape.

The photo itself, sealed inside another clear sleeve, was face down next to the officer's equipment bag.

"Grayson, you remember Sheriff Kovach?" Royce nodded toward the older man in uniform.

Gray stuck out his hand to shake hands with the sheriff. "What have we got, Sheriff?"

"The same type of envelope, which tipped off Ms. Quaid when she was sorting the mail this morning," Sheriff Kovach said. "Hopefully we can grab something off of it since it didn't pass through anyone's hands this time."

Gray picked up the sleeve holding the photo and turned it over.

His mouth dropped open slightly.

It had been taken yesterday in Miami when they were

poolside at the hotel. It was a closeup of Sami Jo standing over Gray before she jumped into the pool. He could make out the scowl on Sami Jo's face and recalled that they'd been discussing Alec Clarke and Luke Dillon at the time. The words *He can't save you* were scrawled in the same red script as the other photo.

It took him a moment to realize Sami Jo was now standing next to him, gawking at the picture.

"He was there?" She looked up at Gray. Her exhaustion was replaced with alarm.

"Looks like he followed you to Miami, kiddo," Royce said.

"Did anything happen while you were there?" Sheriff Kovach asked.

"No," Gray answered quickly. "It was uneventful. Sami Jo did her appearance and that was it."

He could feel her eyes on him.

"We'll send this to the lab. See what turns up." Kovach nodded at the other officer who took the sealed photo from Gray.

"Any word on the other women?" Gray asked.

The sheriff took a deep breath and blew it out. "Angela Guthrie's home in Mooresville was broken into. Luckily, she wasn't home at the time and none of her belongings were taken. But the perpetrator spray-painted a rather nasty message on the wall of her bedroom."

"That's unfortunate," Gray remarked.

"The alarm system wasn't even tripped. She said she thought she armed it but couldn't say for certain." The sheriff shrugged. "We'll let you know if we hear anything."

"Thanks, Ed," Royce said, shaking the sheriff's hand. "Appreciate you handling this."

"Sure thing, Royce." The sheriff then shook Gray's hand and turned to Sami Jo. "You're lucky you have your security agent with you, Ms. McLean. Can't be too careful."

Sami Jo nodded weakly.

"Let me walk you out, gentlemen," Royce said and followed the officers out of the conference room.

Sami Jo settled into the nearest chair, put her elbows on the table, and brought her hands to her face.

Gray pulled out the chair next to her and sat, unsure of what to say. His hand twitched, wanting to touch her shoulder in reassurance. The rest of him wanted to take her in his arms and hold her.

"Thanks for not saying anything about last night." She dropped her hands and crossed her arms on top of the table.

He grimaced. "I didn't think it would go over well with your uncle. He might've fired me and if this guy comes after you, you'll want me to be the one who gets in his way."

She laughed weakly. "You're a real tough guy."

He sat back in the chair. "I do alright for myself."

"You probably see shit like this all the time with what you do."

For the first time since he'd been in her presence, he could see her guard was completely down. She was finally looking at him without hatred in her eyes.

"I've seen worse." He leaned toward her. "But that's why I've been such a hard-ass about all this, Sami Jo. I know how quickly it escalates. I also know if you don't put yourself in harm's way, like walking in the mountains alone or going off with a stranger, you minimize the chance of getting hurt."

She chewed on her lip and sighed. "Well, thanks for not snitching on me. I don't need Royce up my ass any more than he already is. Do you think maybe it was that guy you tossed last night?"

"Probably not. But my office is already checking into his background. We'll see what comes up."

Gray looked up as Royce entered the conference room. The older man's expression was grim. He went to a chair across the table from them and set his hands on the back support.

"What's next, Grayson?" Royce asked. "Do I need to pull her from her events?"

"What?" Sami Jo sat up straight. "Royce, you can't do that. I'll lose my sponsors."

Gray held up his hand. "I don't think we need to go to that extreme. I think if we keep her social interaction to a minimum and she stays by my side, she can fulfill her obligations."

In his peripheral, Sami Jo slumped in relief.

"The alarm system is up and running at her house. The itinerary shows a few public appearances in the next couple of weeks but that should be manageable. I'm not too worried about the rest." Gray folded his hands in his lap. "About that picture, Royce. I'm pretty sure that photo was taken with a zoom lens; there was no imminent danger, just so you're aware. And I kept my eye on her the entire time we were there. She was able to network with some of the other athletes who were at the pool. From what I witnessed, she may have converted quite a few of them into racing fans."

"Good. That's good." Royce nodded.

"Does Mel know?" Sami Jo asked.

Royce gritted his teeth. "She does. She's thinking about taking the kids to Matt's parents' in Tampa for a few weeks."

Sami Jo sat back in the chair with her arms crossed.

Great, there goes that guard of hers—back up again.

"Otherwise the event went well?" Royce asked.

Gray could feel Sami Jo's apprehension.

"It was fine. Typical," she responded.

"Well, keep following Grayson's lead." Royce turned back to Gray. "How do you want to move forward?"

"For starters, I need to grab things at my hotel." Gray glanced over at Sami Jo. "I think it would be wise for me to provide Sami Jo twenty-four-seven protection."

Once again, he felt her stiffen beside him.

———

Sami Jo stared at the glass of bourbon she'd been nursing for the better part of the evening.

From the comfort of her sofa, she'd watched the sky change from blue to orange through her balcony doors. They were now equipped with sensors that tripped an alarm if they were opened by any unwelcome visitors.

The last twenty-four hours had been a bitch but that wasn't why she was drinking.

Grayson Finch was upstairs moving into her guest bedroom. She could hear his footsteps overhead as he unpacked the large suitcase they'd picked up at the hotel after leaving McLean Racing.

He hadn't said much all afternoon. He'd spent most of it on his cell, talking to someone named Cole, while he'd set up his laptop at her kitchen island. She had tried to busy herself by putting away the items in her carry-on and tidying up around the house, but mostly she parked herself on the sofa and watched the ocean waves roll in and out over the sand.

Her cell rang on the table next to her. It was Alec.

"Sami Jo, are you okay? I just saw your text." He sounded out of breath.

"I'm fine. Sorry, I didn't mean to scare you."

When she'd tried Alec earlier, the call went straight to voicemail. She texted him with a message she'd hoped didn't sound too panicked.

Guess who's popular again. Another photo! #overachiever. Call me later.

"What happened?" Alec asked.

She summed up the morning's events without being

too dramatic about it, told him Gray was staying with her until things blew over, but Alec was onto her. "You've got to be freaking out."

The anguish in his voice silenced her.

She didn't reply. Instead, she put the cool highball glass to her forehead.

"Sami Jo?"

"Can we talk about something else, please? Tell me about the tour." Sami Jo finished the contents of the glass and scooted down on the couch. She laid back on the pillow as Alec reluctantly proceeded to talk about the rigorous schedule he'd been keeping and she relaxed as she listened to the sound of his voice.

"Have you been able to patch things up with Melanie?" Alec asked.

"We haven't spoken. She's not dealing with it very well and I know she blames me for all of this. She's worried."

"Frankly, I'm worried about you too."

"Why—because I'm careless and impulsive?" Sami Jo said it with a little more hostility than Alec deserved and instantly regretted it.

"No, Sami Jo, because you're a public figure like me. People want access to us." His admonishing tone quickly changed to concern. "You have to remember, the second you let your guard down is the moment you make yourself vulnerable."

He was talking about Vegas.

"I know. Sorry, I'm a little raw around the edges. It's been a hellish week and I have the Kansas City race coming up. I didn't mean to snap at you. It's just weird having Gray here."

"Probably for the best. Promise me you'll call or text me, I want to know you're okay."

"I will," Sami Jo replied before telling Alec she loved him and hanging up.

Closing her eyes for a moment, she considered that

Alec's unease was warranted. She took her life in her hands every time she hit the track, but something as simple as enjoying her downtime had suddenly become dangerous and she hadn't made the best of choices in the last few days.

A sound from the kitchen startled her.

Gray stood at the refrigerator. His bicep flexed as he put a bottle of water to his lips.

She couldn't deny she felt a lot better having him there. History aside, it beat having a stranger protecting her or being alone. Maybe it was the bourbon softening her resolve or the fact she was in the comfort of her own home, but maybe it wouldn't be as awkward as she anticipated.

Plus, he wasn't bad on the eyes. Her gaze traveled down his lean torso to where his jeans hung low on his hips.

"How are you feeling?" he asked.

Sami Jo quickly met his stare.

"Peachy," she replied.

"How about some water?" Gray opened the fridge and pulled out another bottle.

"It's okay, I'm fine."

Gray crossed the room to her. "Don't be stubborn. You haven't eaten a thing all day and bourbon isn't exactly hydrating."

He handed her the bottle and walked over to the accent chair. She noticed him rub his shoulder as he sat down.

"Do you not like to talk about it?" she asked.

He looked at her, confused.

"About what happened to your shoulder."

Gray began to fidget in his seat and surprised her when he spoke.

"A bullet ripped through my shoulder and I had to have extensive surgery to repair it. That's why I'm retired."

"That must've been awful."

"I'm surprised you didn't hear about it from my Uncle

John or someone in the family."

Sami Jo lifted her shoulders. "Royce is the only one who keeps in touch with them. I haven't spoken to any of them in years."

"With your schedule, you're probably too busy to make it to their annual picnics."

"I think I lost the privilege to attend when my friendship with Gemma ended."

"Oh. I didn't realize you two had been out of touch," he said. "I've been a bit out of touch myself."

"I ditched her the summer you were here and she never forgave me. I don't blame her."

Gray's eyes met hers for a few moments. "You can't blame yourself. I probably own half of that burden."

"It was my choice to hang out with you," she said and chugged some of the water. "Since I've been out of touch with your family, is there a Mrs. Finch back in Chicago?"

"No. Just a Mr. Donovan," he said. Seeing her reaction caused one corner of his mouth to turn up. "He's my business partner. Although, sometimes Cole's like a damn work wife. We served together and he's like your cousin Melanie, always worrying about me."

"That's nice you have a friend like that. Outside of Mel, Alec's the closest thing I have to a best friend."

His expression clouded a bit and she felt the coolness that came across his face. "Well, I have to finish unpacking."

He lifted off the chair and headed upstairs.

Yeah, this won't be awkward at all.

LAP NINE

NOT EVEN TWENTY-FOUR HOURS SINCE he'd moved into her place and playing the dutiful protector was already wearing on Gray's willpower.

When they'd eaten dinner last night, he'd stayed at the island behind his laptop, while she sat on the sofa watching the news in skimpy shorts and the faded Allman Brothers shirt that stretched across her chest. He reminded himself no matter how much as he wanted to lift her onto that island to execute a very dirty fantasy, it would be wrong. And that, despite her actions with Stevens, she was spoken for.

This was his damn job, not a chance to get back together with her. He'd learned that he'd come between her and Gemma, he wasn't going to ruin another relationship.

That morning, Royce and Matt had arrived early to drive them to the airport and the two men had held court with Sami Jo for the entire flight and ride to the track. All Gray could do was hang back and observe. He'd almost welcomed the current reprieve to be *off the clock* while she practiced. And yet, he was feeling a bit of separation anxiety.

As the Kansas Speedway filled with the aroma of rubber and fuel, dozens of people attended to Sami Jo's needs down by pit row. He easily picked her out of the crew—she was the one in the helmet. She climbed into her car and before he knew it, she took off. The rumble of her car's engine practically clattered his teeth as she reached an astonishing speed. When she passed the viewing stand where he was stationed with the rest of her crew, his neck almost snapped as he turned to follow her car.

"You should try to breathe, Grayson. This is all very normal." Royce was standing next to him, laughing.

"Sorry?" Gray said after a moment.

"Son, the look on your face is priceless."

"It's just, she's—"

"Fast? Yeah, she sure is." Royce clapped him on the shoulder. "Just proves to our sponsors we did the right thing bringing on a rookie this year. And a woman, no less."

Gray nodded and took a drink from his water bottle. Even though the viewing area was under a canopy, he felt sweat form under the light sport coat he wore. The thickness of the air reminded him of Afghanistan. He had carried eighty pounds of gear and guns in that desert; he could imagine what it must be like enclosed in a piece of metal wearing those thick fireproof suits. How the drivers could stand the heat was beyond him.

Eventually, he lost track of how many laps she'd taken and attempted to relax as she easily maintained a speed upwards of two hundred miles per hour.

Sun glinted off the hood of the blue number eighteen car behind Sami Jo as it took turn two and started to slide sideways. It crashed into the wall, sending debris across the entire width of the blacktop. Although Sami Jo was nowhere near the car as it spun toward the infield barriers, Gray's jaw tightened.

There were unanimous shouts from the viewing stands next to McLean Racing and an emergency vehicle immediately deployed onto the track as the other cars slowed.

Sami Jo came to a stop in front of her pit crew and exited the vehicle. She took off her helmet and leaned casually against the cement barrier.

She appeared so—calm.

Jesus, watching the actual race was going to kill him.

A few hours later, they were headed back to the hotel so Sami Jo could relax before their dinner with Royce, the other two drivers, and some of the upper management. A few sponsors were in town early and wanted to leverage time with the team. A little *pressing of the flesh* as Royce put it.

Gray had dressed in a navy suit for the occasion and knocked on the adjoining door to their rooms when it was almost time to leave.

Sami Jo opened it in a terrycloth robe. Her hair was still damp from a shower.

"Sorry, I need a few minutes. Want to watch TV?"

"Sure," he said, entering the room.

Her suitcase was open on the side of the bed where the blanket and sheets were still intact. The other side was rumpled and the pillows had an indent where her head had been.

"I napped a little longer than I probably should have," she said as she pulled a dress from the closet.

Gray smiled politely and sat in the chair near the sofa.

"Was that the first time you've seen a race in person?" she asked as she stepped into the bathroom.

"Yeah. I think I've watched parts of a race on television twice at the most. In-person it's certainly an experience."

"Royce said he could tell." She poked her head out of the bathroom. "What did you think?"

"I think it was definitely an experience." He checked his watch. "And I think we're gonna be late if you don't get a move on there, Hot Shot."

There was the nickname again. He needed to stop doing that.

She chuckled and ducked back into the bathroom. "Royce wouldn't know what to do with himself if I was ever on time."

She reappeared twenty minutes later in a black short-sleeved dress with cutout straps that exposed her shoulders. The skirt came to her mid-thigh and Gray forced his focus back to the television. When she turned to the closet, he stole a long look. Her hair was piled on top of her head in a loose bun and thin tendrils framed her face along with dangling gold earrings. She slid into her heels and retrieved a sequined clutch from her suitcase on the bed.

"Okay, we can go," she said, but her face lit up as she reached into her suitcase again. "Hey, can you help me with this necklace?"

Gray rose from the chair reluctantly and crossed the room to her.

"I know this isn't part of your job but the damn clasp always sticks." She handed him a delicate gold chain with a teardrop sapphire pendant and turned around.

He hesitated.

You're right, this isn't part of my job. And you smell terrific.

Reaching over her head, he pulled the chain around her neck and closed the two ends.

"The boyfriend give you this?" he asked and wanted to kick himself.

"No, it was my mom's," she said coolly.

When she turned to face him, he tried to remain stoic.

"My dad gave it to her on their wedding night." She touched the pendant gingerly.

"We're going to be late," he said and headed to the door.

He held it open for her and as she passed by, he caught another hint of her perfume.

In the sedan on the way to the restaurant, Gray fought to think about anything other than the back of her neck and how her skin felt even though he'd tried not to come in contact with it when he put the necklace on her. Luckily, their driver was a fan and had Sami Jo talking about the upcoming race.

She seemed thrilled to chat about how much she loved the sport. He hadn't seen her light up like this since he'd been in town and it reminded him of how she used to be around him. The wattage her smile gave off made him feel guilty for ever wiping that it off her face and bringing her to tears when he'd left her.

It was the only way, he'd convinced himself.

Back then, all he could do was persuade her to hate him. He'd assured himself he didn't deserve someone like her. At the time, he'd blamed their age gap, although now it seemed irrelevant. He'd also argued that he was going back to the military at the end of that summer and he wasn't about to strike up some long-distance thing that wouldn't last.

Now, he hated himself for the way he'd treated her. He'd been harsh—even mean, at the end.

The driver pulled up to Fleming's Steakhouse and opened the door for her. Gray got out and walked a few steps behind her into the softly lit restaurant.

The golden hue of the overhead chandlers throughout the large dining space gave the steakhouse a warmth, despite the air-conditioning that cooled it. Cherrywood walls accentuated the linen-covered tables where customers ate, drank, and talked. None of them noticing the veritable celebrity in their midst.

The hostess, however, recognized Sami Jo instantly. "Right this way, Ms. McLean. Your party is already in our private dining room."

The slender young woman led them down a short hallway to a set of double doors. Inside, a large mahogany table was set for twenty people, and off to the side, guests congregated at a long bar.

Ray Skinner stood closest to the door and tipped his chin at Gray. Sami Jo hugged her teammate as Gray quickly scanned the room.

Matt was at the bar talking to Luke Dillon and a loud laugh erupted from Royce, who stood in the corner with two men. Based on the brief Cole had prepared on the guests, they were the sponsors.

Gray tucked himself against the opposite end of the bar as Sami Jo made the rounds. The only woman in a sea of testosterone—and it didn't seem to faze her.

One of the bartenders stopped over to serve him and he ordered his usual water with lime. As he was squeezing the fruit into his glass, Luke Dillon approached.

"I didn't know we could bring a date," Luke said and Gray shot him a look. "I'm just messing with you, Mr. Finch."

"Now, Luke." Royce seemed to appear out of nowhere and slapped Dillon on the back. "Don't you have some guests to entertain?"

Luke nodded and quickly walked to the other end of the bar toward the sponsors.

Royce turned to Gray and sighed. "He's a good kid. Just easily distracted by bells and whistles. Know what I mean?"

Gray straightened. "I'll try not to make too much noise so he stays focused."

Royce laughed.

"Did you want me here at the bar tonight or should I go sit out in the main dining room until you're done?" Gray asked.

"Oh, nonsense, my boy. We set you a place at the table."

"That's nice of you, Royce. But I'd be fine just standing in the corner." Gray gestured to the area around him.

"Don't be ridiculous," Royce said. "As far as I'm concerned, you're part of the team."

Matt appeared next to his father-in-law. "Better listen

to him, Gray. If I have to play along, you do too. Plus, making light conversation isn't my strongest skill. I need a wingman."

"Yes," Royce nodded. "Don't feel obligated to sit next to Sami Jo. I think she's pretty safe with all of us here."

Royce walked away leaving the two men to talk.

"I'm certainly not sitting by her," Matt said. "She already grilled me about Melanie and the kids."

"They decide to go to your parents?"

Matt nodded. "It's for the best. Nana and Paw-Paw haven't seen the kiddos since Christmas. Will do Mel some good too. She's been worried sick with that second photo arriving."

Royce clinked a fork against a wine glass at the dining table and the guests made their way across the room, settling into the high-back chairs. Gray followed behind Matt and took the last seat available next to him across from one of the sponsors and Sami Jo.

She glanced at Gray as she pulled in her chair then politely smiled at the older man next to her. The gentleman was otherwise distracted.

"Matthew," the man said. "Aren't you going to introduce me to your handsome friend?"

———

Sami Jo stifled a laugh.

Perry Hopkins, Vice President at Hop Distributors, was well-known for being attracted to the overly muscled and well-chiseled version of the male species. And good old Perry probably thought he'd hit the jackpot being seated directly across from Gray.

Matt introduced Gray as their security specialist which, she imagined, intrigued Perry even more since the older man had a thing for dominant men.

Maybe for once, Gray would understand what it's like to be ogled.

She'd known Perry for years thanks to the personal relationship he had with Royce. His company had been a serious sponsor of McLean Racing for over a decade. His brand of alcohol-spiked carbonated water was hugely popular throughout the Midwest and their logo graced the hood of her race car. Ray and Luke both had other Hop logos on the sides of their cars but Perry had invested most of his advertising money in her.

He was also one of the more cordial sponsors they had. But then again, the others were mostly straight older men who spent more time checking out her ass than listening to what she had to say. With Perry, she never had that concern. And anyway, now all of his focus was on Gray.

As the VP chatted him up, her gaze traveled to the navy jacket he wore. It was fitted to his broad shoulders and the pale blue dress shirt underneath stretched across his wide chest.

Perry said something and Gray laughed. His eyes sparkled and met hers.

Perry nudged her with his elbow. "Come on, Sami Jo. No remark on that one?"

Oh shit.

"I'm sorry, Per. I wasn't listening." Her face burned with embarrassment as she felt Gray's eyes still on her. "I'm a little worn out from today."

"See, Gray," Perry said. "No humor with this one. Always so serious."

Crap. They'd been talking about her and she'd missed it while staring at Gray.

"Not always," she responded. "I can be witty."

"No one would ever describe you as witty, Sami Jo," Matt interjected.

Despite Matt's comment, she laughed. "Hey, aren't you're supposed to be in my corner?"

"I'm sorry, but it's true." Matt threw up his hands and their end of the table erupted with laughter.

She glanced at Gray. Damn, his smile was something. She feigned disappointment and picked up the wine glass in front of her, swirling the red liquid around. "As long as you keep doing what you're doing, Sami Jo, we don't care if you're witty or not." Perry picked up his glass to clink it with hers.

"You keep paying to have your logo on my hood and you've got a deal." She touched his glass with hers and winked at Matt.

The wait staff entered the room with trays of food and began to serve the guests around the table. Mountains of steak, potatoes, and steamed veggies wafted up from platters, making Sami Jo's mouth water. After a long day of practice, she was famished.

"Tell me, Gray," Perry said, spearing an asparagus stalk with his fork. "What kind of background gets you into your line of work?"

Gray's expression turned serious. "It was either this or a life of crime."

Perry's fork clattered onto his plate and he emitted a roar.

"Oh, that's rich," Perry said, picking up his fork. "See, Sami Jo. Now that's how you do it."

She shot Gray a look. He grinned and raised an eyebrow in response.

And there it was. The Gray she used to know. The one who used to tease her, then flash a smile that melted any annoyance she might have felt.

"Gray was a Navy SEAL," Matt spoke up.

Perry nodded. "Makes sense. Explains your, um, stature. Did you get tired of repelling brick walls?"

Sami Jo's gaze darted to Gray. He bristled and set down his fork to take a drink of water.

"Not exactly," Gray said. "About five years ago, my team and I were ending our tour in Afghanistan when a missile took out our helicopter. I was injured badly enough it ended my career."

Their end of the table got quiet and Sami Jo realized the entire room was listening. She looked at Gray and despite his intention to conceal it, the horror of what he'd been through was written all over his face.

Perry pulled his napkin from his lap and pushed away from the table. He stood, picked up his glass, and looked down at Gray. "Thank you, son. Thank you for your service."

Suddenly, others from the table rose, expressing their thanks by also raising their glasses.

Gray kept his head down, obviously uncomfortable with the recognition. When he finally looked up, he stared directly at her.

Sami Jo pushed her chair back and stood. She tipped her glass toward Gray, receiving a slight nod from him in return.

"To Grayson," Royce said raising his glass. "I wouldn't trust Sami Jo in anyone else's hands."

Sami Jo swallowed hard. She'd been in those hands. They had been strong, and tender, and—

Jesus.

After dinner, she and Gray rode back to the hotel in silence. While he'd continued to speak with Perry over dinner, now he seemed distracted.

When they returned to her room, he followed her inside and headed to the adjoining door.

"Hey, I have some brandy in my mini-fridge. Would you want to have a drink?"

He hesitated by the door and turned to her. "I make it a rule not to drink on the job. But thanks."

As he went to leave, she found herself grasping for any reason to make him stay. "I'm sorry if Perry made you uncomfortable tonight."

"It's fine," he said over his shoulder.

"It couldn't have been easy—what you went through."

He turned to face her again. "We were ripped right out of the cabin. The missile's impact was like a sudden blast of hot air and the chopper went down into the water. Three of my guys were killed."

Sami Jo stilled and his face contorted as if he hadn't meant to tell her all that. "You're lucky to be alive."

"Yeah. Get some sleep," he said and walked through his door.

He didn't close it completely. A light went on in his room and several minutes passed before Sami Jo snapped out of her trance.

Terrifying images of Gray's ordeal ran through her head for hours while she tossed and turned until she'd rolled herself into a cocoon of sheets and blankets. She dug herself out of the sheets and swung her legs over the side of the bed.

Maybe some of that brandy—

A stern voice broke the silence and she glanced at the digital clock on her bedside table. It read 2:21 am.

She stepped lightly over to the adjoining door. Gray mumbled something but his words were too muddled to understand.

Quietly, she pulled the door open and stepped inside the darkened room. The heavy curtains were open and her eyes adjusted to the band of moonlight that fell over Gray's form on the bed.

As she inched toward him, she saw the sheets had been pushed off and his large frame was revealed in all its glory. With each breath he took, his hard stomach rose and fell. His chest muscles flexed as he shifted slightly and she internally cursed the boxers covering the most interesting part of his anatomy.

Even in the shadows, Sami Jo could see the thick scar across the front of his shoulder. It took an immense amount of willpower not to reach out and run her fingers over it.

"Wait." Gray shifted.

Sami Jo whispered his name and delicately touched his forearm.

Gray said something incomprehensible and before she knew it, he had bolted upright, pulled her across the bed, and covered her body with his own. The weight of him crushed her, but she became very aware of how intimate their contact was.

"Stay down," he grunted, pinning her arms.

She tried to shift underneath him but his body continued to push her down into the mattress. His face was close enough to hers that she could feel the heat from his erratic breathing. He was like an animal hovering over its prey.

"Gray, wake up. It's me."

His body relaxed slowly into hers and his hold on her arms loosened. He lifted his head slightly and his hooded gaze settled on her mouth.

Her tongue flicked out to wet her lower lip and she felt the hitch in his breath.

His hand came up to her cheek and his thumb tugged at her lower lip. Lowering his head, his mouth settled on hers.

It may have been years but she hadn't forgotten the softness and familiarity of his lips.

When they parted and his tongue dipped inside her mouth, she tasted his hunger. A deep growl escaped his throat as their kiss deepened and he settled his growing arousal between her legs. It enticed a heat to rise within her and for just one moment, she wanted to forget the past, even forget the present, and just finish what they'd started years ago.

As if in answer to her desire, Gray slid a hand under her pajama top to caress her skin, making her arch against his touch. This was not what she had intended when she came into the room, but now, she didn't want it to stop.

She spread her legs further apart and felt his erection getting harder against her core. She needed to have him—once and for all.

Breathlessly, Sami Jo's moved her mouth to his ear. "Gray."

He lifted his head and his eyes fluttered open. Even in the dark, they showed regret. His body suddenly went rigid and he pushed himself off of her.

He crossed the room and hit a switch on the desk lamp. She sat up and squinted as her eyes adjusted to the light.

Not budging from his spot by the desk, he ran a shaky hand through his hair. "What the hell just happened?"

The guilt on his face nearly crushed her.

"I think you were having a nightmare. I tried to wake you but you pulled me onto the bed. I imagine that's some sort of fancy military training." Her attempt at humor did nothing to ease her embarrassment.

Gray looked ashen as he stared at her. "Jesus, Sami Jo. I—I didn't mean to."

She stood and fought the urge to run from the room—and the hotel.

Gray composed himself. "You're my client. It's not right. I don't—"

He doesn't want you.

Collecting what little confidence she had left, she said, "Next time, I'll keep my distance." She crossed to the adjoining room, and this time, she made sure the door was completely shut.

She wasn't about to let him hear her cry.

LAP TEN

GRAY WOKE UP A FEW minutes before his alarm was to go off and as he stretched in bed, the memory of what had happened last night hit him.

Sami Jo in his bed.

It caused him to bolt upright.

Fuck.

He dragged his palm over his face, wondering what the hell he'd been thinking.

In his defense, he thought he was dreaming. He'd had nightmares since Afghanistan, although kissing Sami Jo was far from a nightmare. He remembered lying between her legs, his hand under her top and suddenly, other parts of him stood at attention.

When admonished their behavior, her expression had been a mirror image of that night he'd broken things off with her. It wasn't anger on her face, she was hurt.

An apology would be the right thing to do. But how could he say he was sorry for all that?

Gray threw off the blankets and quickly took a shower. Today, Sami Jo would be qualifying for her position in tomorrow's race. He hoped to God what happened last night wouldn't sabotage her focus—or his.

As he dressed for another hot day at the track in a polo

and light pants, he decided he would confront things head-on. Tell her it was a mistake and it wouldn't—couldn't—happen again. As much as he wanted it to.

God, did he want it to.

Suck it up. Do your job.

He pulled on his sport coat, concealing his sidearm, and headed to the adjoining door to her room. He paused when he heard voices on the other side.

It wasn't the television. It was Royce.

He was screwed.

He knocked on the door and took a deep breath, ready for Royce to take a swing at him.

"Gray, perfect timing," Royce greeted him smiling. A bright McLean Racing logo was prominent on his denim shirt. "We're almost ready to head over. Thought I'd ride with you."

Sami Jo stood by the bed in a pair of faded jeans and a t-shirt with her sponsors on it.

"Let's go." She didn't even look up at him as she zipped up a duffel bag, put her earbuds in, and headed to the door.

Royce waved her off. "Don't mind her, Gray. It's her ritual before qualifying. Blasts who knows what into her ears to psyche herself up. She's pretty vigilant in keeping with her pre-race routine."

Gray was afraid to ask what else that entailed. Guess he'd have to deal with what went down last night at some other time.

On the ride over to the track, Royce told Gray what to expect when they got there. First, there would be a random draw to determine her place to qualify. She'd race alone on the track when it was her turn and she'd be timed for two laps.

"It's a lot of sitting around until she goes but we hope she'll place top ten."

Gray gazed ahead at Sami Jo, who sat in the front seat

with their driver. She was very still and her eyes were closed as if she were sleeping.

"Don't expect too much out of her, she practically shuts down until the race," Royce said. "She's like her father that way. He wouldn't speak until he was climbing into the chassis Sunday afternoons."

"Fair enough," Gray said. "Melanie and the kids are doing okay?"

"Sure. It was good for them to go to Tampa. Mel tends to play mama bear with Sami Jo. Been that way since Trudy left us." Royce stared out the window at the cloudless blue sky. "Trudy was like a mom to Sami Jo. Stepped in to help after Lauren died but Trudy was more than happy to do it. We'd tried to have another child after Melanie but it wasn't in the cards for us. Damn shame about Lauren though. Chase loved that woman."

They reached the track and the driver let them off at a special entrance for drivers and staff. Humid air flooded the car as Gray opened the door.

The lobby was buzzing with activity. They snaked their way through the drivers and their families, following Sami Jo, who headed straight for the locker room without acknowledging any of them.

Gray took up a post in the hallway just outside the locker room door as Royce walked over to a group of people congregating around Ray Skinner when his cell rang.

"Gray, it's Uncle John."

"Hey, Uncle John," Gray said, walking over to a quiet corner within sight of the locker room door. "Sorry I haven't had a chance to get over to see you guys. I've been busy."

"No problem, son. Good to hear you were able to take on Royce as a client. Look, I know you've only been in town a few days but your Aunt Fran is dying to have you over for dinner. She promised your mom that she'd make you some home-cooked meals while you're here."

"I appreciate that. Any chance I can bribe you guys to tell Mom I've already been there a few times?" Gray chuckled.

"Wish I could, Gray. But you know how much Fran adores your mom. She'll want to show you some hospitality just to stay in her good graces."

"I understand. We're in Kansas City right now."

"Oh, yes. I know. We watch every Sunday. When are you back? Monday?"

"Well, yes, but—"

"Great. Let's shoot for Monday night then."

Before Gray could protest, Sami Jo was exiting the locker room in her racing suit. She ignored him and walked over to Royce.

"I gotta run, Uncle John. Give my best to Aunt Fran."

"You can give it to her yourself when you see her, son."

Gray hung up and Royce flagged him over.

"Feel free to hang back, Gray. We've got her from here," Royce said and followed Sami Jo through a door to a holding room.

Sure. I'll just hang back and try to come up with an excuse to get me out of a family dinner.

Otherwise, if he still had this job by Monday, Sami Jo would have to tag along.

When it was Sami Jo's turn to race, Gray joined Royce in the viewing booth. It was almost noon and the sun beat down on the faces in the stands. Royce had told him another series was racing that afternoon but most fans made a day out of it and showed up for qualifying.

Sami Jo's pink car shot out of pit row like a bullet. The sound of her motor, even alone on the track, was thunderous. All forty-three cars would be deafening tomorrow for sure.

Her two laps were completed in under a minute and based on the eruption in the booth and the stands, she'd done well. The crew jumped up and down as she returned her car to the pit.

Royce's hands went into the air and he howled. "She broke the record!"

Gray followed Royce out of the booth and down to the track as Sami Jo got out of her vehicle and her crew surrounded her, shouting excitedly.

She removed her helmet, the serious look from earlier replaced with joy. Royce rounded the car to meet her and pulled her into a bear hug. When he released her, her gaze briefly made contact with Gray's, then she was swept up by the applauding crew.

Gray kept within a manageable distance for the rest of the afternoon as Sami Jo proceeded to have lunch with Matt and the other drivers in a small conference room provided by the track. When Matt escorted them to the parking lot later that afternoon, Sami Jo climbed into the back seat. She still hadn't said a word to him.

Matt signaled that he wanted a word with Gray before he got in.

"Can you do me a favor? Make sure she eats something tonight, even if you just order room service."

"Sure." Gray nodded.

"I know it's not typical security duty but today was huge for her. And if anything, she'll be in her head too much to take care of herself."

Gray shook Matt's hand and got in the car.

At some point, she'd have to talk to him, even if it was to pick an entree.

———

The hot water streaming from the showerhead purged the sweat and grime of Sami Jo's day.

Too bad it couldn't wash away the embarrassment she'd felt from Gray's rejection last night.

Thankfully, once she'd gotten behind the wheel of her

race car that afternoon, she'd been able to block all of it from her mind. Focusing on the asphalt was her only option; otherwise, she would've crashed in one of the turns at two-hundred miles per hour. Today's qualifying results were a huge win for her. Not only would she be in the best position on the track tomorrow, but she was also the first woman to break the track record. This was what she'd worked so hard to achieve because nothing she'd earned had been handed to her. It was not only a matter of proving her skills to her sponsors, her fans, or even Royce. It was confirmation for herself that she was truly good at it. Her time today proved she was exceptional, yet she seemed to desire some sort of validation from Gray.

When she stepped out of her car to the cheers from the crowd and the accolades from Royce and her crew, it was his gaze she sought. She didn't know what she'd expected—that he'd run over to her, congratulate her, give her the attention she needed to confirm she'd done something epic? Instead, he'd stood back from the crowd, stoic and detached.

After she dried off, she pulled on a t-shirt and cotton shorts that hung on the back of the bathroom door, and as she brushed out her damp hair, the chaos of emotions heightened.

The familiarity of his touch crept back in, especially when their bodies and lips had made contact. The sensation of how it felt seemed impossible to shake. She'd agonized all night over what had happened, had barely slept, and when she did it was fitful. She'd felt like that eighteen-year-old girl again and all of the heartbreak had flooded back through her.

With Royce's early visit to her room that morning and the meeting with Matt that afternoon, she'd pretty much been able to avoid him. She'd called Alec on the ride back to the hotel to fend off any conversation in the car and when they'd reached her room, she'd escaped into the bathroom still on her phone and sequestered there until she heard Gray shut the adjoining door between their suites. Now she just needed to keep evading him.

Exiting the bathroom, she found Gray standing in the doorway to his suite.

So much for that plan.

He held up a leather-bound booklet. "What did you want for dinner? I'll order it."

"I'm not hungry."

She went to the bed, picked the remote up off of the comforter, and sat on the edge of the mattress.

Gray moved to stand in front of her. "I promised Matt you'd eat. Pick something."

She peered around him at the TV. "I'll do it later."

He snatched the remote from her, turned off the TV, and pushed the booklet toward her.

She took it and flipped through the pages, but his large frame loomed over her and muddied the words on the page.

"Just get me the flatbread pizza."

"That's not enough, what else?"

"That's plenty." She slapped the menu shut and handed it back to him.

He took it to the adjoining door and turned back. "Sami Jo, about last night—"

"Just forget it, Gray. I'm trying to do the same."

He nodded and as he went through the door into his room, Sami Jo picked up the remote and moved to the small sofa. She didn't turn on the TV. Instead, she studied the numbers on the remote. Her fingers brushed lightly over the buttons. She didn't want to watch anything, she just wanted to stop thinking about it. Stop feeling his lips on hers, stop missing the warmth and weight of his body.

She put the remote down and closed her eyes. Exhaustion washed over her as she settled deeper into the cushions.

Focus on tomorrow. Focus on the race.

Eventually, she drifted off and woke to Gray setting a tray on the low table in front of her.

"Guess I dozed off." She sat up and looked at the tray. Both entrees were concealed under metal covers. Two sets of silverware were wrapped in maroon linen napkins and a large piece of cake sat under a clear plastic lid.

"Congrats, by the way," Gray said, nodding at the dessert. "It was a big day for you. You must be thrilled."

As he picked up one of the covered plates and turned to go, something Aunt Trudy used to say came to her.

Never miss an opportunity to show kindness.

Despite her reluctance to admit it, Gray's reaction last night was justified. Did it make her feel like shit? Sure. Was it his fault it happened? No.

Plus, he'd ordered her cake.

Damn you, Trudy.

"If you'd like to stay, you're welcome to. I mean, don't feel obligated but eating alone in a hotel room can be one of the saddest things ever."

The corner of his mouth turned up slightly. "I've always thought that."

He set the plate down and pulled the chair over to the table. He took the covers off both of their entrees and paused.

"Can I just say one thing?" he asked.

"Is it gonna make me regret the invitation?" She eyed him suspiciously.

"Probably," he said, putting the covers to the side. "It's just...the way I freaked out...I was, I don't know...shocked to find you...you know. I had planned to apologize this morning, but Royce was here. I was afraid it was going to impact qualifying today. It didn't but..."

Sami Jo chuckled.

"What's funny?"

"I've just never seen you this tense. Usually, you're so serious and calm."

"Well, this isn't easy for me, Sami Jo. This isn't how I wanted things to play out. But I owe you an apology for more than last night." He ran a hand over his face. "I was a huge jerk to you when I left and I'm sorry. You didn't deserve to be treated that way."

His words settled in. He was apologizing for the break-up? How unexpected. But a huge weight seemed to have been lifted off his shoulders. Maybe forgiving him would make her feel better too. And if he continued to hang around, keeping her safe, she knew she couldn't avoid him forever. He was living in her house after all.

"Yeah, it sucked. I'll give you that much. I spent a lot of time trying to get over that summer. Trying to figure out what was wrong with me."

"There was nothing wrong with you, Sami Jo."

"You made it pretty clear you weren't into me. Not the way I was into you."

"That's not entirely true. But the last thing I wanted back then was a relationship. Hell, I wasn't even looking for a summer fling. I was in Myrtle Beach that summer because I was running away from a bad situation at home. I went there to lay low." He sat down in the guest chair next to the sofa and clasped his hands between his knees, studying them.

"Things with my dad had gone south when he initially found out I'd enlisted," he continued. "He said I was wasting my talents following orders when I should be giving them. We didn't speak to one another for a long time. When I came home after my first tour, I found my ex-girlfriend on my parent's front porch with a two-year-old in her arms."

"You have a kid?"

"No," he said. "I had broken things off with Danielle before I left for boot camp. She didn't take it well, which shocked me because we fought most of the time. Right after I left, she got pregnant, and after things didn't work out with the guy she was seeing, she'd gone to my parents saying the kid was their grandchild. I think she'd hoped they'd talk sense into me to get back together with her. I demanded a paternity test and as expected, it wasn't mine. But it put my family through a lot. Drove a bigger wedge between me and my dad. I thought it was best to get the hell out of there and spend my summer elsewhere."

"I think I can relate to the romanticism of running away," she said.

"As I said, I wasn't looking for anything but from the second you and I met, I was hooked. You were funny and sweet, and interesting. But I didn't want to unload all my problems on you. I was trying to bury them. Being with you helped me forget about a lot of it. I did have a lot of fun that summer."

"If you were having such a great time, why did you end it the way you did?"

"I realized how selfish I'd been. I had taken advantage of you so I could forget about all the shit going on in my life." He looked down at his hands. "In recovery, I'd been thinking a lot about people I've wronged. I don't know, maybe almost losing my life put some things in perspective. I figured taking this assignment would be the perfect opportunity to make up for the way I acted."

"What if Royce hadn't hired you? Were you just going to show up someday?"

Gray shrugged. "I hadn't thought that far in advance. But I'm here and I want you to know I regret how I ended it. I did care about you, Sami Jo, but I'd fucked up most of my relationships at that point. You were just one more. I guess I needed you to hate me as much as I hated myself."

"Trust me, I could be the poster child for fucked up

relationships." She laughed despite herself.

"You seem pretty happy with Alec Clarke," he said.

Sami Jo swallowed. "We're not—together. What you see on the surface is all created by the media. Alec and I are just friends. We've never been a couple."

"Why the ruse?"

"Makes things easier. We're both focused on our careers and neither one of us wanted to be distracted by a relationship. And as Royce would say, the more people talk about you, the better. Our so-called relationship generated a buzz, that's for sure. But it's hard when everyone wants a piece of you. That's why I retreat from all this when I can. I escape to clear my head."

"Not telling people where you are is risky," he said.

"I know." She nodded. "But I won't get any peace if they knew how to reach me. You see how crazy my life is."

"Well, promise me in the future you'll take precautions. You probably won't need to hire security every time but someone should always know where you are."

Sami Jo chewed on her bottom lip. "Do you regret that we never had sex?"

He stared at her for a moment.

"I stand by my argument that it was something you should do with someone you love and I certainly wasn't worthy of anyone's love," he said. "But yeah, I do regret that."

She held his gaze for a moment then laughed.

"Now what are you laughing at?" he asked.

"I don't know, maybe we should've gotten all of this out of the way on day one."

He chuckled. "Yeah, it probably would've saved us a whole lot of drama."

Her thoughts turned serious. "What's going on with the other women who are being targeted? Are they being protected as well?"

"I'm not sure. I'll have Cole give them a call."

"I'm happy to give you a reference if you need me to."

"Are you trying to get rid of me?" he asked.

"No," she said. "But it would be a shame if they didn't have someone watching their back the way you watch mine."

He gazed at her for a long time. "You're precious cargo, Sami Jo. I'm not going to let anything happen to you."

"I'll try not to make your job too tough then."

"I'd appreciate that." He nodded toward her plate. "Now eat, would you?"

She did as she was told, thankful they'd cleared the air.

Now if she could only stop thinking about kissing him again.

LAP ELEVEN

KANSAS SPEEDWAY'S GRANDSTANDS WERE FILLED with race fans hours before the green flag was set to fly. By thirty minutes to race time and according to the jumbo screen across the track, a quarter of the beer inventory had been sold and over fifteen thousand hot dogs had been consumed.

Gray took his spot in the viewing stand above pit row with a headset supplied by Matt that would allow him to listen in on the conversations between Sami Jo and Royce, who was acting as a spotter from high above the grandstands. The sun beat down on the canopy above him as a slight breeze cooled the humid air. In the stands behind him, an audience of all ages gazed down upon the track, their faces shielded by hats and sunglasses and some with their ears protected by large noise-canceling headphones.

He felt much lighter now that he and Sami Jo had talked about their history. Hopefully, it would be much easier working with her now that they'd got it all out in the open. But to say he'd been disappointed to end the night early was the understatement of the year. He could've stayed and chatted with her well into the morning if she didn't have to race today. Once her guard was down and they'd been able to converse without all the snarky exchanges their previous conversations held, he found himself opening up to her and had learned more about her upbringing with Royce and Trudy.

The Alec situation was interesting for sure. Knowing she wasn't in a relationship seemed to ease his mind even if it kept floating back to the idea of taking her in his arms and kissing her—okay, maybe more than *just* kissing her.

He scanned to the track below where Sami Jo stood with her team. As if she felt his gaze on her, she looked up at the booth and smiled. He nodded and continued to examine the crowd on the track. Drivers stood by their cars with their wives and kids and it struck him that Sami Jo had no one by her side to cheer her on, encourage her, or show support.

He turned to Matt who stood at the railing. "Is it okay if I go down there?"

Matt gave him a confused look. "Yeah. Sure, Gray."

Gray pulled off his headset and set it on a chair. He headed to the stairs and down to pit row.

As he pushed through the small crowd of people to get to her, she looked up.

"What's wrong?" she asked when he approached.

"Nothing," he said. "I thought I'd come to wish you luck."

A smile formed on her lips. "You taking pity on me, Grayson Finch?" she asked.

"Well, I did notice all the other drivers are surrounded by family and friends."

"Is that what we are now?" She lifted a brow and grinned. "Friends."

"I sure hope so." He gazed down on her and the way she looked up at him made him wonder if he would be able to keep it in his pants.

The moment was interrupted by the announcer on the

field.

"Good afternoon, Kansas City," a male voice boomed through the speakers on the infield.

The large screen across the track zoomed in on an older man in a NASCAR polo who stood at a podium. After a few opening remarks, he introduced all of the drivers. When he said Sami Jo's name, her face appeared on the screen. She waved as a roar came over the crowd.

Once the lineup was completed, the announcer led a prayer and introduced a retired veteran who sang the national anthem. At the song's crescendo, five fighter jets zoomed over the track.

Gray felt movement at his side as Sami Jo put on her helmet.

He tugged on her arm. "Be careful out there, Hot Shot."

"See you in a few hours." She said and slid in through the window.

When Gray returned to the viewing stand and picked up his headset, Royce was already speaking to her in terms he barely understood.

"Lady and gentlemen, start your engines."

The cars came to life all at once, vibrating the stands as engines revved. One by one, the cars rolled away from pit row and onto the track, following a pace car wrapped in the logo of the race's sponsor. As the vehicles rounded the third turn, the pace car veered off and the green flag was waved. In an instant, all of the cars zoomed ahead, with Sami Jo leading them. By the time they rounded the track again, she was clocked at one-hundred and eighty-nine miles per hour, according to the big screen.

His heart rate went up a tick. With all forty-three cars on the track, it was louder for sure, but the pack of vehicles driving close together at such a high speed was unsettling. After sixty laps, she pulled into pit road to refuel and have her tires changed out. It all happened in under ten seconds. Once the jack was pulled out from under her vehicle, she squealed her tires and was back on the track to play catch up with the lead drivers.

Gray noted her place on the leader board next to the big screen. She had been in the top five for the entire race, now she was trading positions with third and fourth. As she neared the four-hundredth lap, it looked like she was a shoo-in for second place.

In one of the turns, Royce's shouts came through his headset. The car that had been drafting behind Sami Jo was accelerating but as it went past her, the car's front end smacked into the rear corner of her car.

It all happened fast.

The back end of Sami Jo's car slid and slammed into the concrete wall. Another car couldn't avoid the collison and smashed into her front end, ripping off the wheel and most of the sheet metal from the car's nose. Sparks from the dragging metal caused a fireball to engulf her vehicle and debris scattered everywhere. It felt like it took forever before her the car came to a stop on the grassy infield but in reality, it was only about eight seconds.

Gray grabbed Matt's arm. "What's happening? Is she okay?"

"The fuel cell opened up." Matt held up his hand and spoke into his headset. "Sami Jo, you good?"

"Yeah, can I get out?"

"Go ahead. All clear." Royce's voice came through the headset. "Emergency crew is on its way."

Matt turned toward Gray. "She's fine, Gray. She'll be okay."

Gray never felt so helpless in his life. Okay, maybe once—when the chopper went down and he couldn't find his team. But now his hands were shaking badly he had to stuff them in his pants pockets.

He'd promised to keep her safe and right now there was nothing he could do but let the emergency team do their thing.

It took everything not to run onto the track to get to her.

———————

"She's fine, Gray. She'll be okay."

Matt's voice came through Sami Jo's headset.

While Gray's concern was sweet, anger consumed her as she surveyed the wreckage that had once been her car.

She removed her helmet and swore at the sky as two emergency vehicles pulled up alongside the twisted heap of metal. Swirling black and gray smoke danced through the air as the small flames were extinguished by the fire crew.

One of the EMTs exited the red-and-white rescue unit and approached her. "Miss McLean, are you okay?"

"Who hit me? Was it eighteen? Was it Trimble?"

It *had* to be Casey Trimble. He'd flaked during practice, almost hitting her then too. Historically, he was a hot dog on the track and she'd had run-ins with him in the past. Today he'd cost her second or potentially first place.

The young EMT shrugged and led her over to the vehicle to take her away from the scene. Within minutes, they pulled up to the brick infield medical center. Sami Jo exited and looked over at the large screen across the track as it displayed a replay of the accident.

"Dammit!" she shouted as she watched Trimble's car tap the back corner of hers. His vehicle had also spun out into the wall, exploding into pieces, which meant he'd be heading to the medical center where she fully intended to give him a piece of her mind.

The EMT took her by the elbow and guided her into the facility.

Disinfectant permeated the air and the beige linoleum floor glowed under long rows of fluorescent lights. An island of workstations sat in the center of the cavernous room, manned by doctors, nurses, and other medical staff. Exam tables lined one long wall, each flanked by privacy curtains.

The EMT dropped her off at the first table and Sami Jo hopped up on the paper-covered cushion.

"Sami Jo?" Matt's voice echoed throughout the facility.

"I'm here." She pulled off her gloves and threw them down on the rolling tray table next to her.

Matt rounded the corner with Gray behind him.

Gray seemed fraught with worry and his chest heaved as if he'd run his ass off through the pedway to get to the medical center.

"It was Trimble," she said, pushing sweaty strands of hair away from her face.

"Looks like it." Matt came to the side of the table. "Are you okay?"

"I'm pissed off."

"I know. Just let the doc check you out, okay?" Matt patted her shoulder.

Voices from the entryway caused them all to turn as a small group of people followed Casey Trimble through the medical center. He carried his helmet by his side and his tanned features were beaded with sweat. His curly, reddish-brown hair was matted, but his cocky swagger said it all—even though he crashed, he still thought he was hot shit.

He didn't even look over at her as he strutted past.

"Hey," she called out to Trimble as she hopped off the exam table and rushed after him.

By the time she reached him, he was sitting down on an exam table a few sections over. "What the hell, Casey?"

Trimble ignored her.

"Can I get a bottle of water?" he asked in his southern drawl.

"What the hell were you doing out there?" She took a step toward the table but no one budged.

"Come on, Sami Jo," Gray said behind her. His hand landed on her shoulder but she jerked away.

"No, I want to know what this dickwad was thinking?"

"I was thinkin' you should've been behind me, sweet cheeks," Casey said, removing his gloves.

"You've always raced dirty, Casey. And look where it gets you."

Gray's hand came down on her shoulder again. This time, she gave in, muttering to herself as she returned to the exam area.

Matt had walked over to the entrance with his phone to his ear.

"Now who's the tough guy?" Gray said, helping her back onto the table.

"I had it, Gray. I was so close."

"The important thing is, you're okay," Gray said. "You are okay, right?"

"Yeah." She looked down at her charred suit and swore again.

A doctor approached. His tall frame was cloaked in scrubs and a lab coat. "Hi, Sami Jo. I'm Doctor Osborne."

Gray pushed a wayward strand out of her face. "I'll be right around the corner."

The doctor pulled the curtain closed, blocking them inside the small space. "Let's get you out of that suit."

Sami Jo relented and unzipped. She shivered as the air conditioning hit her fire-resistant undergarments and sweat-drenched skin.

Fucking Trimble.

After breaking the record and finally having a good chat with Gray, she'd been feeling invincible. Hopefully, the sponsors would see the crash was unavoidable.

The doctor removed his stethoscope from the pocket of his lab coat and began a physical exam. He took her blood pressure and asked questions about dizziness, weakness, and headache. As the wave of adrenaline wore off, an ache settled all over her body. She was a little dizzy and a wave of exhaustion came over her.

"Everything looks good, Sami Jo," he said once he'd completed his exam. "But I'm going to have you go over to St. Luke's for an MRI, just to be safe. Sit tight."

She zipped up her racing suit as the doctor pushed the curtain open revealing Trimble walking past with his entourage.

Trimble paused and turned toward her. "Next time, I suggest you stay out of my way, McLean. You don't wanna end up like Chase."

Sami Jo opened her mouth to tell him where he could stick his suggestion but a wall of muscle side-swiped Trimble.

Gray held the driver by the front of his fire suit and shoved him into the tray table next to her. Casey's crew did nothing to stop the altercation, which was telling.

"Let go of me, motherfucker." Casey pushed at Gray's chest to no avail.

"Hey, asshole, you need to apologize to her." Gray yanked on the guy's suit, jerking him hard enough that Trimble had to reach out to the exam table for balance.

"Go fuck yourself," Trimble responded.

Gray grabbed Trimble's hand and contorted it in a direction that caused the guy to yelp in pain.

"Okay, okay. I–I'm sorry," Trimble squeaked out.

"Not good enough." Gray applied more pressure and Trimble's knees buckled. Gray continued holding him up. "Do you want me to break your hand?"

Trimble's eyes darted to Sami Jo. "I'm sorry for my incompetence, Sami Jo."

Gray pulled Trimble up and pushed him toward his people with a shove. The man collected himself and stalked past the group toward the door.

As the rest of them slowly walked away, Sami Jo noticed Danny Welliver leaning against the counter at the center island. He raised a hand and waved. Before she could do the same, Gray pulled the curtain closed.

His chest heaved again. His hand went up to push back his hair as a heavy breath expelled through his open mouth.

"My hero," Sami Jo said warily.

Gray stared at her and in an instant, he closed the short distance between them. His hands went up to cradle her face as he leaned in and his lips settled on hers. His kiss only lasted a few seconds but she savored every one of them. His lips were soft on hers and she could smell his musky cologne—or maybe that was just him—and his short beard brushed against her skin.

He pulled back a few inches and studied her face. "I was so afraid you were seriously hurt."

"The doc wants me to get an MRI." She saw the panic wash over him. "Just as a precaution. I feel fine. Just a little jostled."

He removed his hands but remained close. "Jostled? Jesus, Sami Jo, your car spun like a goddamn top. I'm surprised you came out of it without a scratch."

His eyes traveled over her.

Kiss me again.

"It probably looked worse because of the fire. But I'm fine. I just want to get this hospital crap out of the way and go take a hot bath back at the hotel."

The curtain flew open and Royce stepped inside the area. Gray quickly took a few steps back but Royce didn't seem to notice their intimate moment or Gray's flustered reaction.

"There's my girl," Royce said. "Doc said you'll live but we gotta get you over to St. Luke's."

"I can take her, Royce," Gray spoke up.

"Thanks, Gray, because Matt and I need to catch up with Ray and Luke."

"How'd they do?" Sami Jo asked.

"Middle of the pack, as usual," Matt answered as he entered the space.

"You did great, kiddo," Royce said. "Tough luck but don't let it get you down, okay? Text me the MRI results once you have them and go get some rest."

Royce shook Gray's hand and he left the medical center with Matt.

Sami Jo slid from the table and collected her things. "Let's go back to the locker room. I need to change."

Gray nodded and followed her.

As they were leaving, Danny Welliver approached them. "Sami Jo, good to see you're okay."

She nodded. "Thanks, Danny."

"Care to comment on Casey Trimble's behaviors on the track?"

Gray stepped in front of her before she could answer. "Sorry, we're in a rush."

Welliver smiled widely at Gray. "Maybe *you'd* like to comment on why you had your hands around Casey's throat?"

"Give Diane a call at the shop and we'll set up some time, okay?" Sami Jo said, trying to get them out of there before Gray did the same thing to Welliver.

Gray guided her out the door quickly.

Although the race was over, the cheers from the stands were still echoing through the pedway back to the main building. No doubt whoever finished in the top three were standing on victory lane, preening for the crowd and cameras. She should be up there but right now all she could think about was Gray's kiss.

It was on her mind when she changed in the locker room and when they drove over to St. Luke's hospital in Gray's Escalade. Even as she laid prone inside the MRI, the banging and clanging of the machine couldn't distract her from the feel of his lips, his hands on her face, and the look in his eye when they'd been alone in the curtained-off exam area.

People did crazy things in times of tension. Was he simply freaked out by the accident?

Back in the hospital's dressing room, she pulled her clothes on again and looked in the mirror. Their talk last night had been interesting, except she still felt a kind of unease around him.

And the intense desire to have him kiss her again.

Lap Twelve

GRAY HAD HEAVED A BIG sigh of relief when the doctor told him Sami Jo would be fine.

Nothing had appeared on the MRI and her fatigue was most likely due to the trauma of the crash but Gray was still a nervous wreck. She was like a priceless Faberge egg to him now. But he was the one who felt like he was being cracked—cracked wide fucking open.

Back at the hotel, he'd insisted on waiting in her room while she took a bath. He fluffed the pillows on her bed, turned down the blanket, and ordered dinner while she soaked. He even dimmed the lights, making it cozy and serene for her.

This was way outside the boundaries of his job but he couldn't help himself.

Alec isn't in the picture.

The information had scrambled his brain all day and when her car spun out on the track, on fire no less, he'd felt—something. Probably something he shouldn't, but when her car had skidded to a stop and he saw her get out, his heart rejoiced.

Then he'd gone and kissed her.

He heard the sound of the drain open up in the tub and again, he felt some relief.

The door to the bathroom opened and Sami Jo emerged in a big fluffy hotel robe. Towel-drying her hair, she stepped over to the bed.

"Did the maid service come and do this?" she asked.

He looked up, sheepishly. "Uh, no."

"Well, maybe you have a new calling." She chuckled. "But wait, no piece of chocolate on the pillow?"

He laughed. "I can do you one better."

He produced a bottle of brandy from the mini-bar. "This goes good in the tea I ordered for you."

"Score," she said, her eyes brightening. "But Gray, I'm fine. You don't need to dote on me. I'm quite capable."

"I know but I want to dote on you." He held her gaze for a second and glanced at the adjoining door. "Do you mind if I go change? I should be back before room service gets here."

"Please, do whatever you need to do." She plopped down on the bed and resumed drying her hair.

Gray stepped into his room and peeled off his shirt. His cell phone rang as he went to loosen his belt. Seeing it was his mom, he cursed himself for not calling her back after missing several of her calls all day.

"Grayson, is everything okay? We saw the race today, and oh my goodness, that crash."

"Everyone is fine," he said, balancing the phone between his ear and shoulder as he stepped out of his pants. "How are you, Mom? Knee doing okay?"

"It's been better. I'm using a cane now. Your father makes fun of me. Calls me his 'old lady.' But Gray, that crash was horrific. Sami Jo wasn't hurt?"

An incoming call beeped into his ear. He pulled the phone away for a second and saw it was Cole. "She's fine, Mom. But can I give you a call tomorrow? Cole is on the other line."

"That's fine, dear. And don't forget to bring a nice bottle of wine to John and Fran when you see them tomorrow night. Love you."

Shit.

He'd forgotten he'd been invited to have dinner with his extended family.

He clicked over to Cole.

"What's up?" he asked.

"Just checking in. You said you were going to call so I wanted to catch you before I head out for the night."

Gray was forgetting all sorts of promises he'd made, no thanks to the interference of the day—and Sami Jo naked in the next room under that damn robe wasn't helping.

"All good here. Just getting settled back at the hotel," Gray replied, tossing his pants on the bed. "Anything I need to know?"

"Actually," Cole said. "There was an incident with one of the other drivers. The Guthrie woman whose home was vandalized."

Gray stilled as he stood in the middle of his room in nothing but his boxer briefs.

"She was attacked in St. Petersburg after her race earlier today. She was walking to her car and someone approached her from behind."

"Jesus," Gray said, rubbing his forehead.

"They had to airlift her. She's laid up in the hospital with some pretty severe injuries."

"She was alone, I take it?"

"Yeah."

Gray had been thinking about the other women, worried for their safety as much as Sami Jo's. He decided it was time to act.

"Cole, do me a favor. Is anyone between jobs right now?"

"Russ just finished up the detail on the Governor of Georgia's campaign tour. What are you thinking?"

"I think it's time we do a little pro bono work."

Cole read his thoughts. "Okay, boss. And I'll see if that

new hire is ready to spin off on his own. I'll get them in touch with St. James and Guthrie's people and deploy them right away."

"Thanks, Cole." He hung up and tossed the phone on the bed.

Whoever was doing this, targeting these women, had to have easy access to them. Maybe it was someone in the racing circle. He started to think about the Vegas incident when Sami Jo was attacked and considered all the people she must've had around her.

"Gray, room service came."

The door to his room pushed open and Sami Jo stopped short as he turned to face her, half-naked. He guessed her jaw would've fallen to the floor had it not been attached.

"Oh, sorry," she said and backed out of the doorway. "Food is here," she called from inside her room.

Gray pulled a t-shirt out of his suitcase and a pair of mesh shorts. In bare feet, he crossed to the adjoining door and went into her suite.

The tray of food was on the low table by the sofa and Sami Jo busied herself setting up the flatware.

"I'm sorry," she said, shaking her head as she straightened the tray. "I shouldn't have barged in like that."

Something stirred inside him and his conscience wrestled with his libido between what was right and what he wanted. Her—he wanted her. Every inch. He put his hand on her shoulder and turned her to face him.

She looked beautiful like this. Damp hair, no makeup, innocent—and what was that look?

Wanting.

But was he even reading her right? She didn't say anything about the kiss earlier. He knew it caught her off guard. Hell, even he didn't realize what he was doing at the medical center earlier that day until he had his lips on hers. And speaking of lips, she was biting her bottom one and it was driving him crazy. He searched her eyes for something that told him this wasn't the worst idea ever. His hand went to her face and his thumb brushed lightly over her cheek.

"Are you gonna kiss me again or what?" she asked.

That was all it took.

He moved before his conscience tried to stop him. His mouth came down on hers as he pulled her against him. Her arms encircled his neck as her body melted into his. All her womanly curves were soft against his frame and her tongue danced with his as her fingers delved into his hair.

She tasted so damn good.

A deep growl escaped his throat as their kiss deepened and his desire for her strained against his shorts.

Gentlemen, start your engines.

Jesus, he wanted to take her right then and there. Hard and fast. But he also wanted to go slow and enjoy every moment, not rush through something they probably should've done years ago.

Her cell phone rang loudly on the table next to the bed but it didn't matter. If anything, Gray held onto her tighter. The fire alarm in their room could've been sounding and he would have ignored it—nothing was going to stop this.

His hand found the front of her robe and slipped inside where her warm skin waited for his touch. The curve of her waist felt right in his palm. The belt of her robe loosened and his tongue moved down her throat. Her hands glided up his arms and gripped his biceps like she was hanging on for dear life as the terry cloth fabric slipped down and exposed her tattooed shoulder. His lips settled on the ink wrapped around it.

The cell phone rang again and his lips hovered over her skin.

"Maybe you should get that," Gray said breathlessly. The last thing they needed was an in-person interruption from Royce.

Sami Jo nodded and turned away, but not before he got a peek at the pink panties she had on under the robe and the lack of anything else. But it was just a glimpse.

"Hey, Matt," she said. "I was just in the shower. I'm fine. Tell Royce I'll just see you guys in the morning."

She turned slightly to look at Gray, her gaze hooded and her robe still slightly open. She looked down at his shorts where he was practically saluting her and wished Matt a good night.

She placed the phone on the table and Gray froze for a moment.

There'd be no going back if he allowed this to happen. But allowing himself to finally have the pleasure of knowing her body? That would satiate every fiber of his being. Even if it were only for one night.

Before any more skepticism could get in the way, Sami Jo shrugged slightly, allowing the robe to fall to the floor. It pooled around her slender ankles and his breath caught at the sight of her. She was more perfect than he'd ever imagined. The swell of her breasts, the inward curve of her waist, and the decorative ink that swirled around her right hip as it dove under the pink fabric.

"Get over here, Gray." Her voice was soft but demanding.

Conscience be damned, she didn't have to ask him twice. He pulled off his shirt and reached for her. Her hands went to the waistband of his shorts and she tugged them down along with his briefs. Her gaze settled on his erection before looking back up at him.

"Sami Jo, are you sure?" he asked.

Her hands skimmed over his chest, over the muscles that tightened as desire coursed through his veins. One hand traveled down to wrap around his cock and she nodded. "I'm sure."

Jesus, this woman was going to be the death of him.

His mouth smashed into hers, finding her tongue, as his hands came up to run his thumbs over the tight buds of her breasts. She was soft, softer than the hard attitude she liked to portray. She arched against his touch and his cock twitched.

His palms drifted down her torso, his thumbs captured the lace waistband of her panties. He pulled from their kiss just enough to remove the cotton barrier and let them drop to the floor. His craving to consume her and be consumed came to a sudden halt as his gaze traveled to her feminine core. She was goddamn perfect.

"Are you just going to stand and stare all night or are you going to get to it?" she asked.

Oh, he was going to get to it, alright.

Sami Jo decided today's unfortunate events didn't matter.

So what if she didn't finish the race or if her first-place win was obliterated along with her car?

Being in Gray's arms, now *that* was all that mattered.

The heat building between them had her holding her breath at times. She felt overpowered by his sheer mass but welcomed the weight of him as he eased her onto the bed and covered her body with his own. His well-muscled back flexed under her hands as he angled down to kiss the tips of her breasts.

It was like a dream.

No, better than a dream. Better than any race she'd ever won, especially when his hands massaged parts of her body that hadn't been touched by a man in quite some time and certainly never like this. One of her legs came up to wrap around his, and she felt the length of him settle onto her sex.

"Not yet," he murmured into her neck as his tongue

continued to dance over her skin.

Shifting onto his hip, his hand slid over her stomach to her thigh. Long fingers trailed down and back up again, dangerously close to where she wanted him to touch her the most. When his hand cupped her opening, she let out a moan. Slowly, he dipped a finger inside of her and she melted under his gentle stroking.

"Oh, God." His voice was raspy in her ear. "You feel good."

She did feel good. Hell, she felt fucking fantastic. And the more magic he did with his finger, the more euphoric it became. Who knew this tough-natured man, who was a damn Navy SEAL, could be this tender with his caress? When he slipped a second finger inside, she arched upward. Her hand went to his face and she pulled him down to her lips.

She wanted all of him. His tongue, his fingers, everything.

The distant memory of the first time he'd ever kissed her was now replaced by a new one. This kiss, this connection between them, was nothing like it was when she was eighteen. His mouth seemed to claim her, mark her as his own. And when he pulled away, she was on the verge of climaxing. The rush was coming hard and fast. Her core tightened around his fingers as her most sensitive nerves created an explosion that sent waves over her entire body. The pulses barely subsided before he'd removed his fingers to position himself over her.

"You're beautiful," he said as he nestled between her legs, supporting himself on his forearms. "I don't want to leave you like this but I should go get a condom."

Her hand caressed his neck and she shook her head slowly, still coming down from the mind-blowing orgasm he'd given her. "I'm on the pill. And I haven't—well, I haven't in a long time. Unless you—"

She couldn't string words together and he laughed,

pushing the hair from her forehead.

"You have nothing to worry about then," Gray said. "You're safe with me."

I know I am.

Sami Jo parted her legs wider, inviting him in. He reached down and guided himself inside, filling her. Making her whole.

The grunt he made was low and animalistic. And damn sexy.

His eyes locked with hers and she studied his face.

God, he was gorgeous. Even the slight imperfections that had cropped up over time, the minuscule lines that had formed on the edges of his eyes. She got lost in them, especially the way he looked at her now. Her fingers trailed along the outline of his mouth, his short beard prickling her fingertips. His tongue flicked out, wetting his bottom lip. She brought her head up to kiss that lip and tugged lightly at it with her teeth.

"Are you okay?" he asked.

"Never better."

"I'm not hurting you, am I?"

"Not at all."

"It's just, you're so damn tight." His mouth came down on hers as his pace started to intensify.

And he was so damn big inside her, she felt as if they were one body, meant to fit snugly together. She tilted her hips and he seemed to dive deeper. The heat between them was equal to an engine and at any second she was going to combust.

Gray closed his eyes and her head sunk deeper into the pillow as the wave of pleasure rose within her again. Her arms wrapped around him and he drove into her faster until he let out a guttural release from his throat.

They panted in unison as their chests heaved together and his lips came down softly on hers. When he pulled away and rolled onto his side, he pulled her into his arms.

His breathing slowed as his fingers ran over the ink on her skin.

"What is this?" he asked, kissing the spot where his fingers had been. "Does it mean something?"

Sami Jo shifted her body so he could see the design that wrapped over her shoulder and onto her upper back. "It's a tribal design for an angel's wing."

His finger traced the outlines of the markings. "For your dad?"

She nodded and turned back into his arms. "He's with me when I race."

"Like an angel guiding you, looking over your shoulder."

She nuzzled into his neck, kissing under his chin. "I'm surprised you don't have any tattoos, having been in the military and all."

"Never had the opportunity."

She studied the scar on his shoulder and dragged a finger across the marred flesh where he'd been stitched up. "Well, you've earned some sort of stripes for this, I think."

Gray grew still and she propped herself up on her elbow.

"What? You don't think so?" She frowned.

He shrugged and brushed his knuckles along the side of her breast. She lightly pushed his hand away.

"Gray, you saved a man's life, didn't you?"

He nodded. "Cole."

"Then you should be proud of what you did."

"There were other guys there, Sami Jo. Other guys who are dead now." He laid on his back and put his forearm over his eyes. "Can we just enjoy the moment and not talk about it?"

Her gaze traveled up and down his body. He might be a wall of muscle but it was held together with a lot of guilt and shame. Not the sturdiest of foundations but who was she to talk? She was, as Mel put it, chasing her daddy's ghost.

"No, we don't have to talk." She traced the lines of his stomach muscles with her finger. "I'm sure there are things we can do other than talk."

Gray lifted his arm slightly and stared at her. "Are you trying to kill me, woman? I mean, gimme a minute." The corner of his mouth turned up.

"Okay," she chuckled. "Sixty, fifty-nine, fifty-eight—"

———

The second time they had sex, Sami Jo was in charge. It was similar to being behind the wheel. Positioned on her seat and guiding the vehicle. But being like this, with Gray, was more thrilling than speeding around the track.

The temperature in the room had kicked up about a hundred degrees and sweat formed a sheen on their skin. She looked down as she moved on top of him, hitting her in the oh-so-right places. He practically glistened, lying there as he held onto her hips, watching her through half-closed eyes. Her hands reached forward to run over the hard ridges of his chest. Her tongue dipped down to lick the wet skin at his neck. She thrust and a raw grunt escaped his lips.

"Is that good?" She murmured against his skin and thrust again.

"So good. Keep going."

She straightened and every inch of him filled her. The sensation rocketed through her and she thought she might explode. She wanted the feeling to last so she paced herself as she rocked over his hips. Liquid heat began to simmer as she undulated against him. His hand came between them and his thumb moved over the nub just inside her opening. Her vision started to fade as pleasure filled her to the brink. Her thrusts quickened to align with his raspy moans until he was matching her momentum with his hips, pushing up from the mattress, deeper and deeper.

Their release was probably heard by the other occupants of the hotel. Hell, maybe even the next town over.

Sami Jo collapsed into the bed next to him, out of breath, disoriented, and very much sated. The phrase *screwing one's brains out* now made sense to her.

After a few minutes, Gray rolled toward her and propped himself up on his elbow. "I imagine dinner is probably cold by now."

She glanced over at his goofy smile and laughed. "Gee, ya think?"

"Probably too late to reorder."

She lifted her head and looked past him at the clock on the table next to the bed. It was past ten p.m. "Well, I do happen to know of a great late-night taco place around here. That is if you think it's safe for us to go out in the world."

"No offense but I'm willing to risk it for tacos."

"Tacos it is." she sat up on the bed. "I should take a quick shower first."

She left the bed and went into the bathroom, turning on the shower. As the water heated up, she looked into the mirror. Her cheeks were flushed and her hair was pretty wild. She appeared properly—tossed.

Stepping into the shower, she willed herself not to wonder what this all meant but she'd have to be careful. She'd already fallen for him once, having her heart broken again wasn't an option. Maybe, just maybe, she could compartmentalize things.

She had always wondered what it would be like with him.

Check. Amazing.

She understood that eventually his job protecting her would be done.

Check. Short-term at best.

They still needed to remain professional in public.

Check. No one can know.

That was assuming their little sexual escapade wasn't a one-time thing. And God, she hoped it wasn't.

As if to answer her question, the shower curtain slid open and Gray stepped inside with her.

LAP THIRTEEN

G RAY BIT INTO THE LAST taco, practically grief-stricken. The food at La Bodega was unbelievably good; he didn't want it to be his last already.

Sami Jo laughed across the table as she gazed at him. "I've never seen anyone enjoy food that much."

"I was starving. I worked up quite an appetite, I guess." He winked at her, still in a haze from their romp. He was even allowing himself a beer with dinner, feeling like he earned it.

Hell, it just felt right—them together like this. Chatting over Mexican food after mind-blowing sex.

He quieted the guilty voice in the back of his mind. He'd deal with it later. Right now, she was smiling at him and he was eating the best damn carne asada he'd ever had.

"Tell me about this Cole character. How did you put it? Your work wife?" She chuckled, spearing salsa with a tortilla chip.

"Well, he's a technical genius. Or maybe more like a hacker. He could covertly get into just about any foreign terrorist network. At Alliance, he digs into the backgrounds of our clients and anyone who might be targeting them."

"Oh yeah? Did he dig into me?"

"Well you're not exactly a government official or questionable individual who might have mafia ties," he said lifting his beer. He paused with it as his lips. "I was able to get info on you all by myself."

She sneered playfully at him. "Is Cole good-looking?"

Gray almost choked on his beer. "What kind of question is that?"

She shrugged. "I'm just curious because it sounds like you have a little crush on him."

Now he was the one who sneered back. "He's not my type. But I guess you could say he's a bit of a pretty boy."

"Ah, a pretty boy." She laughed again.

"He's a good guy. We work well together. Always have," he said. His smile faded a little. "He helped get me through some shit after everything went down in Afghanistan. He's probably the closest thing I've got to a brother."

When the waitress came by their table to clear their plates, Gray took out his wallet.

"Oh, Gray, let me get this. You're on the clock." She reached for her purse.

"No way," he said. "I've been eating on the McLean dime this whole time. I'll get it."

He handed over his credit card to the waitress and took a final sip of his beer.

"Plus, I can always add it to your tab later." His serious tone turned into a chuckle.

"You're hilarious."

After they settled up, Gray escorted her out to the rental car and opened the passenger door for her. For the few seconds it took him to get around to the other side of the car, he had to wonder if they'd have sex again when they got back to the room. He'd certainly be up for it.

On the short drive back to the hotel, she turned on the radio. Some old Lynyrd Skynyrd song came on and she beamed.

"I love this song," she said. "Reminds me of when I was a kid. My dad and Royce listened to a lot of southern rock when I was growing up. I never appreciated it until I was older."

Her hand traveled over to cover his on the gear shift. She sang along to the chorus of the song. Even though she was by no means a singer, she did alright. The fact that she was comfortable around him, enough to croon the lyrics to "Tuesday's Gone," filled his heart. And suddenly, he had déjà vu. It felt like they were back in Myrtle Beach, years ago, riding around the town in her convertible Mustang. Not a care in the world, no place to be. Just the two of them enjoying the moment.

God, how he wished he could go back and change how he'd treated her. Forgo the feeling of not being worthy of her and the feeling of guilt that had unfurled inside him over the years. All he could do now was enjoy every second he had—

Until you leave her again.

They pulled into the parking lot of the hotel and Gray turned off the engine. He got out, rounded the car, and extended his hand to her. She slowly lifted out of the car and they stood looking at each other. He reached up and pushed a stray strand of hair from her face.

Beautiful. Simply and unequivocally. He felt himself being drawn closer in but the sound of a car door startled them both.

"Hey, you two," Matt walked over from where he'd parked one of the other rental cars and Gray stepped away from Sami Jo.

Shit.

It wouldn't fare well if they'd gotten caught.

"Hey, Matt," Sami Jo said.

"You're out late. I thought you were resting." Matt looked back and forth between the two of them.

"I got hungry. And it was too late to order room service." Sami Jo shut the car door and started to walk with Matt toward the lobby doors.

Gray followed, making every effort to wipe any goofy look he might have had off his face.

"We went to La Bodega," she told Matt.

"Oh yeah, I love that place. I'll have to suggest that the next time we're here. We took the team to Anton's as usual. Royce loves his steak." Matt held the door open, letting Sami Jo and Gray inside.

They headed over to the elevators and Gray pushed the call button.

"Gray, I meant to say thanks for delivering that can of 'shut the fuck up' to Trimble today." Matt snickered. "You lived out a fantasy everyone in racing has. I'd flatten that prick if I could."

"Don't mention it," Gray said as they stepped onto the elevator.

Matt pushed the buttons for their respective floors. The ride was short as his room was on a lower floor. As the doors opened again, he turned back to Gray.

"Thanks for keeping an eye on our girl here," Matt said. "Sleep well."

The doors closed and Sami Jo stifled a laugh.

"You were keeping more than 'an eye' on me earlier." She giggled.

He stiffened. He wanted to tell her that was too close and that they'd gotten lucky Matt hadn't noticed their proximity by the car. And Royce, well, he was pretty sure Royce suspected something at the medical center earlier.

He followed her off the elevator to her room and closed the door behind them once they were inside. The bedsheets were in disarray from earlier and his conscience started to do a number on him.

He must've had a look on his face because Sami Jo walked up to him and stared him down. The corner of her mouth turned up and her arms went around his waist. She rested her chin on his chest as she continued to look up at him. He wanted to throw her on the bed, make love to her, and forget everything. He also wanted to go to the other room and take a cold shower to remind himself of his duty.

"We're alone now, Gray," she said. "So you can either stand there and torture yourself by analyzing all the reasons what happened tonight was unprofessional—"

Was he that transparent? Did she already know him that well?

She pulled away and removed her top, revealing the lace bra underneath. "Or, you can get over yourself and come to bed."

Sami Jo turned away to walk to the bed but he caught her arm and pulled her against him.

———

Sami Jo basked in the pleasure of waking up cocooned in Gray's arms, their naked bodies intertwined. It was the first time in all of this she had felt content.

Gray stirred as the alarm on her cell phone chimed and he pulled her closer against his hard chest. It wasn't the only thing that was hard. His erection pushed against her thigh and she reached between them.

Gray's eyes fluttered open and a small smile formed on his lips. "Good morning."

Without a word, Sami Jo rolled him onto his back and straddled him.

That morning they went slow and were attentive to each other's needs even though they didn't have much time before they'd have to leave for the airport. They showered together and wordlessly got dressed, knowing that soon they'd have to pull apart in front of Royce and Matt. And when the time came to exit her room, Gray took her in his arms and kissed her softly and thoroughly.

"I can't wait to get home," she told him. "It's going to be weird not to be able to reach out and touch you whenever I want."

Gray smiled down and her and swatted her behind. "Come on, we have to get going."

They met up with Royce and Matt in the hotel lobby, where they also found Ray Skinner and Luke Dillon. "That was some mishap you had yesterday. How ya feelin', kid?" Ray asked.

"I feel pretty good."

She noticed Luke giving Gray the once-over and again regretted losing her virginity to the guy. But last night and this morning with Gray had made up for it.

They all ordered coffee to go and piled into the rental cars. Matt took Skinner and Dillon, while Royce climbed into the passenger seat of their car as Gray got behind the wheel. Sami Jo settled into the back seat and stared out the window as Royce talked Gray's ear off about the race.

What an eventful few weeks it had been since he'd walked back into her life. If you'd asked her that first day at Royce's if she thought Gray would make his way into her bed, she would've given a big thumbs down. So many emotions and so much uncertainty flooded through her that she had to force herself to think of something else.

Melanie? Nope. Still not talking to her. And she had to say, she was pretty wounded her cousin didn't reach out after the crash yesterday. Maybe she'd get the number to Matt's parents and get them to make Mel talk to her.

Because being forced to do something you don't want to do always goes well.

She'd just have to wait things out. Hopefully, Mel would come around.

Getting home seemed to take forever, no thanks to the layover in D.C. being extended due to bad weather. They should've been in Myrtle Beach around two but when the plane finally landed, it was just past four.

"Gray, I heard what you did," Royce said from the passenger seat as they were driven from the airport back to her place.

Sami Jo froze. What the hell was he talking about? Did Matt mention he saw them standing inappropriately close to one another at the car last night? Jesus, did he somehow hear them having sex?

"And I think it's a very noble thing," Royce said over his shoulder to her in the back seat. She tried not to look like a deer in the headlights. "Did he tell you his company is providing complimentary protection to Guthrie and St. James?"

She glanced at the back of Gray's head. "That's nice of you."

Royce nodded. "After what happened to Ms. Guthrie—"

Sami Jo frowned. "What happened to Angela?"

"I didn't get the chance to tell her," Gray said.

"She was attacked at practice in St. Pete's yesterday," Royce said. "She had to be airlifted and is in pretty bad shape."

"Jesus," Sami Jo muttered, desperately wanting to reach for Gray but clenched her fists instead. A few pictures were one thing but an attack was a whole new level of oh-shit.

They turned into her driveway and she got out in a daze as Royce said goodbye.

She followed Gray up the stairs to her front door and they went inside.

"I'm sorry I didn't tell you about Guthrie," Gray said. "It's just, last night you seemed—happy. I didn't want to ruin your mood."

Sami Jo headed to the fridge to grab a water and a sound from upstairs caused her to jump.

Gray moved quickly, shielding her, with his gun drawn.

A chill ran through her and she placed her hands on his

back, feeling his back muscles flex under his shirt. Foot-steps overhead caused her to jerk her elbow back, hitting the porcelain canisters on the counter. They clanged together and Gray stiffened.

"Sami Jo? Babe? Is that you down there?" Alec's familiar voice came from the second floor and Sami Jo collapsed with relief against Gray.

"It's Alec." She patted him on the back and slipped out from behind his huge frame.

"How did he get in?" he asked, lowering his gun.

"I gave him the code." At the time, she thought it was a good idea. She had wanted Alec to have access if he was ever in town. "Yeah, it's me."

Alec rounded the corner from the stairs, looking every bit the pop star. The photos and videos on the internet never did him justice. It was no wonder young girls lost their minds over him. His short, jet-black hair was per-fectly coiffed with a strip of shocking blonde highlights on top. A shiny silk leopard-print top sparkled under his black jacket.

Alec's light eyes widened at the sight of the gun in Gray's hand. "I tried calling you."

"Shit, Alec, I'm sorry. My phone has been off since we left Kansas City," she said and walked into his embrace.

He wrapped his arms around her and didn't let go for a long time. "I saw the crash on the news this morning. They didn't say if you were okay and when you didn't answer my calls, I hopped on the jet."

Sami Jo pulled away. "Where were you coming from?"

"Milwaukee. I needed to see that you were okay." He looked over at Gray, and with his arm still around Sami Jo, he put out his hand. "Hi, I'm Alec."

Gray holstered his gun and shook it.

"Sorry to scare you guys," Alec released Sami Jo and leaned against the kitchen island. "Sami Jo told me you had to move in."

"I thought it was best," Gray replied rather curtly.

"You probably know exactly what to do in any situation." Alec nodded toward the gun on Gray's hip.

"Don't you have a show tonight?" Sami Jo asked.

"No, I finally have a break. Hey, how about I treat you guys to dinner?"

Sami Jo grinned. "That would be—"

"We can't," Gray said. "I promised my uncle we'd have dinner with them tonight, and where I go, she goes."

"You didn't tell me about this," Sami Jo said.

But Gray ignored her and opened his laptop.

"Why were you upstairs?" Gray asked Alec without looking up from the screen.

"Gray, seriously?" she said.

What the hell is wrong with him?

Alec grinned over at Sami Jo. "I brought you something, it's in your room. Oh, and Gray, I brought you something too. Check the freezer." He pulled at Sami Jo's hand and led her to the stairway.

When they got to the top of the stairs, Sami Jo tugged at his hand. "I'm sorry if he's being rude. I don't know what's gotten into him."

"I do," Alec replied. "It's all over his face. He's in love."

"Oh, for chrissakes, Alec. Be serious."

"I am. Now, close your eyes." He led her into her bedroom. "Okay, open them."

In the window seat of the master sat a bronzed racing helmet.

"It's from your very first race," he said. "I had your uncle send it to me."

Sami Jo's hand went to her mouth and tears surfaced almost immediately.

"Come here." Alec pulled her into his arms. "I'm sorry you're going through this, babe. I'm just glad you have someone watching over you."

"Yeah. Me too."

"Listen, while I'm here, I need to tell you something." Alec pulled from their embrace, his face riddled with apprehension.

She braced herself for more shitty news but his mouth turned up slightly.

"Do you remember Alicia, the woman that did our makeup for the music video?" he asked. "We've been seeing each other."

"That's great, Alec. I remember liking her a lot. She was sweet."

Alec preceded to tell her how nervous he was asking Alicia out. How they'd talked on the phone for hours each night before going on their first date. That she'd been super understanding of his relationship with Sami Jo.

"I wanted to talk to you before we made anything official. I didn't know how you'd want to handle it with the media and I didn't want to take the attention away from the charity event coming up."

"Shit, I forgot about that. I've been so distracted I haven't paid much attention to my schedule."

"Babe, I don't want you overextending yourself through all this."

"No, I want to go. We worked too hard on that video. Plus, we promised we'd both appear for the meet and greet." Sami Jo said.

"Okay, whatever you want. But if you change your mind, I will totally understand."

"I've missed you terribly, Alec. With all that's been going on and Melanie not talking to me, I haven't been able to think straight. I wish we could just spend the evening catching up." Sami Jo's shoulders sagged. "I can't believe Gray didn't tell me about this dinner tonight."

"I'll make it up to you soon." Alec extended his hand to her. "Plus, I don't want to get in his way. I see the way he looks at you."

Sami Jo's throat got dry. "Don't read too much into it, we—well, I mean, we did—"

Alec laughed at her stammering. "You had sex with him. I know. As I said, it's all over his face. It's kind of adorable."

"It just kind of happened. Let's not turn it into something it's not."

Alec kissed her forehead. "Don't be too surprised when you find out he wants more. He'd be a fool not to."

"Oh, Alec, I don't think—"

He put a finger to her lips. "What is it you always tell people? If you think, you slow down? Well, stop thinking and go for it."

LAP FOURTEEN

GRAY PULLED A BOTTLE OF vodka out of the freezer and by the looks of it, it wasn't a cheap brand.

Now, that was a new one. No one ever brought gifts for the bodyguard.

He struggled with his first impressions of Alec Clarke. He'd met quite a few celebrities and most of them were phonies. The images of Sami Jo on his arm had grated his nerves. Now, seeing the guy in the flesh, got his hackles up again.

They're not together, doofus. The last twenty-four hours should prove something.

He tucked the bottle back in the freezer and heard the sound of footsteps on the stairs.

Alec rounded the corner and entered the kitchen alone. His smile exposed the straightest and whitest teeth Gray had ever seen.

"A car should be coming to pick me up in a few minutes. Sami Jo said to tell you she's jumping in the shower. It's nice you're taking her to your family's place for dinner," he said.

The proper thing to do would be to invite the guy but Gray wasn't sure he was all that comfortable with him just yet.

"Look, I know I don't need to tell you this, Gray, but she's special to a lot of people. Including me. And while I'm sure you've seen all the internet chatter about us, just know that's all it is. Chatter."

Instead of responding, Gray crossed his arms over his chest.

Alec chuckled. "She said you were a bit of a hardass. And trust me, I'm grateful for that. She can be as stubborn as a mule sometimes, she needs someone like you who's got her back. But I think you know there's an amazing and very sensitive woman behind that badass exterior."

"That I've figured out," Gray said. "She doesn't always like to be told what to do."

Alec laughed. "Too true, man. I've had to talk her down from the ledge many times but her heart is always in the right place. She can be loyal if you let her in. I found that out the first time we met."

Same here, he wanted to say.

"She told me all about you," Alec said. "One night when we were hashing through all our relationships. Where we fucked things up, where we got fucked over."

Gray stiffened. Was this guy saying he fucked Sami Jo over? Because although it was spot on, it still hurt to hear some else say it.

"You know, I think the reason why she was keen on developing our fake relationship was that she knew she could never fill the void you left. She may have tried a few times but she never got over you."

The sound of a car outside made Alec smile. "That's my ride."

Gray regarded the man before him. Maybe he'd been a little too judgmental of the guy.

"Just in case." Gray reached into his shirt pocket for his business card and slid it across the granite countertop of the island and outstretched his hand.

"Thanks, brother." Alec picked up the card and shook Gray's hand. "Good to meet you."

"You too. And thank you for the vodka."

He watched the pop star exit the house and looked down at his laptop. The work he'd been pretending to do had just been a distraction. He was finding it hard to focus around Sami Jo since they'd been intimate. Not that he was complaining. She was amazing. But she jostled his brain, especially when they were naked.

He shut the laptop in defeat. He'd have to check emails later when his head clearer.

Sami Jo met him in the kitchen an hour later, dressed in a tan scoop neck sweater and navy capris. The delicate teardrop necklace hung from her neck and her hair was pulled into a braid held together by a gold band.

"Is this appropriate?" she asked, looking down at her clothes.

"Perfect." He had changed as well, into a casual pair of pants and a polo. "Do you happen to have a bottle of wine you can spare? I don't want to go empty-handed and we'll be late if we have to stop."

"Sure. As long as I get to give it to them. Do they know I'm coming?"

He grimaced. "Sorry, but there was so much—"

"Sex?" she said quickly and raised her brows.

He laughed lightly and rubbed the back of his neck. "Yeah."

She sauntered over to him and brought her hands up to his chest. "I guess I can forgive you. But it's gonna cost you."

His cock twitched as he gazed into her eyes. "Oh, yeah?"

"I'll just be sure to throw you under the bus if they say anything." She raised on her toes and planted a quick kiss on his lips. He could smell the soap she used and the perfume she wore, and it intoxicated him.

"Who knew you were this ruthless, Ms. McLean?" He patted her on the behind.

"I like to win. I'll go get the wine," she said, leaving him aching in the kitchen.

On the ride to dinner, Gray reached over and put his hand on her thigh. It felt right even though things had gone from avoidance to touchy-feely rather quickly in the last twenty-four hours.

"What did you think of Alec?" she asked, putting the wine bottle between her feet to balance it.

"I think he spends a lot of money to get his hair to look the way it does."

She laughed and squeezed the top of his hand. "You're not wrong."

He glanced over at her as she stared out the window. Her smile softened him. "He seems like a nice guy."

"He is and the girl he's started seeing is a real sweetheart."

"Won't that make things awkward with the media?"

"We talked about how we can break-up, so to speak. You know, everyone loves a good story but they can also be ruthless and cruel. We'll figure something out."

Gray pulled up to the large brick house that belonged to his aunt and uncle and parked in the circular driveway.

As Myrtle Beach's most successful realtors, their home looked like a museum. The lawn was perfectly manicured, strategically-placed lights illuminated the front facade, and colorful flower beds bloomed under the picture windows.

They followed the path of fragrant hyacinths that led to the back of the house where exposed white bulbs were strung from the pergola over the outdoor dining table. Flames flickered inside the grill on the edge of the patio.

"Grayson," Uncle John called as he exited the house with a tray of meat in his hand.

Gray waved and walked over to slap his uncle on the shoulder. "Hey, I hope you don't mind. I brought someone."

"Sami Jo? Well, look at you." John set the tray down next to the grill and outstretched his arms to her. "I'm glad to see you're okay. We watched your race yesterday and couldn't believe that idiot Trimble."

Sami Jo hugged him briefly and held out the bottle of wine. "Someone needs to ban him from racing."

"Boy, you aren't kidding." John took the wine from her and looked toward the house. "Frannie, honey. Look who's here."

Fran appeared with a platter of appetizers, her curly red hair held back with a decorative headband. When she saw Sami Jo, she shoved the platter into Gray's hand as she passed him.

"Sami Jo, sweetie. It's good to see you. It's been much too long." She hugged Sami Jo then stepped back to look at her.

Gray felt like the odd man out. He hadn't seen Fran in years and yet she was all about his companion.

He cleared his throat. "Am I invisible over here, Aunt Fran?"

Fran glanced in his direction and shooed him away, but then laughed and turned to motion him over.

Gray set the tray on the outdoor dining table and pulled her into a hug.

"How's my favorite nephew?" she asked, her small frame getting lost in their embrace.

"I hope you don't mind feeding an extra mouth. Sami Jo and I are joined at the hip lately."

And then some.

Fran released him and turned back to Sami Jo. "You poor thing. John told me all about that stalker business you're dealing with. It's just terrible."

"Okay, Frannie. Leave her alone," John said, stepping

in. "Can we interest you both in our famous twisted tea? We just set out a fresh batch. Oh, unless you're on duty, Gray."

"I think it's safe for me to have one. But Sami Jo, I'm warning you, more than one can be dangerous," Gray said.

"It's on the kitchen island." John turned to the grill and started piling meat on the cooking grate.

Gray led Sami Jo through the sliding doors into the kitchen where a two-gallon pitcher sat on the counter with clear plastic cups next to it.

"Let me get you some ice," Gray said and selected two cups from the top of the stack.

"Grayson, is that you?" a familiar voice called out from the other room. "And did I see you brought a date—"

Gemma Finch appeared in the kitchen and stopped short.

Her curly shock-red hair had been straightened and cut to her shoulders, very different from when he last saw her. Gone were the bangs that used to cover her bright green eyes. Eyes that now stared across the room at Sami Jo.

"Gemma," Gray said. "I didn't know you'd be here."

If he had, he would've made an excuse not to come.

"Hey, Gem," Sami Jo said, raising her hand in hello. "Long time."

Gemma blinked and looked over at Gray with her mouth hanging open.

Say something, you dolt.

Gemma walked over to the island and put her hand on her hip. The silence that hung between the three of them was severely uncomfortable.

"Does someone want to tell me what's going on here? Or do I have to guess?" Gemma asked. "I hope you're not following him around like a lost dog again, Sami Jo."

"Royce McLean hired me as her security detail," Gray

answered before Gemma could make any more hurtful comments.

Sami Jo spoke up. "I've been receiving threatening photos and there was an incident in Vegas last month. Other female drivers are being targeted as well. One of them is in the hospital after being attacked after practice and—" Gray could see she was rambling. "My firm is supplying bodyguards to all of them."

Gemma narrowed her gaze at him then looked back at Sami Jo.

"Are you still with Alec Clarke?" Gemma asked.

Sami Jo shook her head. "Actually, we're just friends. Can't believe everything you see in the magazines."

"Is that so?" Gemma didn't seem convinced. "Well, he seems like quite the catch. I have his latest release on my phone. Tyler likes to listen to it in the car."

"Tyler?" Sami Jo asked.

"My son. He's two and brilliant. He's got a real ear for music. My daughter, Lizzy, is napping upstairs. She's six months and outside of the curse of the same wild mane of hair I have, she looks like her dad." His cousin seemed almost proud for a moment.

"I always thought your hair was beautiful," Sami Jo stated. "But I love the new cut."

Gemma ignored the compliment and studied her manicured nails. "Where are you staying, Gray? You know, with all of us gone, I'm sure Mom and Dad would be happy to have you here."

"Thanks, Gem. I'm good," he replied.

Gemma gave Sami Jo a once over and smirked at Gray. "Well, I'm glad you're here, cousin. Even if you had to bring work with you. I guess I should go see if Mom needs help."

As Gemma went outside, Gray noticed the crestfallen look on Sami Jo's face. He filled one of the cups from the pitcher and handed it to her. "You okay?"

Sami Jo sighed. "Yeah. It was just—awkward." She downed the contents of her cup and poured herself another.

———

Gray scanned the yard as they stepped out the back door and noticed a tall, slim man had arrived.

He assumed it was Gemma's husband based on his demeanor with Uncle John. And with his perfect hair and a crisp button-down shirt, Gray would bet the guy was an attorney.

"Gray," Gemma called. "Come meet Tom."

She seemed to ignore the fact that Sami Jo walked beside him.

"Good to meet you, Tom." Gray extended his hand and turned. "This is Sami Jo McLean."

"Sure, the race car driver," Tom said. "You'll have to forgive me. I don't know much about the sport. I'm not from around here so I haven't been exposed."

Gemma threw her arms around her husband and grinned up at him. "Tom's a very busy surgeon."

Surgeon. Close enough.

All through dinner of grilled steaks and Fran's famous garlic mashed potatoes, Gemma had kept quiet, intermittently getting up to check on her daughter. And, if Gray was counting right, she was currently inside refilling her twisted tea for the fourth time.

Otherwise, the interactions between Sami Jo and his family had been cordial. Tyler bounced in Fran's arms for a while, then was passed around the table, landing in Sami Jo's lap. Gray watched her interact with the two-year-old, mesmerized. The little boy laughed in her arms, his chubby fingers touching the pendant on her necklace.

"Sami Jo, you're a natural," John said as he headed over to the grill.

"I've had some practice with James and Emma."

"Oh, yes," Fran said. "I remember when James was born. Trudy practically glowed in the dark."

Sami Jo smiled down at the little boy. "Well, James wasn't nearly as jolly as this little guy. His teething years drove us all insane thanks to the set of lungs he had."

Tom reached over and tousled Tyler's hair. "Trust me, you're catching this one on a good day."

The back door opened and Gemma held it there. Her face darkened at the sight of Tyler with Sami Jo. "Tom, I need you to feed Lizzy."

"Duty calls," Tom said and got up. "You okay with him?"

"Don't worry, I went semi-pro with this years ago." Sami Jo grinned up at Tom before he walked away.

Gray felt sorry for him as he went inside and Gemma stalked after him.

Fran leaned from behind and picked up his plate.

"Let me help you." Gray stood and grabbed some bowls. He looked down at Sami Jo. "I'll be back."

"We'll be fine," she said, bouncing Tyler.

He followed Fran inside and immediately heard Gemma's stern tone. Her words were drowned out by the baby's fussing but she was clearly upset.

"Aunt Fran, I'm sorry if bringing Sami Jo caused any problems."

"Nonsense, Grayson." Fran rinsed off a plate and set it in the dishwasher. "She's a pleasure. Always has been. And I know you care for her."

Gray stiffened. "She's my client, Aunt Fran."

"Of course. I'm sure you're doing a fine job."

Gray sighed uneasily. "I hope so. This guy has made it no secret he's been following her. I ended up having to stay at her place just to make sure she's safe."

"You've got to be kidding me," Gemma said entering the kitchen. "You're living with her?"

Gray blinked back without a response.

"Unbelievable," Gemma said and stomped through the kitchen. She headed out the back door, giving Gray a sinking feeling.

He followed her out, witnessing her pulling Tyler from Sami Jo's arms.

"What's going on with you and Gray?" she asked, hotly.

"Gray told you, he's my security detail. Royce hired him." Sami Jo straightened and he saw that headstrong teen in her momentarily come alive. "Based on your father's recommendation, it seems."

Gemma's eyes clouded and her mouth contorted into a frown. "You can act like it's no big deal that Gray is shacking up with you but I know what you're up to."

"We're not shacking up, Gemma. There have been threats on my life. I'm sure you understand how scary that is."

"Don't tell me how I would feel." Gemma's voice was growing louder.

"Gemma, come on. Don't be that way." Gray reached to touch her shoulder.

Gemma shrugged away. "Still trying to get him to fuck you, huh?"

"Gemma, that's enough," Gray said.

Tom had joined them on the patio and Gray gave him a pleading look.

"Gem, honey." Tom took Tyler from her arms. "Come on, Lizzy needs you."

"I don't blame you for still being upset with me even after all these years, Gemma," Sami Jo said. "I was a shitty friend and I've had to live with that. If it's any consolation, I've missed you. Of everything that happened, how I treated you was my greatest regret."

"I should thank you." Gemma sneered. "I found out what true friendship is. I've been much more selective of who I get close to."

"I'm sorry if my being here made you uncomfortable."

Sami Jo alighted from the chair.

"Your apology means nothing to me," Gemma said, swaying slightly.

"Gemma, you're drunk." Gray kept his voice low.

"And you're an idiot, Gray!" Gemma spat out. "Is business that bad you had to sink to this?"

Sami Jo turned quickly and crossed the patio, heading toward the side of the house.

"Nice work, cousin," Gray said. "Tell Fran and John thanks for dinner."

He hurried after Sami Jo, cursing his cousin for being heartless.

Sami Jo didn't look at him as they got into the Escalade and she held her gaze out the passenger window as they pulled away.

It was a few blocks before Gray cleared his throat. "Sami Jo—"

"Don't—"

"Gemma was out of line." Gray reached across the seats and took her hand, squeezing it.

"She'd had a lot to drink," Sami Jo said. "No sense engaging with someone in that state."

"I'm still sorry it got ugly back there."

When they pulled into the driveway, he shut off the engine. Waves crashed in front of them and Sami Jo dragged a hand across her forehead.

"I feel like everything is out of control," she said.

"I know the feeling. Like everything continues to happen despite your attempt to manage it." He paused and leaned back against the headrest. "When Cole and I were recovering we used to say that the days you intended to zig, life would make you zag, and you couldn't fight it. Cole's physical therapy was way worse than mine; I tried to keep some perspective. At least, I could walk, I'd think. Maybe I couldn't lift my arm but my legs worked. It wasn't always easy looking on the bright side."

"I'm hanging onto some of my bright sides. Breaking that qualifying record." She gazed into his eyes. "And you."

He wasn't a bright side, he was a goddamn instigator. He'd made a move that had completely changed the construct of their relationship he wasn't exactly sure it wasn't adding to the insanity.

"Sami Jo, I don't want to make your life any more complicated than it already is." He paused, seeing the disappointment in her eyes.

"I know exactly what I've gotten myself into, Gray. And for now, unless you feel otherwise, it's what I need."

He hesitated to answer because he knew he needed it too. He just didn't want to admit it because then it would be real.

His lack of response was enough to contort her expression into disappointment.

She opened the door and the overhead light flooded the cab.

Crap.

LAP FIFTEEN

SAMI JO WASN'T SURE WHAT discouraged her more—Gemma's remarks last night after dinner or the fact Gray was now ignoring her.

She had gone straight upstairs to her bedroom last night and shut the door. Part of her had hoped Gray would've come to her room, reassure her that he wanted to be with her, and sleep in her bed.

The reality that he wasn't going to chase after her had settled in. If he felt the same way she did, he would've knocked down her door.

It ended up being a restless night.

She may have said she knew what she'd gotten herself into with him but the truth was she was already addicted to him. Addicted to his touch, his mouth, his body on hers, having him inside of her. Giving that up would be devastating and she knew it.

Just like last time.

Rather than stew about it that next morning, she showered and got dressed.

When she stepped into a pair of flip-flops afterward, she heard Gray's voice across the hall. His tone sounded troubled. She opened her door and walked over to the guest room.

He looked up from the bed when she appeared in the doorway, his cell phone to his ear. There was a pained expression on his face and his chest expanded as he took a deep breath.

"Okay, see you when I can," he said. He hung up and stared at the phone.

"Everything okay?" Sami Jo asked.

"That was my dad," he said. "My mom is being prepped for emergency surgery. She fell in the middle of the night and it looks like they can't put off her knee replacement any longer."

"I'm sorry to hear that, Gray."

"There's some concern about her blood pressure being high. I should go see her before she goes under. I might be in Arizona for a few days so I'm going to see if Cole can send one of our best guys to take my place here while I'm gone." His thumb tapped at the cell's screen.

"I'll go with you."

He started to protest.

"Gray, please. I can't just sit here until my next race with nothing to do." She paused as he seemed to contemplate the options. "Plus, I'd feel safer being with you."

His shoulders dropped. "Well, I guess I can't deal with this and be worried about you. You'll have to stay by my side at all times."

"Of course, I will," she said. "I promise. And I'll call Diane to make flights."

Gray threw his phone on the bed. "I'd like to leave as soon as possible."

Sami Jo nodded and went to her room.

She knew flights out of Myrtle Beach were always a challenge. It could take all day to get to Phoenix and she wanted to help Gray out even if things between them were complicated.

She picked up her phone and dialed Alec.

"Hey, sunshine," he said cheerily. "How was dinner

with the family?"

"That's a long story for another time. We're in a bit of a situation and I wondered if you were still in town."

"I just finished breakfast at the hotel and was planning on leaving for the airport in about an hour."

"I need to ask a favor. I would owe you everything." She proceeded to tell him about Gray's mom. "I hate to ask—"

"Say no more. I'd be happy to give you guys a ride. They just have to drop me on the way."

"You're my savior. I promise to pay whatever costs are involved."

"Don't be silly. This is what friends do. I'll meet you at the airport."

Alec proceeded to give her the instructions on where to go and hung up. She quickly texted Diane with some brief details of what was happening and asked her to arrange for a car and hotel rooms in Phoenix. Reliable as always, Diane was quick to respond.

Downstairs, Gray waited in the kitchen with his carry-on.

"I have good news," she told him as she parked her carry-on at the island. "Alec is flying us in his jet. It would've taken forever to get there otherwise."

Gray rubbed his forehead. "Sami Jo, I can't afford flights on a private jet."

"Not to worry. He's got it covered," she said and led them out the door.

In the Escalade, Gray slumped in his seat. "I don't know what I'm dreading more. My mom's surgery or having to interact with my dad."

"Was that the first time you talked to him in a while?"

"Frankly, my first instinct was that he'd dialed me by mistake."

"Good thing you took the call." She reached over and squeezed his arm. "Don't worry about your mom. I'm sure everything will be fine."

———

Sami Jo recognized the mid-size jet reflecting the morning sun as it sat on the private airport's tarmac. Gray parked in the lot next to a small brick building and a woman greeted them when they went inside. She quickly guided them through security and walked them to the plane.

Alec looked up from his seat at the back of the jet as Gray headed over to him and extended his hand.

"I can't thank you enough for doing this."

Alec grinned. "It's no problem. I'm sorry about your mom. If it's any consolation, my grandfather recently had a knee replacement and you'd be amazed how quick the surgery is. Recovery can be a bitch but I'm sure she'll do just fine."

Gray took a seat across the aisle and Sami Jo leaned in to hug Alec.

"Buckle in, girlie. Wheels up." Alec winked at her and looked ahead to the front of the plane. "We're all set, Jim."

The pilot sealed the door, stepped into the cockpit, and the engine came to life.

"Ever fly on a jet, Gray?" Alec asked.

"Can't say that I have."

Sami Jo chuckled. "We're about to ruin you. You'll never want to fly commercial again."

She'd flown in Alec's jet twice. Once when she was his date for the American Music Awards and the other time was when he'd invited her to his Madison Square Garden show last year. There was nothing quite as rock star as flying wherever, whenever.

The jet was in the air in a matter of seconds, quicker than any commercial airline could ever manage, and when the bell dinged overhead, Alec got up and headed to the front of the plane. He grabbed three bottles of water from the mini-fridge and handed them out to Sami Jo and Gray.

Alec sat down again and proceeded to talk to Gray as Sami Jo relaxed into her seat and shut her eyes. The drone of their voices lulled her to sleep and when she woke, they were already in Chicago.

Alec laughed. "Sorry, were we boring you?"

She stretched in her seat. "I didn't sleep well last night." She glanced over at Gray who stared out the window.

As the jet came to a stop, Alec stood.

"Thanks again, Alec. This was too kind of you," Gray said.

"Anytime, brother." Alec leaned over to Sami Jo and kissed her cheek. "Be good. I'll check on you later."

As he left and the door was closed again, Sami Jo switched to the seat Alec had vacated.

"You have quite a friend there," Gray said.

"He's the best and not just because he lets us use his cushy jet."

"Yeah, I could get used to this." He reached for her hand and her heart did a little skip in her chest. "You're a good friend too."

Oh, we're friends again?

Probably not the time to ask.

"Don't laugh but I can't get the mile-high club out of my head," he mused as his thumb grazed across her knuckles. "I mean, bathrooms on regular airlines are entirely too small."

"Maybe for you. You're built like a brick wall." She laughed.

"Are you saying you've tried?"

Heat rose to her cheeks. "Well, no. But I imagine it's a tight squeeze just being in one all by yourself."

"Is this one bigger?" he asked.

Sami Jo glanced at the cockpit and Gray laughed.

"I'm just messing with you." His smile softened.

"After last night, I didn't think something like that would be on the table."

He pulled his hand back. "I'm sorry if I caused you to have a sleepless night."

"There was a lot about last night that caused it to be sleepless."

"I don't regret what's happened between us, Sami Jo. And I would like it to continue. I just don't want you to think I'm leading you on—again."

"I don't think that. I think we're probably making up for whatever we didn't do the last time you were here. But I know this isn't long-term."

He blinked at her. "You're saying the mile-high club is on the table?"

The corner of his mouth turned up making her laugh and feel a bit hopeful again.

———

When they stepped off of the jet, a wall of desert air consumed Sami Jo.

She was always suspicious of the phrase "dry heat" when it came to Arizona's southwestern climate. Frying an egg on the sidewalk might be a myth but she'd bet it would sizzle, at least.

As expected, Diane had a rental waiting for them in the lot of the private airport. The GMC Yukon was already running with the A/C cranked at full blast as they threw their bags in the back and headed for the hospital.

Although status in the mile-high club wasn't achieved, Sami Jo was pleased Gray had expressed his interest in continuing what they'd started in the Kansas City hotel room.

He'd admitted he'd regret if that night—and the following morning—was their last time together. He'd also stated that he'd weighed all the pros and cons of the situation, had considered the consequences, but maybe they could simply be adults about it. Casual sex, no strings, and certainly no broken hearts. They'd agreed that keeping their relationship secret was of utmost importance. No one could know. It would not only look bad for him professionally but her uncle would probably lose it. And her family already hinted they thought she could be a bit irresponsible—sleeping with the bodyguard would be just one more element proving them right.

Sami Jo had concurred. Sure, casual. And okay, no strings. But she couldn't share her uncertainty that her heart would be intact afterward based on last night.

Despite the shroud over all of it, she was satisfied with the deal. She'd have to be.

As they pulled into the parking lot of the hospital, she felt her phone buzz from inside her tote.

The screen displayed a text message from a blocked number.

"Glad to see you made it out of that crash okay. This is why racing is dangerous. That's why I'm hoping you'll stop. You don't want to end up like Angela Guthrie, do you?"

She glanced over at Gray whose scowl indicated he had other things on his mind at the moment—the concern over his mom's surgery, the impending interaction with his dad—and tucked the phone back into her tote.

Despite the obvious threat, it would have to wait.

The hospital's reception desk attendant had them sign in and they headed directly to the surgery wing where the glossy halls hummed with activity. The staff, dressed in different-colored scrubs, buzzed in and out of patient rooms.

When they located Peggy Finch's room, Gray knocked on the open door.

"Mom?"

"Grayson? Is that you?"

Sami Jo trailed in behind Gray and found an attractive

older woman sitting up in a hospital bed. Gray had her eyes for sure and hers lit up at the sight of him.

"I'm glad you're here," his mom said. "I didn't think they'd let me wait much longer."

"Are you in a lot of pain?" he asked, hugging her.

"Oh, no. They have me hooked up to this nifty little morphine drip."

Gray turned. "Mom, this is Sami Jo."

Peggy's smile widened. "Nice to finally meet you, Sami Jo. I'd like to say Gray has told me all about you but—"

"Mom—" Gray warned but Peggy patted her son's arm.

"Don't worry, Gray. I'm not going to embarrass you. But if I do, just blame the drugs."

Sami Jo laughed and decided she liked this woman. She lacked all of the seriousness Gray seemed to own in bulk.

"Where's Dad?" Gray asked.

"He went to grab a coffee. He should be right back," she said. "You got here pretty quickly."

"If it wasn't for Sami Jo, we'd still be in the air," Gray said. "We were able to fly on her friend's private jet."

"Oh, how fancy," Peggy said and gazed at Sami Jo. "Thank you for bringing my son to me."

"Not a problem, Mrs. Finch. I was happy to do it."

"What's going on with your blood pressure, Mom?"

The woman waved off his concern. "It's come down a bit. I'm sure it was elevated from the pain."

"But Dad said—"

"Oh, you know your dad." She looked over at Sami Jo. "The man knows he's screwed if something happens to me and he has to fend for himself."

"I heard that," a deep voice echoed from the hall and an older man entered the room. Despite his grey hair and glasses, he was definitely Gray's dad.

Standing just as tall, the man had a broad chest and the same serious expression Gray usually wore. He crossed the room without acknowledging his son and went to stand on the other side of the bed.

"Sweetheart," Peggy said, addressing her husband. "This is Sami Jo McLean. Sami Jo, this is my husband, Richard." Richard's blue-eyed gaze settled on her. "Sorry if he had to drag you with him."

"Not a problem, Mr. Finch. I'm just glad we made it here in time."

She felt Gray stiffen by her side. "Mom, do you need anything?"

"They've had her fasting so she doesn't get sick from the anesthesia." Richard crossed his arms over his chest and a tension settled in the room.

Even Peggy must've felt it because she ignored her husband's sour tone.

"Sami Jo, we saw your race the other day. Are you doing alright after that crash?"

"Oh, I'm fine, Mrs. Finch. I just got spun around a bit. Our jumpsuits and helmets keep us safe."

"Have you always wanted to race? It seems very dangerous," Peggy asked with genuine concern in her eyes.

"I've been behind the wheel in some shape or form since I was four. I guess you could say it's in the McLean blood."

"You're following in your father's footsteps," Richard stated, glancing at Gray.

"In a way. My uncle and my cousin's husband all raced at one point as well. And even though my father was killed in a race, it didn't affect my love of the sport." Sami Jo paused. She knew Richard had made a jab at Gray's life choices. "It's not for everyone but racing is ingrained in me, just like keeping people safe seems to be ingrained in Gray."

Richard stared at her and dropped his defensive pose.

A nurse in blue scrubs entered the room, breaking the odd silence.

"Are we ready, Peggy?"

"We're all here, I guess it's that time." Peggy looked directly at Sami Jo. "Take care of my boys while I'm gone."

Sami Jo chuckled. Both men were twice her size but she understood the sentiment. "Absolutely."

Gray leaned down and hugged his mom again. "We'll be here when you get back."

The nurse proceeded to disconnect a bunch of wires from machines around Peggy and attached the IV bag to a metal bar at the head of the bed. "There's a waiting room down the hall you'll find much more comfortable. The doctor can meet you there once she's done."

Richard kissed his wife's hand and smiled at her. It was strange to see the older man express love while he exhibited so much contempt toward his son.

A transporter in beige scrubs entered the room and pushed Peggy and her bed out of the room. Gray and his dad stood in the hallway watching the bed make its way down the hall until it was out of sight. There were a few awkward moments as the two men ignored each other and didn't seem to know what to do next.

"Mr. Finch, why don't we go check out that waiting room the nurse mentioned?" Sami Jo asked.

Gray gave her the most confusing look that turned to surprise when his dad nodded and led the way.

The cozy waiting area was empty except for a pair of sofas and four matching chairs that sat around a large oak table covered in newspapers and recent issues of popular magazines.

Richard picked out a chair across the room and Sami Jo sat on one of the sofas next to him while Gray meandered around the room, doing everything but interacting with his father.

"Can we get you anything?" she asked Richard. "Are you hungry?"

"I'm fine. I just had some coffee," he answered.

Sami Jo perked up. "Coffee sounds good. Gray, why don't you go get us some coffee?"

Gray stared at her.

"Don't worry, I'll keep your dad company," she said. He blinked at her, his mouth slightly open. She simply stared back at him, smiling.

Gray relented and headed out the door.

Richard grunted and she almost laughed because Gray made the same sounds when he was discouraged.

"Does he always order you around?"

"He's just in work mode," she said. "He doesn't always bark like that. Only when he's worried. And I know he's worried about your wife. I can tell you are too but I assure you she's going to be just fine."

"She wasn't wrong, you know. I'd be lost without her."

Sami Jo reached over and squeezed his arm. "I'm sure. Women tend to know the truth behind those tough-guy exteriors."

She pulled her hand back and folded both hands in her lap. "Mr. Finch, I know you've just met me, and it's not my business, but I know Gray wishes things were better between you two."

Richard glanced at her and frowned.

"I think he's hurting—a lot," she said, hoping to crack his detached composure.

"I can only imagine what he's told you. But he knew what he was giving up when he joined the military. And not that doing your service for this country isn't admirable but he gave up a bright future. Then he went and got blown up with his team." Richard wiped a hand over his face. "It was my greatest fear. He couldn't even retire with honor. It was a medical discharge. And who does he turn to for help? My brother, John."

"Maybe he didn't think he had a choice," Sami Jo said.

Richard seemed to consider this, but he was just as

stubborn as his son. "He had all the choices in the world. If he regrets them, he needs to get over it. He's a grown man."

"I agree," she said. "But with all due respect, you're both acting like children."

Richard's glare should've sliced right through her but she was determined to face off with the elder Finch to defend Gray. Even if it got her tossed from the hospital.

———

Gray stepped off the elevator with three coffees secured in a cardboard tray, dreading the scene that awaited him.

Being in a room with his dad and all the history they had could prove to be dicey. He hadn't even considered what he would say and now might not even be the time to confront things. His mom was supposed to be the focus here, not their messed-up relationship. Plus, he didn't think he was ready to tackle that one yet.

Thank God for Sami Jo. She seemed to know when to interject herself and he was pretty impressed by how she stood up to Richard about how racing was her choice. Kudos to her, because his dad seemed to back down right away.

He carried the tray down the hall, slowly calculating just how long he could keep himself removed from the situation without being suspicious.

He took a beat outside the waiting room, took a deep breath, then turned the corner.

Much to his surprise, both Sami Jo and his father were—laughing hysterically?

Sami Jo looked up with a huge grin. "Hey, you're back." Gray set the tray on the table.

"What's going on?" he asked, his quizzical gaze on her.

"Well, we may have been having a little fun at your expense." She alighted from her seat, rounded the table, and picked up two of the coffees, taking one back to his dad. "Your dad was telling me about the time you attempted to skydive off the house as a kid."

Gray looked over at his dad who seemed to be suppressing a—a giggle?

His dad slapped his hands together. "Right into your mother's lilac bushes. I've never seen a woman battle more over what to be more concerned about. You possibly breaking your neck or her bushes being completely obliterated."

Gray felt like he'd entered an alternate dimension.

"As I recall, you helped me build the parachute, Dad." Gray picked up his coffee and went to sit by Sami Jo.

Sami Jo's head spun to his dad who looked away guiltily. "Mr. Finch, is that true?"

The man wrung his hands and picked up his coffee. "I thought it was for a school project. I didn't think he'd climb up on the roof and test it out."

"I would've liked to have seen that," she said. "Too bad you didn't video it."

"A friend of mine did," Gray said.

"Joey Simpson," his dad interjected. "I still have a copy on my home computer."

Sami Jo turned to Gray, her eyes bright. "Can we go and watch it? Please?" She turned back to his dad. "Sorry, Mr. Finch, I'm inviting myself over to get a glimpse of that. Do you have any other embarrassing videos?"

"I have tons of videos of Grayson. Even some of his more reputable moments. Like high school graduation and the winning run he hit when he was in the baseball championships." His dad looked away. "I even have some of the videos you sent from Afghanistan."

Gray was surprised since he'd sent them directly to his mom.

"Looked hot there, son," his dad said, finally looking directly at him.

Gray nodded. "It was."

Sami Jo sat back with a look of content on her face. Rightly so, he supposed. She had gotten them talking.

"It got to be about one-hundred and twenty during the summer months. A little cooler in the mountains." Gray pulled out a chair and sat. He leaned his elbows on the table and spun his coffee cup slowly in his hand. "And of course, there was no air conditioning in our tents."

"Do you have more videos? I'd like to see them," his dad said.

"Sure, I can send them to you."

"You two should sit in a race car some time," Sami Jo said. "Not to compare it to your heroic feats in the service, Gray. I mean, you are a national treasure."

"She's a hoot, Gray." His dad muffled his chuckle.

Gray looked at her. She was *something* alright.

"I like to keep him on his toes," she said.

And horizontal.

"Well, I'd be happy to have you back to the house once Peg is cleared." His dad checked his watch. "I don't expect you both to sit around once she's back in her room. Maybe go back to the house afterward."

"I'd be happy to make you dinner tonight, Mr. Finch," Sami Jo said.

"You haven't made me dinner," Gray teased.

Sami Jo waved him off. "We can run to the store and maybe I can whip up a few casseroles to tide you and Mrs. Finch over."

"Thank you, Sami Jo. It's not necessary."

"I insist," she said. "Gives me something to do. And it lets me order Gray around for a change."

She turned and winked at him.

Jesus, how he wanted to lean over and kiss her right there.

LAP SIXTEEN

A FEW HOURS AND SEVERAL CHILDHOOD stories later, Gray was astonished at the change that
had occurred in his dad.

Although his mom was a little groggy, she seemed
delighted to see them on speaking terms for the first
time in almost a decade.

His dad even invited them to forgo the hotel room and
stay at the house. Gray surprised himself by accepting.

On the way to his parents' home, he drove Sami Jo
to the local grocery store, where she flitted about and
bought up ingredients for a few casseroles she intended
to make. They were almost at the house when he reached
over and squeezed her hand.

"Thank you," he said. "This would've been a lot harder
alone."

"Not a problem. I'm excited to make a few recipes. It's
nice to have something to do."

"Well, don't wear yourself out," he said and grinned.

They entered his parents' ranch-style home with groceries in their arms. It had been years since he'd seen the
place and wasn't surprised to see his mom had redeco-
rated a bit. The kitchen countertops had been replaced
with granite and the cabinets were updated. He gazed

out the kitchen window to the patio where his mom's azaleas and oleander shrubs were in full bloom and a new seating area around a fire pit offered great views of the mountains.

Sami Jo started unloading the groceries as he went back out for their bags.

As he reached inside the truck, his cell phone rang.

"Hey, Cole," he said balancing the phone between his ear and shoulder.

"Just wanted to check-in and let you know Russ and the new kid are with the other drivers. Russ has Guthrie."

"Yeah, how's she doing?"

"Still in the ICU. She was pretty banged up. Nothing on the news about it though. I spoke with her team manager and they agreed not to give this guy any airtime for what he did. They're using some excuse that she's sick and that's why she's not racing this weekend. How are things with you? I got your text. How's your mom?"

Gray shut the trunk lid and leaned against the bumper. The setting sun was a welcome respite. "She's out of surgery. We're just back at the house whipping up a few meals for them."

"Sami Jo was cool with going?"

"She insisted. She didn't feel comfortable having us send someone else over to watch her. Honestly, I didn't think we had the bandwidth, and to tell you the truth, she was a big help in getting my dad to open up to me. No great strides but at least we're speaking."

"Gray," Cole said. "You do realize that's the most you've said about her since this whole thing started? Are things that *good* between you two?"

He considered how much to tell Cole, especially if it was all going to end anyway. "Things are fine. She's been behaving."

"And you? Have you been behaving?"

Gray slumped against the car. "As best I can, my friend. Look, I gotta get our bags inside, and start making dinner. I'll text you later."

He hung up and pulled the suitcases behind him into the house. Down the hall were three bedrooms. He peeked into the master as he passed then looked inside the next room. He found more changes had been made than just the kitchen. The guest bedroom had been converted into an office and gym.

He continued down the hallway and stepped into the third bedroom. He set the suitcases off to the side and considered the queen-size bed.

"Hey," Sami Jo said as she entered the room.

Gray ran his fingers through his hair. "I guess their three-bedroom is now a two-bedroom with an office."

She walked over and put her arms around his waist. "Hmm, I wondered about that. I also hoped you weren't going to be all chivalrous and tell me you'd sleep on the couch."

The thought of sleeping beside her again made him hard. At least there'd be a buffer between this room and the master.

"I guess I'll have to explain some things to my dad when he gets home." He tipped his chin down and placed a kiss on her forehead. "We might have a lot to talk about. Don't get angry if I don't come straight to bed."

She rested her chin on his chest. "Then maybe you should apologize in advance." Her brow went up and she pulled him onto the bed.

The springs squeaked slightly and Gray found himself unable to control his lust for her. The meal prep would have to wait.

For now, with her, he was all in.

Sami Jo placed a plate of meatloaf and roasted potatoes down in front of Gray's dad.

With Peggy tucked in at the hospital and on high doses of pain meds, Richard had come home around eight. Sami Jo had insisted he shower, get comfortable, and had Gray pour them all a pre-dinner whiskey.

Now, as they sat around the rustic oak dining table, she thought of her Aunt Trudy and figured this must be what it felt like to take care of a family. Day in and day out, without complaint, Trudy cooked delicious meals for the McLean clan. She always sat down with the family, a sense of pride oozing from her as everyone dug into her home-cooked recipes. And after she was gone, Melanie had taken up the charge. By that time, Sami Jo was out of the house, already on the racing circuit, and only made appearances at dinner when she had the time.

Now, as she sat down across from Gray, she decided she'd make it a goal to have more family dinners over at Royce's house, assuming Melanie would invite her.

Richard commended her cooking and Gray told his dad his assignment with Sami Jo, the other women involved, and how he'd offered those other women pro-tection free-of-charge.

Seeing them talk sent a surge through her heart. Even though she knew she'd have to eventually tell Gray about the text she'd received, she didn't want to break their moment.

After they cleaned up from the meal, Sami Jo showed Richard all of the containers of food in the refrigerator and freezer, then excused herself to go to bed.

Honestly, she was beat. Gray needed time alone with his dad and she was happy to let the two men have it. She stretched out in the bed dressed in just a t-shirt and underwear and looked at her watch. It was almost ten. Which meant for Melanie, it was past midnight. No doubt she'd be asleep by now. And since Mel wasn't one to sleep with a cell phone by her side, Sami Jo picked up her phone and composed a text message.

Mel, it's me. I know you're angry. I know you're probably scared too. I'm sorry. I'm sorry I've been the cause of it. I miss you terribly. I miss talking to you, I miss the kids. And when all of this is over, I want us to spend more time together. I want you to be proud of me but I also don't want you to worry. Gray has been—

She wondered if she should tell her cousin everything. Prepare her for the meltdown Sami Jo would have once he was gone. She'll need her support. She deleted the last three words she'd typed.

Things are going well and I'm glad Royce hired Gray. I want to tell you more but I'll save it for when I see you. Love you, cousin. I hope you and the kids are enjoying your time with Matt's parents. XO

She hit send and considered what a difference a week had made. She went from hating him—not wanting anything to do with him—to having him in her bed. Was she crazy for wanting it to continue? When all was said and done could she go back to her normal life?

Her life wasn't normal—she knew that.

She clicked over to the text message she'd received earlier that day. With all that had happened between Gray and his dad, she'd almost forgotten about it.

Part of her considered she should be thanking the guy for bringing Gray back into her life, but his words chilled her.

"You don't want to end up like Angela Guthrie, do you?"

The screen lit up with an incoming call and she jerked in surprise, jostling the phone and almost dropping it.

Her cousin's name appeared on the screen.

"Mel," Sami Jo answered. "I'm sorry if I woke you with my text."

"I was up. Matt's parents have had the kids up late this week. I was just getting ready for bed," Melanie said.

"I'm—well, what I mean is, I'm the one who should be sorry. I overreacted. But you're right, I was—I am still scared for you."

"You didn't overreact. And you were right. I need to be more careful."

"I heard Grayson had to move in," Mel said. "How's that going?"

"Interesting to say the least. I'm actually in Scottsdale at his parents' house right now. His mom had to have knee surgery. So we came out here to see her."

"Is that standard protocol? A bodyguard taking his client home to meet Mom and Dad?" Mel asked.

Sami Jo chuckled. "We have a lot to catch up on, cousin."

"Ah, you two are dating again." Mel's remark caught her off-guard.

"Again?" Sami Jo tried to play dumb.

"Sami Jo, please. I knew exactly who you were sneaking out to go see every night, what was it? Five years ago?"

"More like seven. Not that I counted."

"Of course you did. You know, I'd often wondered what had happened. You dove headfirst into racing after he was gone. I assumed it either simply ended or it ended badly enough you couldn't talk about it."

"We've worked through some things."

"Mm-hmm, I'll bet." Mel giggled.

"Mel, I miss you. It's good to hear your voice."

Her cousin repeated the sentiment and promised to keep in touch.

———◆———

It felt good to laugh with his dad again.

Gray couldn't remember the last time they'd actually enjoyed each other's company.

His dad had poured a couple of beers into two pint

glasses and as they sat out on the patio, Gray breathed in the dry Arizona air. It was much cooler now and the night sky was filled with more stars than Gray would ever see in Chicago.

"She's a spitfire." His dad's voice broke the silence.

Gray stared into his glass. "You have no idea."

"I like her," his dad remarked. "She's a lot like your mom. She doesn't pull any punches, that's for sure."

"Yeah." Gray tried to suppress a giddy smile in front of his dad. Much like when he was a kid, the good moments—the ones where Gray could let his guard down and be silly—were meant for his mother. His dad had always been the stoic figure in the house. It was probably where he'd picked up his own detached temperament.

"It's okay, Son," his dad said quietly.

Gray peered up from his glass and saw a lopsided smile on his dad's face.

The older man squirmed a little in his seat. "I can tell that you care about her."

Now Gray was doing the squirming. "She's a client, Dad. I work for her."

"That doesn't mean you don't have feelings for her."

Gray opened his mouth to speak but his dad raised his hand.

"Your mother told me about your history with her. She also mentioned your heart was broken the last time you were with her."

"I was the one that did the heart-breaking, Dad."

"And it tore you apart."

Had Cole been talking to his mom? Gray had told her a finite bit of information but never mentioned how he'd felt about it. Still, his dad wasn't wrong.

"It ended badly," Gray said. "It wasn't the right time for us. I was heading back to the military and she was about to start her career in racing. Our age difference at the time didn't seem right and I wasn't about to ask for a long-distance relationship. That whole thing with Danielle had just gone down and—"

"And you were beating yourself up," his dad finished. The older man's shoulders dropped. "Grayson, I wish I hadn't been so hard on you growing up. I hope you understand that I've only wanted what was best for you."

"Dad, I—"

"Listen to me," his dad interrupted. "I was selfish wanting you to love all the things I did. And when you followed your dreams, I felt resentful and was determined to make you feel bad about it. But Son, I honestly am so proud of the man you've become. Your mother shared every email you sent and seeing you in charge of your team, well, I knew you were doing something that mattered to you. When you got hurt, my greatest fear was that I'd lose you and I'd have to live with the regret of how much time we'd lost because I'd been so stubborn."

Gray's mouth set in a thin line. "I've been stubborn too. I've spent the last few years chasing job after job and making excuses to not visit. I've put off mending things between us and I'm sure it's been hard on Mom."

His dad chuckled. "It's our way. Finch men are not the type to gush all over each other. Hell, I don't think we gush, period."

Gray nodded in agreement.

"Can I ask you something without getting gushy?" His dad's smile widened. "Does this life you've chosen make you happy?"

Gray shrugged. "Yeah, I guess. Cole and I work well together. We're making a decent amount of money. We're saving lives if not in the traditional sense. It's not scaling brick walls and gunfire, but honestly, I don't miss that."

"There's more to life than the job, you know? You gotta find someone to share it with. Someone who makes you whole. And I know Cole is your best friend, but he doesn't count." His dad sipped his beer and his smile softened. "Does Sami Jo make you happy?"

He couldn't answer that one. In the time they'd been together, he felt all kinds of emotions around her. Happy was one of them, but he also felt guilt and maybe a little fear that something might happen to her.

"Sorry," his dad said. "it's none of my business."

"No," Gray said. "She's, well, she's special to me. I do care about her. I'm just trying to separate my feelings from the job I need to do."

"I'm going to give you some advice that you can take or leave," his dad said and leaned forward. "Don't separate the two. If you care for her, you'll work that much harder keeping her safe. You deserve some happiness, Gray. If it means chasing after the girl, chase away. Don't let your work ethic get in the way. Your mother and I wouldn't be together if I hadn't broken a few Human Resources rules along the way."

"What do you mean?"

His dad sat back. "Your mom was my secretary at the office when I first started."

"Really? I thought you two met at a party."

"We did," the older man smiled sheepishly. "It was a party her coworkers threw for her after I fired her."

Gray's shock registered and his dad laughed.

"I fell in love with your mother the minute I met her at her little desk outside my office. And there was no way I was going to be the executive who slept with his assistant. So, I found her another job in the company, on another floor, for a different department. I brought her into my office, told her things weren't going to work out for her, and that she was being transferred. Then I asked her out."

"How come you never told us that version of the story?"

"Your mother still thinks it's scandalous," his dad said.

"But I think secretly she's grateful for the way things went down. She moved up in her department pretty quickly after that, and well, she had her executive fiancé a few floors away. I think she loved that we kept our relationship under wraps for as long as we did. We'd sneak away during our lunch hours, meet at a café where we knew no one else would catch us. It was very cloak and dagger."

Gray laughed. That sounded like his mom alright.

"The funny thing was, after she quit the firm and we announced our wedding, no one seemed surprised." His dad shook his head. "We Finch men might appear to be aloof, but we have a tell."

"Yeah? And what's that?" Gray asked.

"Go look in a mirror and you'll see what I mean."

———◆———

The next morning, Sami Jo woke to sounds coming from the kitchen and an empty bed. She pushed off the covers and threw on a pair of shorts.

She found Gray making breakfast in the kitchen. Bacon sizzled on the stove as he whisked eggs in a bowl while his dad sat at the island reading the newspaper.

"Morning," she said.

"Good morning, Sami Jo," Richard said. He was dressed in casual pants and a polo with the Tommy Hilfiger logo on it. "Sleep okay?"

"I did, thanks."

Gray motioned to the cabinet where he stood. "There are mugs here if you want coffee."

He had the goofiest look on his face as she approached and he surprised her by giving her a quick kiss as she went to reach for the cabinet.

Did he tell his dad about us?

She poured coffee into the mug and went to the island. "Any word on how Mrs. Finch is doing?"

"I called her room this morning. She sounded great," Richard said. "She's looking forward to seeing you again, Sami Jo."

"She had that same effect on Fran," Gray said. "She was more interested in seeing Sami Jo than me."

"When can she come home?" Sami Jo asked.

"Probably tomorrow. They want to get her started on physical therapy right away." Richard folded the paper up and placed it to the side of the table. "Where's your next race?"

"The next two are in Charlotte."

Gray poured the eggs into a pan and took a sip of his coffee. "Think you'll be okay after what happened on the track on Sunday?"

"Absolutely. The only person that needs to worry is Casey Trimble." She joked but then remembered the text she'd gotten. Casey had been shitty toward her after the crash, telling her to get out of his way. She considered how he might have the means to find out where she was at any given time. His trust fund certainly gave him some leverage.

Now, however, might not be the time to bring it up. Gray seemed to be in such a good mood. His dad too. Plus, today was still about Gray's mom and his getting to spend some time with her.

She'd have to wait to share her suspicions about the test when it was more convenient.

LAP SEVENTEEN

G RAY HAD TO ADMIT, SITTING in coach was a let-
down after flying in a private jet.

They'd spent most of the day at the hospital with his
mom, who seemed to light up whenever Sami Jo spoke.
She even whispered into his ear when he hugged her
goodbye that he should *take special care of Sami Jo.*

He knew what that meant but he didn't have the heart
to explain to his mom that their situation wasn't perma-
nent. Still, as they sat on the plane, he reached over to
hold Sami Jo's hand during takeoff.

"Thank you," he said to her once the plane had leveled
off. "You have no idea how good it was to mend things
with my dad."

"I was happy to. It meant a lot for me to be able to just
be there for you."

He stared at her. Her lips curved up and he wished
they were already back at her place to savor the little bit
of time they had before they were off to Charlotte for
her next race.

For now, he'd be content just sitting with her.

The flight connected in Dallas and when they finally
landed in Myrtle Beach, the sun was starting to set. Diane
had arranged for a car to take them to the private airport

to pick up Gray's truck and when they arrived, they threw their bags in the back and headed toward her house.

"I was thinking," Sami Jo said after they'd been driving for a few minutes. "Maybe you should investigate Casey Trimble."

Gray stiffened. Trimble was the guy he throttled after the race the other day. "Why would you think that?"

"Besides the fact that he's a colossal jerk. His comments at the medical center were pretty direct. And I was thinking this morning, he'd have the resources to have me followed if he wasn't doing it himself. He comes from money and he's got a huge chip on his shoulder because I'm getting ahead of him."

"Those all could be acceptable motives and I can certainly have Cole look into his background, I just don't think it's him."

"Why not?"

"He doesn't fit the profile."

"And what's the profile?" she asked.

"Most likely, this is a male, maybe thirty to fifty years old. They may be connected."

"So far that all sounds like Trimble."

"There's most likely something driving them to do this that might be tied to some sort of trauma or obsession. Something tells me the only obstacle Trimble's ever faced is a bad hair day. Every message has been designed to show you that this guy thinks he's in control. He's trying to distract you," Gray said.

"He thinks I'll stop racing."

Gray glanced over at her. She had pulled out her phone and was scrolling through her texts.

"Why do you say that?" he asked.

"'This is why racing is dangerous. That's why I'm hoping you'll stop. I don't want you to end up like Angela Guthrie,'" she read.

Gray quickly pulled onto the shoulder and slammed

on the breaks. The truck skidded on the gravel, throwing them forward as the truck stopped suddenly.

"What the fuck, Sami Jo."

"I know, I wanted to tell you sooner, but with everything that was going on—"

He wrenched the phone from her hand and looked at the messages. "Why didn't you tell me the second you got this?"

"We had just gotten to the hospital and I wanted you to have time with your mom. I was planning on telling you."

Gray pulled his phone out and took a picture of the message and texted it to Cole, telling him he'd call once they were back at the house. He muttered more curse words and tucked both phones in his pocket.

"Can I please have my phone back?" Sami Jo asked.

"No," he fumed and pulled back onto the highway.

Rage flooded his body. He was angry with her for withholding this information but maybe angrier with himself for allowing his adolescent-like hormones to interfere with the job he was here to do. He'd allowed it to happen. She cared about his feelings, about him, and she'd put herself in danger by not telling him about the text sooner.

They pulled onto her street and she shifted in her seat to face him. "Gray, I—"

As they turned into the driveway, the last bit of sun lit up the side of the house and they both stared at the words spray-painted across the garage doors.

Found you, bitch!

———

When the sheriff pulled up in front of the house, Gray saw that Royce had also arrived, parking behind the squad.

The men exited their vehicles and walked over to speak

with him while Sami Jo was still inside the truck, where he'd ordered her to stay. Just to be safe, he'd removed the keys and locked her inside.

Sheriff Kovach made a few notes after Gray had shared the text Sami Jo had received last night. "I'll have an evidence team come over and check this out. Looks like he took out the camera over the garage. Surprised you didn't get an alert."

"Suffice it to say, Grayson, it's probably not safe to stay here." Royce crossed his arms in front of his chest. "Why don't you two come to stay with me? We have room."

Gray nodded.

"We'll increase the patrols for both houses," Kovach said. "Especially with all of you in Charlotte this weekend."

"Maybe we should have her sit out this next race," Royce said, his eyes darting over to the truck. "Claim an illness or blame the crash from Sunday. Concussion or something."

"I think that's exactly what this guy wants," Gray said. "He'd probably see it as a win."

"Well, maybe we just give him what he wants," Royce said.

"And as soon as she races again, it'll start all over." Kovach tucked his notepad in his top pocket.

"You're right about that," Gray said. "We keep it business as usual. Sheriff, any chance you have some connections in Charlotte? Maybe I can get a little help from some plain-clothes officers."

"Let me reach out to one of my colleagues." Kovach shook hands with both men and headed over to his squad to call it in.

"Royce, she's gonna want to pack up her stuff. Would you mind coming in with us?" Gray asked. "She could probably use your support."

Truth was, he needed Royce there. He couldn't face

Sami Jo alone right now because he knew what he needed to do.

Back at Royce's house, Sami Jo threw her flip-flops across the bedroom that had once been hers growing up and flung herself onto the bed like an upset teenager.

In the interest of her safety, she and Gray had moved into Royce's house. When they'd arrived, he'd placed his bags in the room across the hall from hers and set up his laptop downstairs in the kitchen, where she imagined he'd stay.

His attitude had changed and he'd completely shut her out after noticing the graffiti on her garage doors. Scratch that, it was after seeing that damn text message that had done it.

She almost wished she'd never mentioned it. He had immediately become withdrawn, had gone into work mode, and did everything but talk to her directly. There was a big difference between being professional in front of others and being downright cold.

It was as if they were back to where they were a week ago. And reality gave her a hard slap in the face that whatever they had been doing these last few days was probably over.

She was determined not to let heartbreak kick in— especially while he was still around. But it was already consuming her. Maybe to put some perspective on the matter, it wasn't like they'd been having sex for several weeks. It had been what? Three or four times?

If anything, she should consider it an itch that should've been scratched years ago. If it was that effortless for Gray to move on, so be it. She'd show him just how meaning-less it was to her as well.

She wasn't going to mope about.

She slipped from the bed and headed downstairs.

Royce stood at the island in the kitchen with a glass of bourbon in his hand while Gray sat across from him behind his laptop. "The sheriff secured four men for the weekend. They all have extensive training in protective services," Gray said. "We'll meet them when we arrive."

"Are you talking about Charlotte?" Sami Jo asked as she retrieved a highball glass and a bottle of Makers from the cabinet.

Royce was the one who answered. "You just worry about the race. Gray's on top of this."

"I'd still like to know what to expect," she said.

"We'll run a tight schedule," Gray said, his gaze transfixed on his screen. "I've rented a house that's a few miles away from the track and the men I hired will stay there with us."

"My own personal army, huh? Is all that necessary?"

"This guy is following the same cadence he did with Angela Guthrie, according to the sheriff. First, there were photos, then her house was trashed, then she was attacked." Gray's eyes never met hers, as if she wasn't even there.

"Hang on, wouldn't he have shown up on the cameras around my house?"

"He was smart enough to take one out with a pellet gun. All we caught was a figure dressed in all black with a ski mask," Gray said. "And you would've gotten an alert but we were on the plane at the time."

"He's pretty ballsy doing it in broad daylight," Royce said.

"Guthrie was attacked in the middle of a parking lot and the sun hadn't even gone down yet," Gray said. "This guy is determined, to say the least."

"Well, Grayson, I know we're in capable hands. Now, if you two don't mind, I'm going to go do a little work and turn in." Royce leaned over and kissed Sami Jo's cheek.

"I'm glad to hear you and Melanie finally spoke."

"Yeah, me too."

Royce said goodnight and walked out of the kitchen, leaving her alone with Gray who clicked away at his computer.

"Are you hungry?" She alighted from the stool and went to the fridge, insistent on carrying on as if nothing had changed. Inside was a container of leftover pizza, a few apples, and a jar of preserves. She felt bad that in Mel's absence she hadn't thought to stock her uncle's fridge as they had for Gray's parents.

When he didn't respond to her question, she turned to face him. "Gray?"

He grunted a response and she slammed the fridge door. The action got him to glance up.

"Is this how it is now?" she asked. "Are we back to stilted conversations and frosty interactions? Because you need to warn me. I don't switch on and off as easily as you do."

Gray sighed and shut his laptop. "What do you want me to say?"

"I don't know but am I wrong in guessing things have changed between us?"

"It's the way it should be." He averted his eyes. "Being together was irresponsible, foolish, and ultimately, pointless."

She blinked as his remarks cut into her but she wasn't going to break.

"Well, I guess it was fun while it lasted," she said coolly and left the room.

It was only muscle memory that propelled her to the stairs and up to her room because she was fighting back tears as her heart constricted in her chest.

She certainly wasn't going to let him see how upset she was.

LAP EIGHTEEN

A STORM FRONT WAS ROLLING IN over Charlotte and clouds whisked across the sky like they were in a hurry to get somewhere else.

Somewhere else was also where Sami Jo wanted to be right now. Since completing her practice run earlier that morning, she'd been cooped up in the rental house with Gray and four other guys who looked like they spent all of their off-hours at the gym. She didn't catch their names but they sure as shit knew who she was. They were all armed but dressed casually so they'd pass for racing fans.

Two of the men were from the local police department. They had been on the force ten years each. Both had wives and kids and seemed generally pleasant. The other two had military backgrounds and were serious, brooding men of few words probably cut from the same cloth as Gray.

The rental house was exactly in the middle of nowhere and most likely been a farmhouse at one time. Its rustic exterior was painted white and wood beams held up the roof to the front porch which was complete with an American flag mounted near the stairs. Inside it had been modernized with new appliances, leather and wood furniture, and attractive vintage fixtures with a two-story stone fireplace. From her perch on the sofa in the great room, she had views of the grassy landscape of the backyard that seemed to go on forever.

Since the hired guns were also staying in the house, they had commandeered the only two guest rooms, leaving her the master. She wondered where Gray would sleep or if any of them would sleep at all.

Gray ordered pizza for the team that evening. The men all crowded around the island, grabbing slices as Gray went over the agenda for the next two days of qualifying and the race when his speech was interrupted by a loud crack of thunder.

An emergency alert came across the screen in the great room that severe thunderstorms were heading their way with possible tornado-like winds.

"A slight change of plans for tonight then," Gray said. "If the weather picks up, take posts inside the house. Just keep an eye outside."

They all nodded in agreement.

Sami Jo took a slice of pizza over to the sofa and watched the weather map. Red patches passed over the area showing that the crux of things would happen in the next hour. Another thunderclap struck and she was sure she felt the house shake. The lights flickered a bit but stayed on. The cable for the television, however, went dark.

After all of the men had cleared out of the room, Sami Jo stood. She approached Gray who stood behind the island in the kitchen where he had a bird's-eye view of the great room and both the front and back door.

"I'm going to take a hot bath," she said. "Is that okay?"

He barely glanced up at her. "Don't take too long."

She bit her tongue and headed to the master suite.

Inside the attached master bath, a clawfoot tub sat in the middle of the hardwood floor. Sami Jo ran the faucet, dug a bottle of bath gel from her toiletries bag, and poured a healthy amount into the hot water.

As lightning flashed outside the frosted windows, another crack of thunder followed. She lit a few of the candles around the tub and on the shelf by the window. Stripping out of her clothes, she dropped them to the floor and slowly slipped into the tub.

The muscles in her back were extremely tight after practice. She relaxed into the tub as the bubbles formed around her. Kicking off the water with her foot, she sank deeper and a bright flash of lightning knocked out the power. The light from the candles gave the room a soft glow and the whole house seemed to have gone quiet except for the heavy footsteps coming down the hall.

She'd left the bathroom door open a crack and heard Gray call to her.

"Are you okay?" he asked, slowly pushing the door open.

His eyes scanned the room and fell on her, his gaze taking in the bubbles. He retreated slightly and looked away.

"It's nothing you haven't seen, Gray. Don't be bashful."

"It's inappropriate, Sami Jo. Especially with the team here." Gray glanced over at her. "I just wanted to make sure you're okay."

"Well, I'm not okay," she said, deciding she wasn't going to let him off that easy. "I'm tired of waiting for this asshole to do something short of photos and spray paint. I mean, you probably don't come cheap and now we have that goon squad hanging around. I think I should go back to my original opinion that all of this is completely unnecessary."

Even in the candlelight, she could see the twitch in his jaw. She lifted an arm out of the water and whisked off the soapy bubbles.

"Hurry up," he said. "I can't keep checking on you like this."

He turned and left the bathroom, leaving Sami Jo smirking at the area he'd vacated.

———

Although the storm had cleared up overnight and the power was back, Sami Jo's thoughts were still dark. But at least now, she had come up with a plan. She knew she had to try to get this stalker of hers to come out of the shadows even if her conscience warned her of the risk she was about to take.

The first thing that morning before heading to her qualifying race, she had called Danny Welliver to see if he was available for an interview. Lucky for her, he'd jumped at the chance to speak with her even though she insisted it happen over video chat.

When she broke the news to Gray, she thought he'd be less inclined to berate her like a child since she'd concealed her whereabouts.

She was wrong.

Gray exploded.

"Are you out of your mind, Sami Jo?" he shouted across the great room of the rental house causing the two off-duty policemen to cringe and turn away. The other two men ignored their interaction.

"It's not like I invited him here," she said, patting powder on her face as she sat on the sofa dressed in a windbreaker with her sponsor logos across the chest. Her tablet was set up on the table in front of her next to a bottle of water, ready for her to log in. "I'd appreciate it if you all made yourself scarce while I do this. Maybe you can walk the perimeter or whatever it is you guys do."

Gray tipped his chin at the four men who exited the house but he didn't budge.

"Why, Sami Jo?" Gray asked.

"Why what?"

"Why the interview all of a sudden? It wasn't on the

schedule."

"Danny has been hounding me for months and the biggest race of my life is a week away. I need to do this. Especially after getting knocked out last week."

Gray stared down at her for a moment. "I'm going to be right outside that door." He pointed toward the front door.

When the door slammed behind her, she let out a sigh and went back to primping in the compact's small mirror.

It was the first time she'd been completely alone in the house and even though Gray was right outside, he felt miles away. This was exactly the feeling she had dreaded—that once things were done between them, she'd feel empty and broken.

If only he wasn't so stubborn about the whole situation, so bound by his honor to protect her, maybe things would've been different. But apparently, he could turn off his feelings for her.

Or maybe he never really had them.

She set the compact on the table, picked up her tablet, and logged onto the video chat application.

Danny appeared on the screen and smiled. "Hey, Sami Jo."

"Hi, Danny," she said. "I appreciate the short notice and sorry we have to do it this way."

"I'm just happy you called. I didn't think we'd ever get together."

"Do I look okay? No glare?" she asked.

"You look perfect," Danny said. "I have some basic questions lined up but since you reached out I figured you might have something specific you wanted to cover."

"I do." She chewed on her lower lip and proceeded. "Off the record, Danny, I have a stalker."

Danny's brows lifted. "Oh, wow. I'm sorry to hear that."

"That's why I couldn't meet you in person. I'm at a safe house, I guess you would call it."

"And you want to talk about your situation in our interview?"

"I'd like to, yes."

"Okay, well, let me see how we can casually roll it into the conversation." Danny reached out and seemed to be clicking away at his keyboard. "I'm recording, but don't worry, I'll edit everything down. Ready?"

She nodded.

"I'm here today with Sami Jo McLean, and you all know, I've been anxious to speak to the racing phenom since she hit the track. Sami Jo, thanks for taking the time."

"It's my pleasure, Danny. I hope you don't think I was avoiding you." She gave him a million-dollar smile. "I'm quite busy these days."

"Yes, and we all know why. You're at the top of your game for your first year out. How did last week's crash play into your goal of winning a championship?"

"It can happen to the best of us, I guess. Unfortunately, it could've been avoided. But I'm still going to get out there tomorrow and give it my all."

"It looked like you were tapped by Casey Trimble," he said.

"I was. I suspect Casey has the same goal as I do. To win."

"Are you making excuses for him?" His brow raised as he grinned.

"By all means, no. I'm sure he had his reasons for doing what he did. But there's a level of respect we all show each other on the track."

"You're being very gracious, Sami Jo," Welliver said, narrowing his gaze at her. "I've seen footage of you going at drivers who don't stand up to that level of respect. Why hold back now?"

"Where would it get me, Danny? And honestly, scream-ing at my competition isn't the legacy I'm trying to live up to."

"You're referring to your father, Chase McLean, who died twenty years ago in the same race you're about to compete in next weekend."

"That's right. I'm really looking forward to paying tribute to my dad."

"How do you manage your expectations? Especially after a crash last week?"

"You can't let it affect your mindset or your will to win," she said. "I'd be lying if I didn't say it's not challenging but you have to approach each race as a new one. You just gotta stay focused."

"What's your routine to prepare for a race like this?" Danny asked.

"It's tough when your time is filled with other events, not that I'm not grateful for those opportunities. I love interacting with the public but to stay grounded I try to make time for myself. The last few weeks that's been nearly impossible to do."

"You mentioned you have a bodyguard."

She laughed. "You could say I have the equivalent of a personal militia with me. I'm on some psycho's radar right now. It started with some threatening photos. My home was vandalized just the other day. So yeah, for my safety, I have a bodyguard. Frankly, I think whoever is doing this is a coward."

"A coward?"

"Obviously, he has an issue with women. Right now, he's hiding behind his photos and his cans of spray paint. If he thinks that's gonna keep me off the track, he's got another thing coming. I'm not going to stop racing."

"Is that the equivalent of 'come at me, bro?' Because it sounds like it." Danny asked.

"Call it a guilty fascination but I'd like to know what's going on inside this person's head that makes him think he has any power over me."

Danny nodded. "You do have that legacy to live up to, after all."

Welliver took another twenty minutes to ask questions about her family, her crew, and those first races in her teen years, then wrapped things up. "Sami Jo, I appreciate the interview. Are you sure about all that stuff you said?"

She picked up the bottle of water and sat back on the sofa. "Between you and me, Danny. I just want all this craziness to end."

"It has to be weird being followed around."

"You don't know the half of it. I just want things to go back to normal."

"What's normal for a female race car driver who's at the top of her game?"

She thought for a moment and laughed. "I have no idea. But I'll let you know when I figure it out."

"Well, thanks again. I'm going to try to piece it together before the race next week." His eyes lit up. "Oh hey, I'll be at your boyfriend's video release party next week. I guess I'll see you there."

"And you'll see me in the video. Alec's PR is betting on a two-for-one. His fans based in Charlotte are most likely race fans too."

"Smart marketing on their part. Good luck tomorrow."

"Thanks, and Danny, sorry about making you wait so long to chat. Let's keep in touch," she said.

"We will." He smiled.

After she logged off, she gave herself a mental pat on the back. She'd tell Gray before it aired, but hopefully, by publicizing this, the guy would finally show his gutless face or stop altogether. Maybe then, the whole thing would be over with, Gray would finally be out of her life, and she could move on.

LAP NINETEEN

SAMI JO SHIFTED GEARS UNDER a clear sky as the road advanced under her race car.

Somewhere in the stands of the Charlotte Motor Speedway, around the viewing booth and pit row, the team of plainclothes officers was sweeping their areas as Gray had commanded.

Earlier that morning, Gray had been the epitome of a drill sergeant, barking detailed instructions to his soldiers before going to war. He'd been curt with Sami Jo the few times they had to interact, but that was fine with her; she needed to remain in her zen-like state for the race and concentrated on the task at hand.

Matt and Royce spoke into her headset as she headed into the final lap. Fortunately, she didn't need to worry about Trimble because he was trailing big time. And while the three cars in front of her contained the best in the pack, she skillfully maneuvered ahead of one of them and Royce spoke into her ear.

"Sami Jo, you got this."

As she sped past the checkered flag, Matt confirmed third place. Third place wasn't the worst place to end in, but she had wanted first.

As the cars slowed on the track and she pulled into pit

row, her team cheered. She exited her vehicle and pulled off her helmet, smiling at their excitement and returning the high-fives they extended. Gray was by her side within moments but she kept the grin plastered on her face as he escorted her to victory lane.

The cheers from the stands were deafening as the two other drivers who placed first and second joined her. Alex Foster and Kurt Hamlin were NASCAR legends and pride swelled inside her as they helped her climb onto the podium. Flashes from cameras went off as the three linked hands and raised them over their heads.

After the ceremony concluded, the two drivers hugged her and said a few words of encouragement. Everyone knew all the reasons why next week's race mattered most to her. Foster and Hamlin were too young to have known her father but they were hopeful she would achieve the same results as today, if not better.

Sami Jo buzzed with delight on her way back to the locker room with Gray in tow. She changed into a pair of jeans and a cotton shirt with an embroidered peach on the front before they headed to Gray's Escalade and left the track.

On the ride back to the rental house, she received a call from Alec, congratulating her. His charity event was only a few days away and she looked forward to having her friend around, even if it was only for one night. And when her phone rang again, it was Melanie letting her know she had watched the race and couldn't wait for her to come home.

"I got back last night," Mel said. "The kids stayed behind with his folks. There's a nice man from Gray's company here before you get worried."

"I can't wait to see you, Mel. Let me see how soon I can get out of here."

When Sami Jo hung up, she texted her uncle that she was going to head straight back to Myrtle Beach rather than wait for them.

"I'd like to get on the road as soon as we can," she told Gray who had yet to speak directly to her all day. "Mel's back and I'd like to get home to her."

"Fine," was his only response.

Back at the rental house, Sami Jo packed her bags and they were on the road again within the hour. The scenery whizzed by as she stared out the passenger window, a smile on her face despite the friction between them.

"Congratulations, by the way," Gray said after an hour of silence.

Her smile faded. "Thanks."

She could feel the irritation roll off of Gray in waves but honestly, she wasn't looking for a fight. She just wanted to get home to Melanie. Pushing the button on the side of the passenger seat, she reclined it and closed her eyes. She was physically exhausted and the hum of the road under the Escalade's tires lulled her to sleep.

When she woke, Gray was pulling off the highway in Myrtle Beach. She repositioned the seat and stretched.

"Your phone buzzed a few minutes ago," he said.

She picked up her cell from the cup holder between them and saw a text message from Matt.

Call me ASAP.

Matt answered on the first ring.

"Got some bad news," he said. "Angela Guthrie died from her injuries."

Sami Jo's stomach clenched. "Oh my god, Matt. That's horrible."

"I wanted to let you know before it hits the media. Can you let Gray know? We'll see you in a few hours."

"Sure," she said and hung up.

While she'd never met the woman, Sami Jo had the deepest respect for Angela Guthrie. It was a tragic loss. She, along with many others, had paved the way for women in racing.

"Angela Guthrie is dead." She stared out the window, contemplating how many times had she been vulnerable to this loon.

The mountains, Miami, her home, and who knew where else he had followed her to?

She suddenly felt regret for calling the guy out in her interview with Welliver. Maybe she could convince Danny to edit out that portion because there was no denying how real this had all become. A woman was dead, for chrissakes.

She quickly texted Diane to send Welliver an urgent message to call her.

As Gray pulled into the driveway of Royce's house, tears threatened at the corners of her eyes and as she looked up and saw her cousin leaning in the doorway of the house, she crumbled. She threw the door open and raced up the stairs into Melanie's embrace. The tears for her fallen colleague and the remnants of her relationship with Gray surged like a wave through her.

———◆———

Sami Jo sat on the sofa in the living room of Royce's house dunking a tea bag into her mug over and over again.

Melanie sat next to her and shook her head.

"I just can't believe it," her cousin said.

"Which part?" Sami Jo asked.

"All of it," Melanie said warily.

Sami Jo had told her everything, including what had transpired between her and Gray. Melanie had been sympathetic, not once making Sami Jo feel bad about her behavior even when she had told her about Miami and Chris Stevens.

They had kept their voices low because Gray was in the kitchen with his coworker from Alliance who had been guarding the house in their absence.

"You were right, Mel. I've been too reckless," Sami Jo said, setting her tea on the table next to her. "Especially with this thing with Gray. I feel stupid. I let myself fall for him again."

"Sometimes we can't help ourselves," Melanie said. "You know, I never intended to marry a race car driver."

This was news to Sami Jo.

"Trust me, I was adamant about not dating drivers. Especially someone on Daddy's team," Melanie remarked. "I didn't want anything to do with the business. I saw how much it consumed his life and I figured I'd find myself a nice lawyer."

"Is that even a thing, Mel? A *nice* lawyer?"

Melanie chuckled. "Well, probably not. But I took one look at Matt and all bets were off. I was head over heels and all my rules went right out the window."

"Sure, but Matt reciprocated your affections. That's the difference here."

"Not at first. Courting the boss's daughter is not every man's dream. For all his death-defying moves on the track, Matt was apprehensive to even look at me the wrong way for fear Royce would kill him." Melanie paused and looked toward the kitchen. "I'm willing to bet Gray is apprehensive, too."

"I'm pretty sure he was just curious about what he'd missed out on years ago. I was too but I couldn't quite compartmentalize it like I thought I could."

The front door to the house opened and Royce's voice echoed in the foyer.

Melanie lifted from the sofa and Sami Jo followed her into the kitchen where Gray stood with Decker, the man he'd hired to watch the house. Decker wasn't nearly as imposing as Gray but his hard expression showed he was all business. Dressed in a black suit, he looked every bit the part, even with his graying hair and the deep lines around his eyes.

Royce entered with a grim look on his face.

"Hi, sweetheart," he said, wrapping his arms around Melanie. "How are the kids?"

"They're probably getting spoiled as we speak," Melanie replied.

Royce turned his attention to Sami Jo. "Hey, kiddo. You okay?"

Sami Jo leaned against the island and nodded, feeling Gray in her peripheral.

"Well, before we get to it, I need to say nice job today." Royce smiled warily and walked over to where Gray and Decker stood. "Thanks for being here."

Decker shook Royce's hand and took a step back to allow Gray to do the same.

"Matt might be a while but we can proceed." Royce turned to the cabinet to pull out a couple of glasses and the bourbon.

"What's going on?" Sami Jo asked.

Royce brought a glass over to her and poured a shot. He set the bottle down and put his hand on her shoulder.

"We've decided it might be best to pull you from the rest of the season," Royce said. "Or at least until they catch this guy."

"You can't do that, Royce," Sami Jo pleaded.

"It's for your protection," Gray piped in.

Sami Jo's head whipped around to look at him. "You stay out of this."

Royce removed his hand from her shoulder and stuffed it in the back pocket of his jeans. "We're going to set you up somewhere no one will find you until this blows over."

"What then? This guy wins? He gets me off the track and gets what he wants? No way. The next race is too important, Royce. I'm not giving in." She started to pace the kitchen.

"Honey, we can't keep going like this," Royce said.

"We can't continue to employ a team to protect you."

Sami Jo stopped and looked at Gray. His mouth was set in a thin line.

She turned to Royce. "We don't need a team. Between you and Matt and me staying here, I don't need the extra security. I'll lay low, whatever it takes, but I am not missing a race. I didn't come this far to walk away."

"It's not about the money," Gray said. "I'm happy to do this pro bono if we have to. But this isn't sustainable, Sami Jo."

"Then why don't you just pack up your shit and go already?" she asked.

"Sami Jo," Royce said sternly. "You should consider yourself damn lucky to have Gray around. Angela Guthrie wasn't as fortunate."

"I refuse to run and hide. I have a charity event with Alec this week in Charlotte and then the race. I'm not missing either of those things." Sami Jo picked up the bourbon and tossed it back, looking pointedly at Gray. "Do what we pay you to do or consider things done here. Either way, I'll make do."

Sami Jo turned on her heel and stalked out to the porch, hoping he wouldn't follow her out.

Gray pushed through the door to the porch and Sami Jo's shoulders sagged as she slumped into a chair.

He stared down at his hands. They had touched intimate parts of her and while he'd never regret it, he couldn't do it again. And if he couldn't do it again—

"I think it's best if I implement my replacement. Decker is a good man and he'll follow along with whatever you need. I can get you through the week while he's brought up to speed, then he'll be at your disposal going forward."

She didn't even flinch. No sign his words had even registered. Was this a relief for her? He couldn't blame her if it was. Frankly, as much as it killed him, perhaps he'd find a sense of relief after he left. In the meantime, he still had work to do.

"Please reconsider dropping out for the rest of the season," he said.

"You know I can't." Sami Jo looked over at him. "My uncle's business is hanging by a thread."

Gray nodded. "I'm willing to bet he'd rather see you safe and lose everything than put you in harm's way."

"It's my career. I don't know who I am if I'm not racing. I'm sure you can appreciate that."

"I can," he said and straightened. "The military was my career. But I got hurt and had to give it up. I didn't have a choice, you do. Sometimes you have to do the right thing even if it means losing the thing you love to do."

"Is that what you're doing now?" she asked, gazing up at him. "The right thing?"

He chewed at the inside of his cheek. It sure didn't feel right.

"Sami, Jo," he began and let out a deep sigh. "My attraction to you has been my greatest weakness and I can't let it get in the way of your safety."

Sami Jo stood and the hate that clouded her face mirrored her expression seven years ago. Wordlessly, she crossed the porch and headed inside the house, leaving him alone with the decision he'd made.

He pulled out his phone and walked over to the stairs. The breeze off the water did little to ease his mind as he dialed.

Cole answered. "Yeah, boss."

"Clear Decker's schedule until further notice. I need him here."

"Sure thing."

"And find me a gig to start the week after next."

There was silence on the other end of the call.

"You catch that, Cole?"

"I'm confused," Cole said. "Decker's staying and you're—"

"Coming home. I'll be back Sunday night after the Charlotte race."

"Okay, but don't you want a few days to decompress?"

"No," Gray responded. "And before you start interrogating me, save your breath. I'm training Decker and then I'm done here."

The interrogation would come, Gray was certain of that.

"And let me see the invoices before you send them to Royce McLean," Gray said.

At least Cole knew enough not to question him on that one. Gray wasn't ready to admit he was planning on tearing them up.

———

Hours later, Gray sat at the kitchen island alone, having relieved Decker for the evening. They'd reconnect in Charlotte in a few days for the event Sami Jo was going to attend with Alec.

He liked Brian Decker and respected the older man's work ethic. Decker was a family man, married thirty years, and expecting his first grandchild. He'd been with Gray since the beginning and had always provided excellent service to Alliance's clients. He had Uncle John to thank for the introduction as Decker and John had been old college buddies.

He often wondered if John would've been eager to assist in getting him the job had he known how Gray had destroyed Gemma's friendship with Sami Jo. It wasn't a topic that ever came up; he assumed John didn't know.

Now, Gemma was on that list of relationships he needed to mend. Man, he'd really fucked things up.

He pulled out his phone and texted John.

Hey Uncle John, thanks again for dinner last week, and sorry we slipped out abruptly. Wondered if you could send me Gemma's number when you have a minute.

Almost instantly, John texted back.

Sorry things went down the way they did. I didn't realize Gem still harbored such resentment toward Sami Jo. Hope to have you both back soon. Tell Sami Jo congrats on her win today.

John texted Gemma's number and Gray dialed.

"Hello," Gemma answered cheerfully.

"Gem, it's Gray."

"Hey," she said, her tone somewhat reluctant.

"Sorry, I know it's late. I just wanted to apologize for how things went down at your folk's. If I had known you were going to be there, I would've opted out. I didn't intend to reopen old wounds and while we're on that subject, I'm sorry I inserted myself into your friendship with Sami Jo. It was wrong of me."

"Don't apologize, Gray. I shouldn't have acted that way—both times. I was jealous that she wanted to spend time with you that summer. How can I blame her? You're a great guy."

"No, Gem, I'm not. I treated her like shit."

"I should've been there for her after you left. A true friend would've forgiven her and given her a shoulder to cry on. And I should apologize for my behavior at dinner. I had too many twisted teas and it reminded me of how badly I handled everything. But it's pretty obvious you guys figured things out."

"It's not how it looked."

"Oh, I thought you two were together again. I mean, I saw the way you two were acting at dinner."

"Let's just say I have a tough time learning from past mistakes and I've made a mess of things again. I'm going to be leaving after her next race. If you can find it in your heart to give her a call after I'm gone, I think she'd appreciate it."

"Okay. But promise me you won't be a stranger. I do

miss you, cousin."

Gray hung up and stretched. He just needed to get through this next week without incident and he'd be out of Sami Jo's life forever.

Again, he reminded himself that it was the right thing to do.

But it made him feel like shit.

LAP TWENTY

A S LUCK WOULD HAVE IT, Decker's daughter went into labor the day he was expected to meet Gray in Charlotte for the charity event.

Gray insisted the man be with his family and that he'd see him in a few days for the race.

It had been a brutal week. With nothing to do but hang out at Royce's house, he did his best to stay out of Sami Jo's way. Now, as they stood in the VIP balcony at the Charlotte House of Blues, where two hundred and fifty attendees gathered on the main floor below, talking over the popular hits coming out of speakers over the stage, he couldn't take his eyes off of her.

Admittance to the private meet-and-greet came with gold-level donations to Alec's charity, most of which were made by CEOs and company presidents. No doubt they'd donated the hefty sum to get their teenagers in— the ratio of graphic t-shirts and glitter nail polish to suits was ten to one.

In a steely-blue suit and fingerless black leather gloves, Alec commanded a crowd of young girls who hung on to every word he said as Sami Jo stood next to him. Her hair was twisted up and regrettably, Gray's gaze was drawn to the flesh-colored panel underneath the black lace dress. The slit up the sides of her short skirt didn't leave much to the imagination. She was a bright *fuck me* beacon in high heels.

Despite Decker's absence, there were more than enough bodyguards stationed around them. And Alec's manager, a blonde woman named Claire, was a total badass with his schedule.

She signaled to Alec from across the room, motioning to wrap it up.

"Hey, everyone, thank you for coming." Alec reached for Sami Jo's hand. "We appreciate your generosity and hope you enjoy the show."

As they exited, the small crowd applauded and Claire guided them through the door to the back stairwell as Gray and the other bodyguards followed.

As they approached the door to the green room, three men emerged and Gray instinctively grabbed Sami Jo's arm.

She gave him a sharp look. "Stand down, soldier. They're from *Hello Hollywood.*"

Gray spotted the camera that one of the men carried by his side and released her arm.

Forming a semi-circle, the two-man crew set up the shot as the third man pasted on a huge smile and lifted a microphone to his mouth.

"Hello, Hollywood, it's Flynn, and I'm coming to you live from the House of Blues in Charlotte at a charity event hosted by Alec Clarke, where he'll premiere his new video 'For Your Amusement.'" He turned slightly toward Sami Jo. "We also have NASCAR darling, Sami Jo McLean. Tell me, Sami Jo, how was it to work with Alec?"

"It was great, Flynn. As you're about to see, he knows how to push the envelope."

Flynn leaned toward Alec. "I understand you two have a bit of *naughty* fun in the video, Alec."

"You'll have to stick around and watch it." Alec winked at Sami Jo then mentioned the charity he supported.

"Everyone wants to know," Flynn said. "When are you two tying the knot?"

"Well, maybe someday," Sami Jo said and smiled sheepishly at Alec. "Just not to each other. Despite the rumors, Alec and I are just close friends. Have been since day one."

"Are you saying you two aren't an item?" Flynn asked.

"No," Alec said. "We're more than that. We're family."

When the interview wrapped up, Claire gestured to Sami Jo. "Your outfit is hanging on the back of the bathroom door in the green room. We'll meet you at the stage entrance in twenty minutes."

Wordlessly, Sami Jo turned into the nearby doorway with Gray in tow.

The ten-by-ten room was sparsely decorated with a worn leather sofa and a small table that held bottles of water and a bucket of champagne. Sami Jo headed directly into the bathroom and Gray leaned against the wall as he waited for her to change.

The truth was out about her and Alec on national television. Sami Jo was a free agent, free to find someone—someone else. She'd have men lined up around the block and the thought made him bristle.

The door to the bathroom opened and Sami Jo emerged in a black and white velvet cape-like dress that resembled a glittering checkered flag. Her bare arms poked through two slits in the fabric. The hem was shorter than the dress she'd previously had on, making her legs look a mile long as she stood on three-inch black patent heels.

"How do I look?"

"Maybe you should ask Clarke's manager."

"Oh, come on, Gray. Let's pretend we're friends for just a minute before you're off to your next assignment. What would you say to your friend if you saw her dressed like this?" Sami Jo did a quick side to side twirl.

"I'd say you look like you belong on a race track as the first car passes the finish line."

Sami Jo stepped toward the door. "You ain't seen nothin' yet."

They made their way to stand behind the soundboard with Claire as Alec headed out onto the stage.

"Ladies and gentlemen, thank you for coming out tonight. I am pleased and honored to have worked with such a fantastic crew on the video you are about to see. What do you say? Let's get to it!" Alec stretched out his arms and the crowd cheered.

He stepped offstage and the lights went down. A thumping beat began, shaking the walls of the venue. A large monitor on the soundboard showed the video being broadcast onstage. It opened up to quick images in sync with the rhythm.

Neon lights reflected onto the hood of a race car. Its headlights turned on, cutting to a man's black motorcycle boot as it lifted into the passenger side. The camera panned up the closed passenger door to the window, where Alec Clarke sat with his head back and his eyes closed. His arm came out the window and he splayed his fingerless-gloved hand over the door, slapping it to the beat. As he lip-synced the first verse, a hand with long, red nails reached up and caressed his face, insinuating a woman's head was in his lap.

Gray almost rolled his eyes but he realized the woman was Sami Jo.

The scene blurred to the camera facing the front of the car, where she sat behind the wheel as if she were driving. Her fitted racing suit was unzipped down to her waist and Gray had to wonder what kind of two-sided tape kept her from falling out of it. Alec was singing to her, rocking toward her as if he were ready to pounce.

Sami Jo mouthed the female backup verse, *"I'm here for*

your amusement."

In the next shot, Sami Jo and Alec were standing next to the car, facing each other. Alec's black shirt was ripped open and frayed, and he slowly pushed Sami Jo's racing suit over her shoulders, exposing her bare skin. Sami Jo's arm was strategically placed to conceal her breasts as she ran her hand up Alec's chest to his chin. Her thumb tugged on his lip as she mouthed the verse again.

The scene cut and Sami Jo was lying on the hood of the car in a revealing checkered flag bikini with her back against the windshield and her legs crossed. She looked stunning and Gray's cock twitched.

Another cut and Alec stood at the front of the car with his back to the camera, pushing her legs apart as he climbed over her. If Gray didn't know any better, he would've had his doubts about their "friendship," because the next scene insinuated they were having sex on the hood of the car.

By the end of the video, Sami Jo sat behind Alec on the hood, her legs wrapped around his waist as he twisted the checkered bikini in his hand. She sunk her teeth into his shoulder and a satiated expression filled Alec's face as the scene faded to black.

Cheers erupted from the audience as Alec took Sami Jo's hand and walked her onto the stage.

"Sami Jo McLean, everyone," he said into the mic and the crowd went wild.

Alec lifted her hand to his lips and kissed the back of it. Taking his cue, Sami Jo reached up to unclasp the cape. With one swift flick, she opened it and let it drop off her shoulders. Alec caught it and pulled it away, revealing the same checkered flag bikini she wore in the video.

More cheers filled the venue and this time, Gray swore under his breath.

Alec said a few words about the director of the video, his charity, and how great it was working with Sami Jo who cocked an eyebrow at him and leaned into the mic. "I think you better sing something for these people, Alec. It's a bit chilly in here."

She took her cape from him and waved as she walked offstage. She took the stairs carefully and strutted past Gray toward the green room, not bothering to cover up. He shut the door behind him once they were inside and Sami Jo headed into the bathroom.

Yep, leaving her in Decker's capable hands was the right thing to do. Decker was happily married; there'd be no chance the old man would try to live out the fantasy currently flashing through Gray's head. And someday, another man—a better man—would come along and steal her heart. The heart he'd managed to break time and time again.

Before he could further discredit himself, there was an abrupt knock at the door.

He smoothed his hands over his hair and opened the door slightly.

"Hey," Danny Welliver said, standing in the hallway. "I'm—"

"I know you are," Gray said.

"I was hoping Sami Jo had a quick minute since I'm here. She left me a message the other day and I have the edit from our interview to show her."

Gray turned back to look at the bathroom door. Images of her stripping out of the bikini taunted him. He turned back to the doorway to find Alec's manager was standing behind Welliver.

"Mr. Finch, sorry to interrupt. I was hoping you might have a few minutes to chat before you leave. We have some artists performing at a festival in a few weeks and could use a few extra bodyguards."

Welliver brightened. "I'm happy to sit with Sami Jo."

"We'd be right across the hall," Claire said, looking hopeful.

Gray looked back at the bathroom door then at Welliver. Cole had backgrounded the guy, he was legit. And goddamn it, he just needed a minute away from her sexy ass.

"Okay, sure." Gray let Welliver inside the green room. "Just stay here. No one in or out."

Welliver saluted Gray. "She'll be safe with me."

———————

Sami Jo stood in the bathroom, fumbling with the clasp of her necklace, failing to get it hooked together, and frowned.

It stirred up memories of the night in the Kansas City hotel room, Gray's breath on her neck, his fingers brushing over her skin.

She wished she could let it all go.

The last few days, she'd tried to act as if he were already gone, or that nothing had happened between them. She had hoped seeing her in the video, and in the checkered bikini, would've stoked something in Gray.

He was all business. And after Sunday, he'd be gone for good.

She kept telling herself that at least she'd finally gotten the one thing she'd always wanted, but now, she was left holding a bag of emotions she couldn't sort out.

Giving up on the necklace, she clutched it in her hand and slipped into her heels.

She opened the bathroom door, half-expecting Gray to be standing where she left him, with a scowl on his face, but the green room was empty. A twinge of relief fell over her as she stepped from the bathroom, the chain wrapped around her fingers.

The air moved in her peripheral and a cloth-covered hand came up to her mouth. She smelled the ether just before everything went black.

Lap Twenty-One

SAMI JO OPENED HER EYES to a muted darkness. Flat on her back with her legs bent to the side, she was covered with a blanket that went over her head. She shifted and felt the bindings around her wrists. Her hands were tied in front of her while her ankles were also bound. The back of her head ached and her heart started to race as she realized she'd been knocked unconscious in the green room and taken.

The floor vibrated underneath her.

She rolled side to side so the blanket fell from her face and the inside trunk of an SUV came into view.

Struggling to free her hands, she heard a faint whistle coming from the front seat that sent chills up her back.

She rolled again to look over the top of the backseat. A man sat behind the wheel but she couldn't make out his eyes due to the glare of oncoming traffic sending sparks into her vision. On the backseat were cameras and lighting stands.

Danny?

She looked up again, straining to focus, and Welliver's gaze met hers in the rearview.

"You're awake," he said cheerily.

It suddenly became clear. He had been in Miami, he

had press access and was able to get into most racing events, and he'd hurt Angela Guthrie—

Her heart kicked up a notch.

"Danny, what's going on?"

"I'm taking you someplace safe, Sami Jo. You were in terrible danger."

"Where's Gray? Is he okay?"

"He left you along to go talk to someone. Guess he isn't that great of a bodyguard after all."

"Why am I tied up?" And how did he get her past all those people at the House of Blues?

"Can't have you doing anything stupid, Sami Jo. Just lay back and relax. We have some driving to do."

"Pull over right now, Danny." She kicked out at the back tailgate when he didn't respond. Her heels slammed into the door.

"Hey, keep it up and I'll knock you out again. I don't want to have to do that."

Tears stung her eyes but she wasn't going to fall apart. She had to stay focused even though the world was still topsy-turvy.

How could he have done this? And why? And where the hell was Gray?

Danny drove for what seemed like an hour and Sami Jo kept quiet, considering all the ways she could get away from him. The SUV turned off the highway onto a bumpy road and trees whizzed by through the smoked glass. It was too dark to make anything else out and the tears threatened to come again. She blinked them away and rolled quietly, forcing the blanket off.

Danny brought the SUV to a stop and shut off the engine. When he opened the driver's side door, a bright light flooded the vehicle, temporarily blinding her. She shifted so her feet were facing the trunk lid and she shimmied close to it, bringing her knees to her chest.

When the trunk lid opened, her feet shot out but Welliver moved too quickly for her to make contact.

"Now, is that any way to treat your savior?" He put his hands on his hips for a moment then reached in to grab her.

Sami Jo struggled as he pulled her out of the SUV but he held her firmly as she teetered on her heels. When she twisted in his grip, he slapped her and the sparks went off in her head again.

"See what you made me do," he said, pulling a folding knife from his pocket. "Now, I'm going to cut the ties around your ankles. Don't try anything funny, Sami Jo. I don't want to hurt you."

He bent over.

"Like you hurt Angela." She sneered down at him.

He stood back up abruptly without cutting the bindings. "You're a quick study. Now, don't move."

He bent over again and released her ankles with a quick jerk of the blade.

She looked around and saw mostly forest to her right. Tall trees blocked out the sky—there were so many of them. To her left was a large field as far as the eye could see.

"Where are we?" she asked, knowing they were legitimately in the middle of nowhere.

"Someplace safe," he said, taking her arm.

A log cabin sat dark several yards away. The trees around it kept it partially hidden; no one would even know it was there.

Her ankles wobbled as Danny steered her down the dirt path toward the cabin. A couple of times she lost her footing but he grabbed her arms and steadied her.

"Those are some dangerous shoes, Sami Jo." He said as if they were old friends.

"I'd like to gouge your eyes out with them," she muttered.

Welliver shoved her ahead and she stumbled, hitting the

dirt with a thud. The wind was momentarily knocked out of her and she tasted blood.

Welliver's hands went under her armpits and he dragged her backward toward the house.

She screamed into the night as Danny chuckled.

———◆———

Gray stood in the empty green room, his heart thudding so hard in his chest that he heard it in his ears.

There was no sign of Welliver, but more importantly, no Sami Jo.

As he rechecked the empty bathroom, something sparkled at his feet.

Her pendant.

He picked it up and held it in his hand. The chain seemed delicate, fragile, and beautiful in his palm—like her. But she wasn't that simple, was she? She was strong, and caring, and—

He loved every bit of her.

He'd probably always loved her but he had pushed her away.

He didn't have the time to think why she'd gone with Welliver if that was what she did. However, the necklace on the floor made him suspect that she might be in danger.

He tucked the necklace in his pocket and pulled out his phone to instruct Cole to work his magic. To see if Welliver had used his credit card, to trace his phone, maybe see if there was any info on his vehicle. If they got lucky, it had GPS tracking on it.

Rushing out of the green room, he ran into Claire, Alec's manager. "Mr. Finch, there's a gentleman that needs to speak with you."

"I'm sorry, I need to find—"

"He saw Sami Jo leave."

A roadie dressed in all black approached them, the red

bandana tied around his forehead moist with sweat.

"I was just telling the lady here that I was up on the lighting rig and I happened to look down as some guy was dragging that McLean woman from the green room. I assumed she'd been over-served."

"What did the guy look like?"

"He's that sports show guy from cable television. Kinda slim, brown hair." The roadie wiped a hand across his brow. "She looked in pretty bad shape. But like I said, people tend to get black-out drunk sometimes. They headed down the back hall out to the alley about fifteen minutes ago."

Sami Jo had only had one glass of wine in the VIP area. Welliver must've done something to compromise her consciousness.

"Thanks," Gray said and turned toward Claire. "I'll be in touch."

He didn't wait for a response because every second counted, and when he got his hands on Welliver, he was going to choke the life out of him.

And when he got his hands on Sami Jo, he was never going to let her go.

He raced down the hallway and out into the alley but it was empty. He rounded the building and headed to the valet booth.

The attendant behind the counter was scrolling on his phone.

"Ticket?" The uniformed man barely looked up.

Gray slid the ticket for his rental across the counter. "Do you keep license plate records?"

The attendant nodded, pulling the keys off the board. "Yep, helps us track keys and cars."

"I need to see the list of cars that left in the last thirty minutes."

The attendant finally looked at Gray and shook his head. "I can't do that."

Gray pulled out his business card and placed it on the counter.

The attendant glanced at it. "You're not the police."

"No, but a woman's life is in danger."

"The girl from the alley?" a voice behind him spoke.

Gray turned to find a young man in a similar valet uniform standing a few feet away.

"I pulled an SUV around to the back of the joint before the owner of the vehicle brought her through the alley door. Gave me a nice tip for doing it."

The attendant behind the counter, the kid's boss no doubt, sighed in frustration.

"She looked wasted," the young attendant said.

"Did you get the make and model?" Gray asked.

"Ricky, that's enough," the man behind the counter said.

"There's a twenty in it for you if you give me the info and get my car here quickly." Gray turned to the counter. "And there's another twenty in it if you give me that license plate."

Less than ten minutes later, Gray was on the road.

"Anything?" he asked Cole over the truck's Bluetooth.

"Nothing on Welliver's rental and his cell is off," Cole's voice came through the truck's speakers.

As Gray got onto the highway, he heard Cole clicking away at a keyboard. He hoped he was, at least, going in the right direction.

"Hang on," Cole said. "Nothing listed for Daniel Welliver, but there's a real estate listing under an Elaine Welliver. Died twenty-three years ago, along with Brianna Welliver, age four. Survived by her husband, Ashton, and son—Daniel."

He gave Gray the address and he typed it into his GPS.

"Died from what?" Gray asked.

The clicks from Cole's keyboard came through the speakers again. "A press release states Elaine and Brianna died in a car accident. Daniel was with them. Let me check police reports."

Gray watched the GPS reroute him in the other direction.

Crap.

He turned off the next exit, got back on, and headed north.

"Elaine was chased by police doing about one hundred miles per hour," Cole said. "Looks like she lost control and slammed into a tree."

"Sounds like she was running."

"I'm not pulling up domestics between her and the husband but that doesn't mean she wasn't trying to get away from him." Cole surmised.

"Send me as much as you can. I'm on my way to the address."

Gray hung up and stepped on the gas, hoping he wouldn't be chased by the police as well. Nothing was going to stop him from getting to Sami Jo.

Assuming she was even there.

Lap Twenty-Two

SAMI JO HAD LOST HER heels at some point. Most likely they were still in the middle of the gravel driveway where they had been pulled off her feet as Danny dragged her to the cabin.

Her feet bled and her whole body ached from hitting the ground when Welliver had shoved her.

He kept saying he didn't want to hurt her but his actions said otherwise.

Sami Jo sat tied to a creaky high-back chair in the middle of the small living room. An antique lamp in the corner of the room gave off very little light, but she could make out the shabby furniture that was like something out of goodwill. A dilapidated fireplace stood against one wall where Danny stoked the fire with a metal poker.

He turned and studied her. "It can get cold at night and you're not exactly dressed for it."

"Danny, what's this all about?" She tugged her wrists against the bindings holding her to the arms of the chair.

"It's for your own good, Sami Jo." He replaced the poker in the stand next to the hearth.

He moved over to a tattered armchair and sat.

"What does that mean?" she asked.

"Well, it's obvious you have no respect for your own

life." He frowned as he shook his head. "I was hoping the crash last week would've taught you a lesson, but you got right back out there, didn't you?"

Welliver cocked his head with what looked like genuine concern.

"Racing is my career, Danny. It comes with risks."

"Risks you choose to take."

She didn't have an answer to that.

"Why would you put yourself and the lives of others in that kind of peril? I mean, Sami Jo, life is precious. You, of all people, know that. Your dad was killed in a race. Did you learn anything from that?"

"If I stop racing, will you let me go?"

Welliver folded his hands, positioning his index fingertips together, and raised them to his lips. He pulled his hands away and pointed those fingers at her. "You and I both know you're not going to stop."

"Danny, why are you doing this?"

"The only way you'll stop is if you can never race again. And the only way that happens is if you physically can't drive."

Fear washed over her and tears formed on the edges of her lids. "Danny, please let me go."

He stood and she jerked against the chair.

"I like you, Sami Jo. But I have to say your interview the other day made me realize that you'd have to be dealt with. On camera, you literally asked *the guy* to come at you. You were awfully eager to put yourself in harm's way. Why would you do that?"

She looked away, ashamed to admit she had done it to get Gray out of her life.

"There is a reason, isn't there?"

"We couldn't continue to afford the cost of a bodyguard," she lied.

"Apparently, he wasn't very good. You got away from him a few times."

How does he know about that?

"When he moved in, I was concerned he'd get in the way, but I got to you anyway," Welliver said.

"Yeah, you won. Now what?" she asked, jutting her chin out at him.

Danny laughed. "Always so bold, Sami Jo. I like that about you. It also explains why you think you're such hot shit on the track."

"I don't think that at all," she said. "I just happen to have some skills and probably a bit of luck on my side."

"That just proves my point," he said. "That's why you need someone to save you from yourself. To stop you before your luck runs out."

A tear ran down her cheek and she glared at him through her watery gaze. "Why are you doing this?"

He stopped and turned to her. "What's that sentiment? If I can save just one life, it'll make up for the ones I couldn't."

Her gaze cleared and she stared at him. "What do you mean? Who couldn't you save?"

"Trust me, Sami Jo. You'll thank me later." Welliver winked at her and strode toward a doorway across the room.

"Danny, please," she pleaded, but he was already gone.

Immediately, she started pulling against the straps. She rocked back and forth, hoping the chair's instability would help, but she was too tightly bound and she was starting to lose feeling in her feet.

A door somewhere inside the house slammed and tears rolled over her cheeks. She considered what Welliver meant to do to her that would keep her from racing again. Did he mean to physically or mentally impair her? The thought forced her to fight against the bindings again, but it was no use.

Her not being able to race was like not being able to breathe.

A door slammed again and Welliver entered the room. She stilled but her breaths came in huge bursts.

He carried a roll of plastic under one arm and had a duffle bag slung over his other shoulder. He dropped everything to the floor in front of the fireplace and left again. The door slamming behind him again.

Sami Jo looked at the items on the floor.

In the crackling fire, she saw the duffle bag was open, and inside, a large silver hacksaw that made her scream in terror.

———

Gray had parked the truck a quarter-mile away from the address Cole had given him.

He walked through the thick forest quietly with his gun drawn.

A dim light flickered in the window of the cabin that appeared through the clearing and he moved around to the back of the property. He watched Welliver exit the back door of the house and head to a shed about seventy-five feet across the weed-covered yard.

Welliver seemed to be moving things around in the shed by the sounds of it and Gray took the opportunity to move quietly to the side of the house. He got to the side window and the sight of Sami Jo, alive, filled him with relief. Then he noticed she was tied up and her cheeks were wet with tears.

Gray rushed to the front door and tried the handle. Much to his surprise, it was unlocked.

He stepped over the threshold and snuck across the entryway to the living room where Sami Jo was being held. The slam of the back door forced him to conceal himself next to the doorway.

"Danny, you don't have to do this," Sami Jo said, her voice raspy and pleading.

There was a thud and he could hear Sami Jo's sobs.

"You know, you sound like my mother. God rest her soul," Welliver said. "She'd say those exact words to my father right before he'd beat the hell out of her."

Gray peeked around the corner. Welliver was standing at the fireplace, hovering over a large duffle bag. There was a large plastic bag spread out on the floor and off to the side was a hacksaw. Gray stepped back into the shadows as Welliver looked up at Sami Jo.

"For years she stayed with him, putting herself, and me and my sister, in harm's way. When she finally tried to escape, she took off in her little Honda with us in the back. My father chased after her. She was never gonna outrun that Porsche of his. I don't know what she was thinking. She wrapped the car around a tree. The impact killed her and my sister, but I made it out alive."

There was a rustling of heavy items in the duffle bag and Gray stepped into the doorway, raising his gun.

"Don't make a move, asshole," Gray said and Sami Jo's head whipped around. He could see a bruise on her cheek and blood on the carpet under her bare feet.

Rage bubbled up inside him.

That brief second of looking at her was all Welliver needed. A shot was fired and Gray was hit in the shoulder.

Sami Jo let out a scream.

Gray went down but as he hit the floor, he aimed his gun and capped Welliver in the chest.

"Gray!" Sami Jo cried out.

He grunted and sat up, the pain searing down his arm. What were the odds he'd get hurt twice in the same location? He looked over at Welliver, who was writhing on the carpeting in front of the fireplace. Gray got up and stumbled over to him, kicking the gun away.

"Gray, are you okay?" Sami Jo asked through tears.

He grunted and looked down at Welliver. "What were you gonna do to her, you son of a bitch?"

Welliver coughed up blood through his sneer. "You

must be the worst bodyguard ever. Leaving her alone like that."

"Well, I'm never leaving her again." Gray turned and went over to Sami Jo. He dropped to his knees, placed the gun on the floor next to her chair, and attempted to untie her ankles. Searing pain shot down his arm.

"Gray, you're hurt," she said.

"This is a graze compared to the last time," he looked up and gave her a half-smile.

With her feet free from the bindings, he went to stand up, but the pain in his shoulder was blinding.

"Gray, behind you!"

He hadn't heard Welliver get to his feet, and Sami Jo's warning was inconsequential as something came down on his head and he blacked out.

———

Sami Jo watched Gray fall to the floor for the second time and anguish took over.

Welliver was a blurry figure as he stood over Gray holding the poker for the fireplace in his hand. He raised it again over his head to strike again and that was when Sami Jo made her move.

With her feet free, she was able to stand up and took the chair with her, charging at Welliver. She turned at the last second, crashing into him.

The action broke the chair and although the armrests were still attached to her wrists, the rest of it fell to the floor. Welliver landed with his back in the fireplace and his shirt quickly caught on fire.

He didn't scream. His head had hit the stone frame and knocked him out.

Now that she could reach them, Sami Jo yanked at the straps around her wrists and the armrests dropped. She turned to Gray who was slumped on the floor. There was blood in his hair where Welliver had struck him.

The warmth of the fire behind her increased as Welliver's body was consumed by the flame.

She had to get Gray of there.

Reaching for his gun, she tucked it in the holster on Gray's hip and felt for his pulse. He had one but it was weak.

"Gray, come on. We have to go."

When he didn't respond, she shook him, trying not to focus on the blood oozing from his shoulder.

The fire was spreading and soon the house would be engulfed. She rolled Gray over and grabbed his jacket lapels.

"Get up, Gray! Get up, we have to go!"

He roused a little and she pulled at his jacket to sit him up, feeling the heat of the blaze behind her.

"Get up, soldier!" she yelled into his face. "You did not save me just to end up dying. I won't allow it."

With all her might, she slapped him across the face.

His eyes fluttered open and he looked at her through glazed eyes.

"We have to go," she said and stood.

He attempted to get up with her but staggered as he tried to get his footing. She held onto him and was able to maneuver him across the room and out the front door. It slammed behind them and when they got about ten feet from the house, it slammed again.

Sami Jo and Gray turned around together and saw Welliver, on fire, heading in their direction.

Sami Jo reached toward Gray's hip, pulled the gun from the holster, and aimed at Welliver.

Before he could reach them, however, he fell to the ground.

And within moments, Gray slumped onto the grass beneath them.

Sami Jo got down on her knees. "Gray, stay with me. Where's your phone?"

He pulled it out of his jacket but because it was in the top pocket where Welliver had shot him, it was shattered. She looked up at the house, which was now overrun with flames. She imagined Welliver's car keys were somewhere inside, melting under the heat of the fire. If she didn't get help soon, Gray might die. "What about your car? Where is it parked?"

"I meant it," Gray mumbled.

She looked down at him as he laid in the grass. His jacket was soaked with blood and his eyes were half-closed.

"You meant what?"

"I—I've been so stupid." A long-labored breath pushed through his lips. "I'm never leaving you again."

Her chest constricted and tears came to her eyes again, fearing he wouldn't be able to keep that promise.

"I love you, Sami Jo." Gray's eyes locked with hers for a moment and then he closed them. His head rolled to the side and he was unconscious again.

"Gray, you need to stay awake." She shook him but he wasn't responding.

She laid her body next to his and put her arm around him. She listened for his heartbeat. It was slow and by the wheezing sound in his lungs, she feared he was taking his last breaths.

"Gray, please. Don't do this to me. I love you too. More than anything."

There was no way to know if he could hear her. He wasn't moving.

LAP TWENTY-THREE

SAMI JO WASN'T SURE HOW long they stayed like that. She was having trouble hearing his heartbeat and his breaths were coming slow and shallow. As quiet as the area was, the sounds of frogs and crickets seemed loud. They were as deafening as a roaring engine.

It was then she realized it wasn't the sounds coming from the forest but something else.

A helicopter.

She raised herself off of Gray and looked to the sky. Smoke from the fire inside the house billowed overhead but through the black fog, a chopper appeared. She got to her feet and started waving her arms, shouting to the pilot, praying he saw them.

The helicopter lowered onto the grassy field and two men in EMT uniforms exited the door with a stretcher. They ran toward her.

"Ms. McLean," one of them yelled over the noise from the chopper. "Are you okay?"

"I'm fine but Gray was shot and took a blow to the head. I don't even know—" She caught herself before saying the words *if he's still alive.*

The man nodded at her and crouched over Gray. He checked a few of his vitals and he lifted him onto the stretcher with his partner's help.

Sami Jo followed them to the helicopter and one of the men helped her up and strapped her into a seat.

"How is he?" she asked as the other man attached an oxygen mask to Gray's face.

"Still alive, but barely."

Sami Jo felt ill. She looked out the window as squad cars approached the burning house along with three fire trucks.

"The police are going to want to speak with you," the older EMT said. "But they know where to find you."

"How did you know where we were?" she asked.

"Cole Donovan called us," the EMT said and put his headphones on, giving the pilot the okay to take off.

They lifted into the air and Sami Jo prayed silently that they'd make it in time.

———————

For hours, Sami Jo had laid back on the gurney in the emergency room wishing the tears would just stop.

She didn't think she had that much left in her system but every time she felt a lull, the emotion would rocket through her. And it kicked into high gear when Royce entered the room.

"Sweetheart, my god." He raced to the side of the bed and put his arms around her.

She clung to him and he rubbed her back. When her sobs subsided, he pulled away and looked at her.

"I'm glad you're alright." Royce was tearful too. He wiped his eyes and shoved his hands in his pockets. "Any news on Grayson's condition?"

"They took him right into surgery. He lost a lot of blood." She looked down at her hands. "I have something I need to tell you, Royce. I—I'm in love with him."

"I know."

She looked up at her uncle and he smiled down at her.

"And this isn't the first time you've loved him," he said.

"How—did Melanie tell you?"

"Girl, I'm not blind. I knew you were up to something that summer he came to town but Trudy told me to stay out of it. And I could tell by the look on your face when he was on the porch a few weeks ago that you hadn't moved on. And I imagine that he loves you too."

Sami Jo nodded. "He told me before he passed out."

"Well, Melanie didn't have to say a damn word. We all knew," Royce said. "Matt confirmed it when he caught you two in Kansas City if you were wondering."

"That's funny, he never acknowledged it."

"Sami Jo, we know enough to let you find your way on your own. You've always been headstrong like your daddy. You see something you want, you go for it. We just try to stay out of your way."

"You know what I want right now?"

"What's that, darlin'?

"I want him to be okay. I can't lose him again." Tears burned her eyes again and she blinked them away. "I need to get a hold of his family and Cole, his business partner."

"Matt is taking care of that," Royce said. "You just rest."

A young nurse in blue scrubs entered the room and held up a pair of socks. She was the same woman who had cleaned up the scrapes on Sami Jo's feet and applied ointment to ward off any infection.

"I know they don't go with your outfit but at least they'll keep your feet warm." She smiled and leaned down to put them on for Sami Jo.

"Any word on Grayson's situation?" Royce asked the woman.

"Nothing yet but that reminds me." The nurse reached into her pocket and pulled out a chain. It was Sami Jo's pendant. "This was in the pocket of his pants."

Sami Jo took the pendant and held it in the palm of her hand.

He had found it. He had found *her.*

He had to find his way back.

Two more hours passed and since Sami Jo had been released from the emergency room, she sat in a waiting area on the surgery floor with Royce and Alec, who had arrived not long after Royce. He'd been in the room as she relayed to the police what had happened with Danny Welliver and now sat next to her with his arm around her shoulder.

"Alec, you don't have to stay. It's getting late and you have a show tomorrow night."

"Don't be silly. Do you want something to drink?" He motioned to one of his security guards who had been stationed at the door.

"You've asked me five times. I'm fine."

The guards parted to allow a doctor to enter the room and Sami Jo sprung from her seat, padding over in the socks the nurse had given her.

"How is he?"

"He's just coming out of recovery but he's heavily sedated. We did some massive repairs to his shoulder. Looked like he'd had surgery there before."

Sami Jo nodded. "He was injured when he was with the SEALs."

"Well, we have one of the best orthopedic surgeons in the country here and he did a great job. The recovery will be long but he should feel a lot better with the job Dr. Scholl did. He did lose a lot of blood so he's not out of the woods just yet."

"Can I see him?" Sami Jo asked.

"Give us some time to get him to his room. I'll have someone come for you." The doctor smiled and quickly left.

Sami Jo melted into Alec's arms as they went around her.

"He's going to be fine, Sami Jo. I just know it." Alec

pulled away and squeezed her arms.

She took a deep breath. "Thank you for being here."

Royce clapped a hand on Alec's shoulder. "Seriously, son. Why don't you go get some rest? We've got this."

"Promise me you'll call me when you know more. Doesn't matter what time," Alec said.

Sami Jo nodded and went to drop into a chair as Royce walked Alec to the door.

He crossed the room to her and sat next to her. "I know this isn't the time but you have practice tomorrow. What do you want to do?"

"I have no idea. I know if I don't practice, I don't race. But honestly, being with Gray is more important than anything else right now." She realized what she was giving up by missing the race she had fought so hard to compete in. But there would always be another one.

Royce reached out and patted her knee. "Let's just play it by ear then."

When a nurse stopped by and told them Gray's room number, they rushed down the hallway that led to his room and Royce waited outside while she went in.

Sami Jo held her breath as she entered.

The room was dimly lit. His large form was covered with a blanket and he had wires, an oxygen tube, and an IV attached to him. For as strong as he was, seeing him like this made him look vulnerable and she didn't think she could stand it.

Gauze covered his shoulder and a strip surrounded his head. His chest rose and fell evenly to the beat of the beeping machines in the room.

Sami Jo reached out and touched his hand but he didn't stir.

She didn't know how long she had stood there before the door to the room finally opened and a nurse walked in.

"His family is here," the woman said.

John Finch entered and frowned at the sight of his nephew. Behind him was Gemma.

Sami Jo's heart sank at the sight of them both. On some level, she felt guilty for putting Gray in this condition, even though it was Welliver who had hurt him. Her eyes welled up and she turned away.

She felt an arm go around her and she turned to find Gemma standing next to her, comforting her.

Gemma's face, rather than being filled with hatred and contempt, showed sympathy and compassion.

Sami Jo folded into her embrace as her tears flowed.

———

"I absolutely think you should race," Gemma said to Sami Jo as they sat in the hospital cafeteria. "You can't let that guy win, even in death. And Gray would want you to, Sami Jo."

Sami Jo nodded and studied the coffee cup in her hand.

"Gray might be here for a few days. And one of us will be here when he wakes up," Gemma continued. "If he found out you skipped the most important race of your life for him, he'd never forgive himself."

Sami Jo gazed up at her old friend. "God, I've missed your counsel, Gem."

Gemma sat back in the chair and sighed. "We've missed out on too many years."

"I'm sorry I flaked out on you that summer. I was in love with him."

Gemma arched a brow. "Was?"

Sami Jo wasn't sure how to respond. She had just gotten the equivalent of some much-needed forgiveness from Gemma. If she admitted how she felt now, would it spiral her friend back to hating her?

Gemma's lips turned up and she laughed. "Good thing you don't play poker, Sam. You'd suck at it."

Sami Jo laughed uneasily.

"Hey, after all this, you two are definitely meant to be together." Gemma leaned forward and placed her hand on Sami Jo's arm. "I would be pissed if you guys screwed it up again."

The corner of Sami Jo's mouth turned up as some relief spread through her.

Lap Twenty-Four

WELL, DADDY, HERE WE ARE again.

Sami Jo stood on the track next to her car as the national anthem played to a sold-out crowd of race fans.

She had spent two long days of practice and qualifying as Gemma had given her hourly updates on Gray.

Although Gray had finally woken up, Gemma said that he'd been adamant Sami Jo not come to the hospital. When Sami Jo asked why, her friend didn't have much of an answer for her. She figured two things had happened. Gray realized he'd said the L-word in a state of confusion and trauma—he probably thought he was going to die—and he was pushing her away because he hadn't really meant it.

What was the phrase? If you love something—

She'd always been the one set free, now it was her turn to let him go if that was what he truly wanted.

At least until after the race. Then she fully intended to go to the hospital. Even if it was to say goodbye.

For now, this was where she needed to be. On the track.

Her thoughts kept wandering to her father. His presence was everywhere, which was lucky for her because she needed him watching over her today.

Positioned second, Sami Jo knew if she could stay

focused, she just might have a chance to win this damn race.

The sun beat down on all of the cars are they roared to life.

When the pace car rolled off the track and all the cars sped up, Sami Jo stepped on it. She had a couple hundred miles before her and all she had to do was what she'd been born to do.

Kurt Hamlin, the second-place winner from last week, was in first for most of the race. A few times Sami Jo slipped to third and then fifth, but as the race neared the finish, she caught back up to him.

As the last lap laid ahead of her, a voice spoke into her headset.

"You got this, Hot Shot."

Gray. Gray was there.

Sami Jo put her foot down and kept up with Hamlin, but as the checkered flag flew, she still wasn't able to pass him.

She had finished second.

By the time she reached pit row, her heart was beating like a drum. When it was safe to do so, she climbed out of the car and searched the viewing booth. She caught sight of Matt, who pointed down, and that's when she saw him.

Gray stood at the cement barricade next to her new bodyguard, Decker. The bandage on Gray's head was gone but his arm was in a sling.

Sami Jo raced over and hopped the barricade, knowing things could go either way. But the smile on his face told her he wasn't there to say goodbye.

She wrapped her arms around him and her lips met his. When he grunted in pain, she realized maybe she should go easy on the affection.

"Sorry, did that hurt?" she asked.

"I'll be okay," he said. "I was afraid I ruined your chance for first by talking into Matt's mic."

"Are you kidding me? I tried to go faster to get to you."

Gray laughed. "Wasn't this race important for you to win?"

"You're more important than any race, Gray. And before you can say anything else, I love you."

"I heard you the first time," he smiled. "The other night."

"I thought you were already unconscious." She smiled through her tears. "How's your arm?"

"Turns out Welliver did me a favor. The orthopedic here was able to fix what they couldn't overseas and they said I won't have much pain once I'm recovered. But are you okay? That was some horrific shit Welliver put you through."

"As long as you're okay, I'll be fine." She chewed on her lip. "What now, Gray?"

"Now, we figure out how I can open up an Alliance office in Myrtle Beach, and I guess I'll need a place to live." He smiled down at her and pulled her closer. "Know where I can find a nice beachfront property?"

"I know just the place." She kissed him again. "I love you, Gray."

"I love you too, Hot Shot."

"Sami Jo." Royce appeared at their side. "I hate to break up the reunion, but you have a second-place trophy to accept."

"You better go." Gray kissed her forehead and released her. "We'll have all the time in the world after you go accept that trophy. I'm counting on you to nurse me back to health."

She gazed up at him and her love for him filled her.

"Race of your life, Hot Shot, and you got second," he

said. "How do you feel about that?"

Sami Jo thought for a moment. "With you here? It sure feels like first."

AUTHOR BIO

Kelly Duff is an award-winning romance author who has been writing about strong women and hunky heroes since she was eight-years-old. Inspired by music and thanks to a career in the radio business, Kelly tends to weave her experiences from the green rooms and back-stages of concert venues into her romance novels.

When she's not wrangling her two fur babies, Kelly and her husband are usually binge-watching TV shows or listening to music. They live in the burbs outside Chicago.

———

Connect with Kelly:
www.KellyDuffWrites.com
@kellyduffwrites
instagram.com/kelly_duff_writes/
facebook.com/KellyDuffWrites

Made in the USA
Monee, IL
30 January 2021